# CATNAPPED

## A Klepto Cat Mystery

## Patricia Fry

Matilija Press
PMB 123
323 E. Matilija St.,Ste 123
Ojai, CA 93023
www.matilijapress.com

# *Catnapped*

## A Klepto Cat Mystery
## by Patricia Fry

ISBN 978-0-9911065-1-6

Cover Art: Bernadette E. Kazmarski
Cover layout: Dennis Mullican
Page layout: Dennis Mullican

Printed in U.S.A. by: Create Space

**Other Novels by Patricia Fry**
Cay-Eye Witness
Sleight of Paw

# A Klepto Cat Mystery
# Book One: *Catnapped*
## by Patricia Fry

## Chapter 1

Savannah saw something scurry past her in the near darkness—*a cat! It's one of the missing cats. How frightened he must be in this desolate spot where nothing is familiar—where danger is imminent.* Now she could relate to the cat's fear. It had become personal. If only she could find a way to keep her kidnapper at bay until help arrived. But no one knew where she and Aunt Margaret were—no one would come in time.

　　She thought about the circumstances that had landed them in this terrifying predicament—a situation that could very well end in torture and death for both of them.

***

It was a week and a day earlier. All but one occupant in the old Forster home slumbered peacefully. He couldn't (or wouldn't) sleep. He'd rather explore. He's considered nocturnal, after all. No, he isn't a werewolf or a vampire, but a mere cat—an incredibly curious cat.

　　*What the...?* Savannah raised up on one elbow, tilted her head and listened for a moment. *Must have been dreaming or hearing things,* she thought as she scrunched back down under the warm blankets.

　　"Screeeeeeech!"

　　*There it is again. It's coming from downstairs.* "Aunt Margaret," Savannah whispered under her breath as her feet hit the floor. There was just enough moonlight shining through the sheer curtains to illuminate the small lamp at her right. Savannah switched it on and reached for her robe, grateful that she had packed the newer one. No one ever saw her lounging in her favorite, well-loved robe. Not if she could help it.

She rounded the last post at the bottom of the staircase and rushed toward the guestroom, wondering what calamity had occurred at 5:30 a.m. "Auntie, are you all right?" she asked as she peered into the room around a slightly ajar door. In the dim light from the bedside lamp, Savannah saw her aunt sitting on the edge of the bed still in her nightshirt, staring down at Rags.

"What happened?" Savannah asked hesitantly as she entered the room.

"Oh nothing. He just startled me; that's all. Right, Ragsdale?"

"Are you sure? It sounded like you saw the ghost of old Grandpa Forster," Savannah quipped.

"No, Vannie. I heard something scratching around in that dresser over there. You know, we get all kinds of vermin and critters out here in the country." She winced. Then, looking up at her niece, she continued, "That's something you don't have to deal with in the big city."

"I didn't realize you were so squeamish, Auntie. What kind of vermin are you talking about, anyway?"

"Oh, you know, snakes, raccoons, mice. I don't mind these animals, but not in my house." Margaret shuddered.

"So there's a snake in here? Or a mouse?" Savannah asked.

"I'm getting to it," she snapped playfully. "Do

2

you want to hear my story or not?"

Savannah nodded submissively while suppressing a smile. "Yes, please go ahead."

"Okay, so I turned on my little lamp here and I saw something moving in my lingerie drawer. I don't know why I left it open. Just forgetful, I guess. And with this danged broken foot, I'm not taking care of business like I usually do."

"Which is why I'm here, right?" Savannah smiled. Then creasing her brow into a frown, she asked, "So what was it in your drawer?"

"There he is right in front of you." She pointed at Savannah's cat, who seemed to be the epitome of innocence at the moment. "I saw something dive for cover under my pink slip. Well it started moving around and I didn't know what was about to jump out of there. It scared me. I mean, how would I escape if it decided to attack?" Margaret asked, her face tingeing pink as she relived the experience.

"When the creature popped out of the drawer with a pair of my pantyhose trailing across its back, I wasn't sure what I was seeing. I didn't have my glasses on, and the bulb in this tiny lamp is so dim. I couldn't tell what it was—a possum, an alligator...or maybe a wild boar!" Her eyes grew larger along with her imagination.

Savannah couldn't contain her urge to laugh. "Oh Auntie, you're exaggerating. When is the last time you had an alligator or a wild boar anywhere near this house? And since when are you afraid of Rags?" she asked, reaching down and roughing up the fur on the cat's head.

"Since he disguised himself and snuck up on me in the dark." She chuckled, watching the cat roll from side-to-side on his back while wrapping his front paws

3

around Savannah's out-stretched hand and kicking it playfully with his back feet. "Anyway, I thought we closed my bedroom door last night—didn't we?" She cocked her head slightly to the left, her bobbed brown hair swaying across her shoulder.

"Yes, I closed it. But, unless you lock it, Rags can open it." She pointed over at the door, saying, "He's an expert with those lever door handles of yours. No room in this house is safe from him unless the door's locked. When he wants in or out, he just jumps up, hits the lever, and the door opens." Savannah stared off into space for a moment and then continued, "I almost lost him once when Travis and I spent the weekend at friends. They had those lever door handles, and he just helped himself outside one night while we were sleeping."

*That was a mistake,* she thought. *I vowed his name would not cross my lips nor would thoughts of him enter my mind. Not for a while. Yet, it may not be possible, what with Travis having been so much a part of my life. Not now, Savannah,* she willed herself. *Not yet. It's too soon. Let the memories die. It's best.*

"Uh-oh." Margaret patted the top of the bedside table.

Savannah's attention now on her aunt, she asked, "What?"

"My glasses…where are my glasses? I always set them on the table next to me when I go to bed."

"Well, since this isn't your bedroom and you're not used to being in this guestroom, maybe you changed your routine. Did you leave them in the bathroom? Let me look." Savannah promptly returned, saying, "I didn't see them in there. Are they in that drawer?" Savannah followed her gaze over to the bedside table and pulled on the knob.

4

"I don't think so. I did a little reading before going to sleep and I'm almost positive I put them right here." Margaret pushed her Kindle to one side and felt around the base of the lamp.

"Maybe they fell behind the table," Savannah offered. But her efforts to locate the specs behind or underneath it were fruitless. Suddenly, Savannah let out a sleepy sigh and looked down at the cat, who was by then lying on the bed next to Margaret enjoying a series of tummy scratches. "Okay," she scolded, "what did you do with them?"

"I told you, I put them on this table. I know I did," Margaret insisted.

"No, Auntie, I'm not talking to you. It's Ragsdale. You see, there's something I forgot to tell you. He's a…"

"Eeeeoooo, what's this?" Margaret grimaced as she pulled something out from beneath her heirloom quilt. Savannah stared at the perforated tube her aunt held in her hand and watched as white cream oozed from it. "It's my body lotion!" Margaret exclaimed. "How did it…" she started. She shook her head in disbelief. "Why is it in my bed? Am I losing my mind?"

"Ragsdaaaale!!!!" Savannah dragged out the cat's name for emphasis.

"What does he have to do with this?" Margaret asked. "He's a cat!"

"He's a kleptomaniac," Savannah said with a deep sigh.

"Huh?" Margaret responded, her mouth open as she stared down into the green eyes of the striking grey-and-white cat. "Rags put this here? And he stole my glasses? Do you really think so?"

"Oh yes, Auntie!" Savannah twisted her shoulder-length, almost-blond hair into a knot on top of her head and walked over to her aunt's closet.

"You said he was a good cat—no trouble—like Layla." Margaret glanced over at her own cat, who was curled up in a cozy leopard-print cat bed across the room.

Savannah turned abruptly to face her aunt, looking as innocent as she knew how. "I said he is litter-box trained, he comes when you call him—most of the time, he has his own bed, he travels nicely in the car, and he's fun to be around. What I didn't tell you is…" Savannah hesitated, guilt washing over her face, "he loves plastic tubes, especially if they contain perfumed lotions. And he steals things." Savannah paused while Margaret digested this new bit of information. And then she added, "If he were human, he'd be doing time for burglary—big time!"

Savannah opened the closet door, picked up one of her aunt's shoes and examined it. "Are you missing some jewelry? There's a watch in your moccasin."

"Heavens, he *is* a bad boy." Margaret gazed over at the empty accessory dish. "I wore that yesterday and put it on this little tray when I went to bed."

"It looks like he also took something out of your lingerie drawer." Savanna held up a pink satin-and-lace bra. "Auntie, I didn't know you wore such pretty underwear."

"Sure I do," she snapped playfully. "You never know when you're going to…" The look of astonishment on her niece's face stopped her in mid-sentence.

"How old are you, anyway?" Savannah asked.

"You're only as old as your hormones declare, my dear. Why do you think I'm so eager for this danged foot to heal? I'm not through dancing, yet."

"You don't need sexy underwear to go dancing,"

the younger woman reasoned—a mischievous cadence to her voice.

"Oh, you'd be surprised," Margaret said with a wink. "If your mother knew what was good for her, she'd be out dancing, too." She took on a more serious tone. "It's been six years since your daddy passed and she's a mighty attractive fifty-five-year-old."

Margaret was right; the Brannon women had lucked out in the good-looks department with their clear skin, dark hair, and brown eyes. Savannah was the only offspring with almost blond hair—*dirty blond*, she called it. She had always felt short-changed in both gene pools. She missed out on the dramatic coloring from the Brannon side and didn't get quite enough of the Jordan's fair genes. She liked having the light eyes and height from her father's side, but had always been unhappy with her rather drab hair color. She was thrilled when she discovered the process of highlighting. Now she considered herself a true blond—she even wrote *blond* on her driver's license application.

"What's that?" Margaret stopped mid-room on her crutches as she made her way slowly to the bathroom.

Savannah turned toward the sound and listened. "I think someone's at the door."

"What time is it, anyway?"

"Well, it's starting to get light—must be sixish."

"Who stops by at this time of morning?" Margaret asked, not expecting an answer. And then she added a postscript: "I guess I really wouldn't know; I'm rarely up at this hour."

"You go pee and I'll go see." Savannah laughed at her unintentional rhyme and headed toward the living room. Rags traipsed along beside her, darting across her path a few times with his tail high. When they reached the large room, he jumped up on the sofa, slid across the coffee table, and hopped over to the ottoman.

"Who's there?" Savannah asked as she peered through the windowpane alongside the heavy wooden front door. She could see a man silhouetted against the tangerine backdrop of the sunrise. But the details in his face were unclear through the stained glass, and she didn't recognize his lanky frame. But then she didn't actually know many people in Hammond, anymore.

"I'm Max...a neighbor," he said through the glass.

Savannah opened the door a crack and asked if everything was all right.

"Oh yes. I was just walking by and noticed lights on; wanted to make sure Maggie's okay. I knew she just broke her foot and all."

"Yes, she's okay." Savannah wasn't sure what to do next. *Do I invite him in at this early hour or what?* she wondered, not knowing her aunt's relationship with him.

As if he were reading her mind, he said, "You must be Maggie's niece. She told me you were coming to help her out for a while. Your aunt helps me a lot over at my place, you know."

Savannah *didn't* know. Not yet, anyway. Certainly her Aunt Marg would fill her in on everything she needed to know and probably a lot she would rather not know. But she had only arrived just yesterday and there'd been no time to discuss the neighbors. Savannah, along with Helena, Margaret's housekeeper, had been busy moving her aunt to her temporary bedroom downstairs. Helena had stayed with Margaret for a couple of nights after the accident—both of them sleeping on the living room sofas. While there,

8

Helena made enchiladas and a pan of brownies to keep Margaret and her guest from starving before someone made a grocery-store run. There were also some fresh tomatoes from the garden Margaret's handyman Antonio tended out behind the Forster home.

While Savannah contemplated how to handle the early-morning visitor, she heard her aunt roll up behind her in the rented wheelchair. She opened the door wider and stepped aside.

Margaret peered around her niece to see who she was talking to. "Oh Max. Come in and have a cup of coffee. I see you've met, Vannie—um, Savannah. She's a cat person, too," she said over her shoulder as she turned the chair and wheeled it through the living room and dining room toward the large country kitchen. Savannah and Max followed.

The over-sized cat strolled into the room behind them. He sidled up to Margaret when she stopped near the kitchen table. She reached down to stroke his fur. Looking over at Max, she said, "This is Klepto, AKA Ragsdale."

"What a handsome devil," he said, "with that plush grey tuxedo he's wearing. He's a good-sized cat, isn't he?"

"Yes, he can out-reach most cats," Savannah said as she added more water and grounds to the coffeemaker in order to accommodate their guest.

"And probably leap tall buildings," Margaret added with a hint of sarcasm.

Savannah gave her a playful smirk and then turned to Max. "So you have cats?"

"A few." He winked and then squatted down to get a better look at Rags. "A klepto, you say? What does he steal?"

"I'm still looking for my reading glasses,"

Margaret complained.

Savannah feigned a sheepish look and then changed the subject. "Auntie, where's the princess? I thought I'd wait and feed the two kitties their canned food together. Rags can nibble on kibbles for now."

"Sure. She's probably still enjoying her beauty sleep. Or she's hiding out. She doesn't like strangers much, but she usually acknowledges Max."

"It isn't me, it's my cats. She likes to get acquainted with them, even if only by proxy," he said with a wide grin. He looked over at Savannah. "She has a love affair going on with the enticing feline scents on my shoes."

"Well, she was one of your strays—poor little thing." Margaret turned toward Savannah and said, "When he brought her to me, Vannie, I thought she was a drowned rat. I had to feed the scrawny kitten with an eyedropper. It was touch-and-go for a while. Now look at her—well, you saw her last night. Isn't she a beauty?"

"She sure is," Savannah agreed. "If I hadn't had Rags fixed, I'm sure he would be interested."

"I don't think I'd allow that union," Margaret quipped. "Not with this bad boy cat."

"Well, I think Rags and Layla would make beautiful kittens together," Savannah insisted.

Max suddenly took on a more serious demeanor. "And that's what we don't need—random breeding just to make beautiful kittens. There are already more cats than there are people to love them."

The two women nodded in agreement.

Savannah walked over to the sideboard. She selected three mugs and carried them to the counter, placing them next to the coffeepot. She then removed a chair from around the kitchen table so her aunt could roll up closer. Max took a seat next to Margaret, and Savannah sat opposite him. She looked over at Max. "You know, when I first began to hear all the hype encouraging people to get their cats spayed and neutered, I was actually afraid that cats would become extinct and there would be no more kittens. I mean, a world without kittens—how dismal is that?"

Max looked down at Rags, who was rubbing against his leg. He ran his hand over the cat's coat and gave him a scratch behind the ear. "Dismal indeed," he agreed. And then he leaned back, his eyes focused on something behind Savannah and said, "I was a relative latecomer to the *movement*—if you would call it that. But my grandmother was a woman before her time when it came to the welfare of cats. She was known as the *cat lady*, and I don't think in a kind way. Now she would probably be considered a *hoarder*."

Savannah put an elbow on the table and rested her chin on the palm of her hand. She looked over at Max and asked, "When was this?"

"She had cats from the time I was a small child—in the late 1950s. She was always hauling a cat to the vet to be spayed or neutered or to be treated for an abscess, worms, broken bones—you name it. And it didn't matter if it was her cat or not. Many of the cats wound up as her cats. She had big wire cages out behind her house, full of cats. I loved it. When I was a kid, going to Granny Jeffers was like visiting a zoo—a cat zoo." He paused for a few seconds as if relishing the memory.

Savannah stood and walked over to the counter. "So how did she end up with so many cats?"

"Word got around and people started using her yard as a dumping ground for stray cats or cats they no longer wanted."

"Or maybe cats just found their way to her," Margaret suggested. She looked up at Savannah and explained, "We're finding that stray or abandoned cats seem to have a way of locating colonies where they can get fed and be relatively safe."

"Well, Granny Jeffers sounds like a kitty angel," Savannah said while placing two mugs of steaming coffee on the table. "Cream?" she asked.

"No, black," Max responded. "Thanks."

"You don't use cream, do you, Auntie?"

"Just a tad of sugar." Margaret reached for the cut-glass sugar bowl. And then she said, "Max has followed in his grandmother's footsteps. He has quite a wonderful facility next door."

"Oh, so you rescue cats?" Savannah asked, sitting down at the table with her cup of coffee.

Max wrapped his hands around his coffee mug and stared into the black liquid. "Rescue, treat, rehabilitate, adopt, relocate—whatever it takes."

"He's one of those kitty angels," Margaret quipped.

"If only we could save and protect them all," Max said, suddenly turning sullen. He then glanced up and sat back in his chair. "Sorry ladies, I didn't mean to gloom up your morning."

\*\*\*

Meanwhile in another part of town, two fourteen-year-old boys stood on a corner. The taller one pulled his jacket collar up around his ears which were covered by a dark knit cap. He peered up and down the street. "So do you think that guy will show?"

The second boy scrunched his hands deep into the pockets of his hooded sweatshirt. "Heck, who knows. He's one creepy guy. But the work's not bad for the pay."

"Yeah, if we don't get caught." The first boy looked up in time to see a vehicle slowing. "That's him. You get in first."

"Why?"

"Just friggin' do it," he said in a loud whisper as the automobile stopped alongside the pair and the passenger door swung open.

"Git in, kids; we don't have all day," the man inside said impatiently. He didn't seem to notice the elbow-nudging and face contortions of his two passengers as they silently communicated their disgust at his body odor.

*This is one day I'll be glad to get to school,* thought the taller boy. *This guy friggin' stinks.*

The smaller boy had the displeasure of sitting closest to the grubby man. *Phew! I hope we score and earn some money fast. I can't wait to get outta here.*

The driver was silent, as well, caught up in his own thoughts. *Stupid kids. Stupid job. I'm gonna git what I'm owed one way or t'other, so I don't hafta do this shit no more.*

\*\*\*

"It's okay, Max," Margaret crooned while leaning forward and placing a hand of comfort on his arm. "We'll get to the bottom of this. You know we will."

"What's going on, Auntie?" Savannah asked quietly.

"We'll talk about it, later. In fact, you may learn more about human nature before the week is out than you ever wanted to know." She gave her niece a knowing wink.

*I should have expected there would be more to this visit than playing nursemaid for my aunt,* Savannah thought to herself.

"Well, good morning, Lady Layla," Max said in a sing-song voice as Margaret's faux golden Persian strolled in, looked around the room, and headed for Max's shoes.

Rags, who had been lounging nearby, jumped to his paws and greeted her, as well. At least he tried to be cordial. His attempt at rubbing up against her was met with a hiss.

The visiting cat seemed puzzled by Layla's reaction to his friendly overtures and he sat down, cocked his head, and stared at her, as if contemplating his next move.

*Time to intervene, lest we wear out our welcome,* Savannah thought. "Auntie, why don't you two visit? I'll be down in a minute. I want to hear more about your cats, Max. Come on, Rags." She motioned for the cat to follow, as if he actually understood. Maybe he did, for he ran after her into the living room and bounded up the stairs ahead of her. When she neared the top of the wide staircase, she noticed that he sat waiting for her on the landing. "Show off," she said with a laugh. She stared into his quizzical face for a few seconds and then, in a more serious tone, she asked, "Now I want to know, where did you put Auntie Marg's glasses, you naughty boy?"

As Savannah rounded the corner into her guestroom, Rags leaped onto the bed, walked over to the headboard and stretched up as tall as he could toward the window. She put her hands on her hips and scolded, "Rags, move on. I want to make the bed."

He responded by jumping in the middle of the bed, rolling onto his side, grabbing a wad of the sheet

14

between his front paws, and kicking at it playfully. Savannah wanted to be annoyed, but couldn't help laughing at his antics. She picked up the pencil she'd used to work a crossword puzzle the night before and tossed it on the floor. Just as she thought he would, the frisky cat dove off the bed after it. She took that opportunity to pull the blankets up and cover them with the handmade quilt that had adorned the spare rooms in Aunt Marg's homes for years. Savannah had lost track of who made the now slightly faded patchwork quilt—a great-grand or great-aunt somebody. But she remembered having seen it in every house her aunt had lived in since Savannah was old enough to notice the intricate design of the pretty pastel-print fabrics. In fact, the pattern became imprinted in her memory the summer old Jed Forster died in a barn fire on the property.

The Brannon siblings and their families had all converged on Tom and Margaret's home for a weeklong stay. Savannah had just turned eleven; her sister Brianna was nine. The two girls shared this room with their twin girl cousins Melanie and Roxy, while the boy cousins slept on the screened-in porch. Each set of parents had their own rooms. Since Savannah was the oldest of the children, she got her own bed. The others shared beds and used sleeping bags. At that time, Savannah was devouring *Nancy Drew* and *Hardy Boy* mystery books. She was practically addicted to suspense and anything mysterious. And she had a rather morbid curiosity about the details of her great-uncle's demise. She took every opportunity that week to listen when the adults spoke about the details of the deadly fire that had occurred a month or so earlier. One detail she wishes to this day she hadn't heard was the speculation and possibility that someone had set the fire on purpose and killed the old man.

That was her first lesson in the dangers of eavesdropping. Yes, she remembered the quilt. *I could probably describe every inch of it if I had to in a court of law, after lying awake staring at it every night that week afraid that the murderer would come back and burn me alive inside this big, old wood-frame house,* she thought. *I wonder what ever happened to the clue we found the day we were digging around out there in the fire area. We should have told someone about it, but we didn't want to get into trouble for going near the burned-down barn. It was off-limits to us kids, and way too tempting for a junior sleuth like me to ignore.*

As Savannah pulled a soft blue tee shirt and a pair of her comfiest jeans out of the suitcase, she remembered something else. Her two boy cousins, Jake and Jimmy, hid the clue the day they all left for home. *Oh my gosh, I remember where they hid it. Could it still be there?*

Her thoughts were interrupted by her aunt's voice over the room-to-room intercom. "Savannah, your coffee's getting cold and Layla is hungry."

"I'll be right down," Savannah called into the speaker. *I should unpack and hang up my clothes,* she considered. And then, *Later,* she decided. *I want to hear more about Max's cats.* She stopped, a thoughtful look crossing her face. *And what did Auntie mean about getting to the bottom of it? The bottom of what? It's obviously something about cats...and human nature. Max and Aunt Marg seem so concerned. What could be going on?*

She rushed into the bathroom to wash up and brush her teeth, then took the knot out of her hair and ran a brush through it while Rags lapped at the stream of water coming from the spigot. She secured her hair

16

in a ponytail and hurriedly donned the clothes she'd set out. With the cat leading the way, Savannah jogged down the staircase. Her first stop was at her aunt's temporary bedroom. She turned over shoes, poked around in the bathroom again and lifted the dust ruffle to look under the bed. She peered into the various little dishes and other containers on the two dressers and checked the drawer and shelves on the nightstand.

*Oh wait, Auntie Marg saw Rags climbing out of her lingerie drawer. What was he doing in there—depositing something?* She pulled the drawer open and felt carefully through the silky unmentionables—*bingo!* She worked her fingers through some folded fabric and pulled out a pair of glasses. *Boy, will Auntie Marg be pleased. I saw her relying on these a lot last night as we looked through some old photo albums.* Savannah smiled. *That was a nice walk down memory lane—seeing pictures of the family when I lived here many years ago. That was before Margaret married Tom Forster.*

Margaret was the only Brannon left in their hometown. She'd followed her second husband back there after meeting him at a class reunion. He was a member of an earlier graduating class and had come to the reunion with his younger cousin. He and Margaret hit it off right away. She'd been single for five years, when they married. After his parents died, they moved into the old Forster place to take care of his grandfather, Jed Forster. Fourteen years later, Margaret became a widow, and, when there was no opposition from other family members, she inherited the property.

*I can see why no one else in the Forster family wanted this old place. It's charming and all, but there's so much upkeep. Auntie always did like a challenge.* Savannah sighed as she looked around the room—one of several that had yet to be refurbished.

"What are you doing, Rags? Get out of that drawer," Savannah said as she put the glasses on her own nose so she could scoop up the persistently curious cat. She noticed a pair of panties dangling from one of his claws. "Let go, Rags, darn it!" After helping Rags retract his claw from the silky undergarment, she dropped the cat onto the bed with a slight reprimand. She then bent down to pick up a piece of paper she'd seen drop out of the drawer. *It appears to be something a child wrote,* she thought, until she looked more closely.

"YOU DO NOT BLONG!" Savannah read while peering over the rim of her aunt's purple-framed reading glasses. There was a crude drawing of a skull and bones under the wording. *Blong?* Savannah pondered. *Oh, Belong. "You Do Not Belong." What does that mean?*

"What's taking you so long, Vannie?" her aunt called from the kitchen. "Your coffee's cold now."

"I'm coming, Auntie," she replied while placing the strange note back into the corner of the drawer.

She was still subdued and solemn as she entered the large kitchen, so was taken aback when her aunt began to chuckle. "Hmmm, they actually look good on you," she said. "Where did you find them?"

"Oh." Savannah stopped and shook her head slightly, attempting to regain her bearings. She'd have to ask her aunt about the note, later. Definitely, she would do that. There had to be an explanation. "Your glasses..." She lifted them off her face and handed them to her aunt. "Rags put them in your lingerie drawer."

"Ragsdale..." Margaret scolded. "What are we going to do with you? I have enough trouble keeping
18

track of things without you moving them about. Max, in all of your wanderings with cats, have you ever known a klepto?"

"Yes, one." His ruggedly chiseled face took on a pensive look. "She belonged to my ex-wife. She once stole my wallet and I never did find that sucker. I had to cancel my credit cards and get a new driver's license...and maybe it wasn't the cat at all, but Rebecca capitalizing on the cat's behavior. Before that, all Miss Kitty took was jewelry, tea bags, and Post-its." He started to laugh and then said, "She had a fixation with the fax machine. When she'd hear it ring, she'd run in there and wait for the fax to roll out." He became animated as he continued, "She loved paper. If we weren't around to stop her, she would carry the fax off and shred it." Max took a swig of coffee then set his cup down before saying, "The cat had some endearing qualities, but Elmer and I were not all that sad to see either her or my ex-wife go."

"Elmer?" Savannah asked, while dropping dollops of cat food from a can on two little plates.

"The other family cat," he explained.

After putting the cats' breakfast on their placemat, Savannah tasted her coffee and then headed for the microwave to warm it up. She picked up the carafe and offered a refill to Margaret and her guest.

"Just a little," Max said.

"So tell me, Max, where do your cats come from? Are they strays? Do you work with local shelters or cat colonies?"

"See, I told you she was savvy about rescue operations," Margaret boasted. "She's a veterinarian, you know."

Savannah placed the carafe back on the warmer with her right hand while waving her left one in front of her attempting to erase what her aunt had just said. "Not a practicing one, yet." She took her cup out of the microwave, then turned and leaned against the kitchen counter. "I work in a large clinic in Los Angeles as a tech."

Max nodded and smiled. "Cool. Do you specialize or is it an all-animal clinic?"

"We have a variety of patients—dogs, rabbits, iguanas, boas—you name it. Personally, I'm partial to the cats." Savannah twirled a few loose strands of her hair around her index finger. She then added, "I adore horses, but not so much from a medical perspective—more as a rider or handler. If I had the land, I could see myself opening a horse-rescue facility."

Max chuckled. "Now there's an ambitious goal." He looked over at Margaret. "Can you imagine cleaning up after a dozen or so horses every day and trying to teach them manners in order to make them adoptable?"

"Well, I'll tell ya, there are days when it seems like we're cleaning up after horses and there are some cats that come with some mighty big challenges," Margaret reminded him.

The trio remained silent, all eyes on Rags, who was cleaning himself up after his meal.

"Why are you standing, Vannie? Sit down. Relax," Margaret insisted. "We have a big day—er… week ahead."

"Well, Auntie, someone has taken over my chair and her name could be Goldilocks," Savannah cooed as she peered into Layla's sweet face as the little cat licked one of her paws and rubbed it over her ear.

She reached down and began scratching the little cat under the chin. Once Layla was completely relaxed—eyes closed, chin raised and purring ever so softly—someone else joined in. Rags reached up and rested his paws on the chair seat, watching the resident cat with interest. Savannah lifted him away from the chair. "Okay, down you go, Ragsy. Let's sit over here, shall we, boy?" She pulled out an empty chair and sat down. Rags continued to stare at Layla.

"Max has a way with cats," Margaret interjected. "I've seen him take wild ones and domesticate them into pets. It's uncanny watching him work. He's our very own cat whisperer. Maybe he can whisper in Ragsdale's ear and change his thieving ways," she said while laughing out loud.

Max reached out to smooth the cat's fur as he sauntered past on quiet paws. "I wouldn't change a thing about this guy. He's one-of-a-kind—so confident and curious. He seems to be interested in everything and everyone around him."

"Yes, he doesn't miss much. Likes to be in the loop. I give him outdoor time at home in order to help him burn off some of that energy. Otherwise, he keeps me awake at night racing around the room, bouncing on the bed, playing with things and breaking things." Savannah chuckled. "I've had to Rags-proof my apartment since acquiring him because he was so bent on reorganizing it."

"How does he get along with the neighbors?" When Savannah looked puzzled, Max explained, "I mean him being a cat burglar and all…"

"Oh that. Well, I do spend many weekends walking around the neighborhood with a basket full of stuffed toys, sunglasses, bikini tops and bottoms, pencils, gloves, kids' shoes, socks—just about anything he can carry. The funny thing is, he walks along with me as if helping me find the rightful owners. Yes, he is a kick. Keeps me laughing."

Savannah leaned toward Max. "You must smile a lot in your line of work—finding homes for so many stray and feral cats. What a satisfying pastime."

"Yeah, they aren't all warm fuzzy success stories," Max admitted with a hint of melancholy. "But we do all we can to place each of them in forever homes."

"And he keeps some of the cats, don't you? You've had Sammy and Grizwold forever."

"Yes," Max responded, "and Missy, Gretchen and Big Boy. They're all virtually unadoptable. Missy's almost blind, Gretchen never did become gentle enough, even to work as a barn cat. Plus she isn't much of a hunter, so would not survive long. Big Boy and Grizwold—well, I grew too attached to part with them. They are good for the cats we bring in. They mentor those that need a good role model in the behavior department. Sammy's disabled." Max grinned and said as if sharing a secret, "Just don't tell him that. He gets around on two paws every bit as well as any able cat."

He took a sip of coffee and then asked Savannah, "How long will you be here? Maybe you'd like to come over and see the place."

"I'd love to," Savannah gushed. "I'll be here for as long as Aunt Marg needs me." She smiled toward her aunt, saying, "…a week or ten days, maybe, if she can put up with Rags and me."

"Or vice-versa." Margaret smiled. Her demeanor then took on a more serious tone. "Max, speaking of challenges with cats, how did things go at the emergency meeting last night? Have any of the cats been found?"

"I'm afraid not," Max said, leaning back in his chair. He let out a long sigh. "We seem to be at a dead end with that situation." He looked hard at Margaret.

"I'm really concerned." He then glanced over at Savannah and asked, "Has your aunt told you what's going on?"

Margaret was quick to respond, "Not yet. We'll have a little talk later today."

Promptly, Max stood, drained his coffee cup, and walked over to the kitchen counter to set it down. "Thanks for the coffee and the visit." He nodded in the direction of the ladies as he made his way toward the side kitchen door. "I have work to do—I want to make sure that Glen and Becky get the pens washed out with bleach. We had a suspected case of feline leukemia come in yesterday. Someone put a kitten in a common pen instead of isolation. I think it was one of our new volunteers." He started to leave and then turned. "Oh Maggie, can you and Savannah still pick up the kittens at the vet this afternoon?"

"Sure, Max. We'll be there after two. Okay with you, Vannie?"

Savannah's voice oozed with enthusiasm, "Kittens? Absolutely!"

"Great, then you'll be able to tour the place," Max said with a wide smile. "See you later," he called over his shoulder as he started to open the door to leave. But, he hesitated. "Hey there, big guy, I don't think they want you outside."

Savannah jumped up and darted toward the cat, who was rubbing himself against Max's legs. She picked him up. "Rags, no you don't. Goodbye Max," she said as the door closed. She gently tossed the cat out in front of her and watched him trot off. "Hmmm, interesting man," she said. She then turned to face her aunt and asked with an impish twinkle in her eye, "Is he the one you wear the silky lingerie for, Auntie?"

"Maybe and maybe not," Margaret teased. "Hey,

I have to see the doctor this morning. You don't mind driving me do you? If the swelling has gone down enough, I might get a cast."

Savannah rubbed her stomach. "What about breakfast? I'm getting hungry. Can I fix you something?"

Margaret pushed herself away from the table. "I'll treat you at my favorite place downtown. How about that?"

"Okay. Here, let me help you." Savannah took hold of the handles on the back of the wheelchair and started to push her aunt out of the kitchen.

"Ooooomph! Rags!" Margaret scolded as the cat jumped up on her lap and sat down ready for the ride. "Now that's one lazy cat." Both women laughed out loud.

*** 

"So things went well with your doctor, Auntie?"

"Yes, I'm thankful I don't need surgery. The thought of having a pin rammed into my bone turns my stomach." Margaret shuddered, as she rested the crutches next to her against the plastic booth seat.

"Well, if you continue to do what the doctor orders, you'll most certainly avoid that discomfort. So take advantage of me while I'm here. No monkey business," Savannah warned good naturedly.

"Whatever do you mean—I've been good, haven't I?" The older woman looked coyly at her niece.

"Surprisingly, so far," Savannah agreed. "But you do have a reputation, you know."

Margaret opened her mouth to protest when the server appeared with menus and a pot of coffee. "This conversation is not over," Margaret threatened from

24

across the table in a hushed voice.

"Hi Maggie, what happened to you? You were on all twos when I saw you at the auction last week."

"Good morning, Iris. I'm afraid I broke something in my foot a couple of days ago while out in the yard. Didn't seem like a big deal at the time, but x-rays showed a fracture. So my niece, Vannie, drove up from LA to help me get around."

"Oh, nice." She paused and then said, "I mean, Sorry to hear about the accident, but nice to have a visitor because of it. Hey wait," the waitress stared at Savannah and pointed in her direction with a menu, "aren't you Gladys's and Ted's daughter?"

"Yes," Savannah said, obviously surprised.

"This is Savannah. Savannah, Iris and I went to school together many years ago," Margaret explained.

"Hi. You know my family?"

"Hell yes. Didn't everyone? I think every teen in town worked for your father's company and his father's before that for at least three generations. Those Jordans helped to give many a kid work-ethic training and spending money." She looked down and shook her head. "It was a shame when your dad sold the company. It never held the same values again."

Savannah was touched by the waitress's genuine display of remorse. Before she could comment, Iris perked up and said, "I remember when you and your sister used to come in here for lunch with your dad now and then." An inquisitive look on her face, she asked, "Are you the vet or the doc?"

"I work as a vet tech in a large animal hospital," Savannah said trying not to sound like she was apologizing for not running her own practice, yet.

"Order up!" someone shouted from the window behind the counter.

Iris twisted her body in that direction. "Oh, that's me." She quickly laid the menus on the table and asked, "Coffee?"

"Uh, I think I'll have a glass of orange juice—and water, too, please," Savannah said.

"Coffee for me," Margaret stated. "With cream."

As Iris walked away, Savannah asked—a puzzled look on her face, "Cream?"

"Sometimes yes and sometimes no." She leaned in toward her niece and whispered, "The coffee here's strong. I have to cut it with something and they don't serve hard liquor." Margaret sat back, picked up her menu and gave it a quick look. "By the way, I recommend the blueberry waffles."

"Fresh blueberries?"

"Yeowza, picked this morning—or maybe yesterday…"

"Mmmm, sounds good. That's what I'll have, then."

"Me, too." Margaret placed her menu on the table edge. She then looked across at her niece in a piercing stare and demanded to know, "Now what do you mean I have a reputation? Who says?"

"Oh, your older sister, your younger sister, Uncle Ray…" Savannah started.

"Baloney. They're just a bunch of fuddy-duddies with no sense of adventure."

Margaret had always been the most daring of the three sisters. Even her brother, who was four years older, couldn't match her bravado as a child.

"Yeah, that's probably it," Savannah patronized. "They're just a bunch of fuddy-duddies." She then leaned toward her aunt, her demeanor more serious. "So what's up with the group Max was talking about? What were you going to tell me later?"

26

The two women pulled back from their conversation while Iris placed their drinks in front of them. The waitress then took a pencil from her dyed red hair and wrote down their orders.

When Iris left, Margaret looked over at her niece. *Dare I talk to her about this? She already thinks I'm a bit over the edge.*

"Come on, Auntie, I'm going to find out one way or another. What's going on?" Savannah prodded.

After stirring a little cream into her coffee and glancing around the room to her left, Margaret took a swig, put the cup down and leaned forward toward her niece. "We have reason to believe that someone is snatching cats."

"What cats?" Savannah asked, way too curious to feign disinterest.

Margaret turned in her seat and looked around the restaurant. After making a mental note of who was there, she settled back down in the booth and said, "Let's eat and then I'll take you for a drive, and show you what's going on."

"How about if I take you, since you can't drive right now?" Savannah reminded.

"Yeah, yeah. You drive. Whatever..."

Savannah relaxed in the plastic booth and scanned the room with her eyes. Yes, she remembered this place. She felt so grown up when she'd come here for lunch with her dad. "Isn't this where we had your surprise birthday party a few years ago, Auntie?"

"Yeah, some surprise, all right—for you and your mother. That'll teach you to try second-guessing me. Gladys may have a predictable lifestyle, but that isn't me," Margaret blurted.

Savannah remembered all too well traveling the 500 miles north with her mother and being stood up.

Unbeknownst to them, Aunt Margaret had chosen that week to take a cruise with an eligible bachelor she had met at a ballroom-dancing class.

Savannah's eyes rested again on her aunt. *Yes, she is an adventurer—always was and always will be, no doubt*, she thought with a smile. The only one who came close to inheriting Margaret's penchant for adventure was Savannah's own younger sister. Brianna lived on the edge as much as any med student might. She was a fun-loving, energetic young woman. She didn't just give lip service to causes, she got out there and worked toward what she believed in at the moment. She'd even been arrested a few times, which didn't sit well with their mother. Aunt Margaret, though, snuck in a high-five and a "you go, girl," when she'd hear about one of Brianna's escapades. Margaret had even tried to convince her less Bohemian sister to let Brianna follow her heart and hitchhike through Europe one year, staying in backpackers' hostels. Savannah remembered her aunt saying, "How do you expect this girl to sow her wild oats before marriage if she continues to live under your thumb? And believe me, this girl has wild oats to sow."

Savannah usually enjoyed watching her aunt intervene on behalf of herself and her sister. Her mom could be overprotective, even when the girls became of age—especially after their dad passed away. Aunt Margaret could always suggest a more interesting alternative to Gladys's typically rigid perspective.

Savannah, although certainly moved by conflicts between good and evil and right and wrong, generally weighed the consequences of her actions with a more precise scale than her younger sister did. Savannah was known to snatch kittens from bullies more than once, fully prepared to defend a kitten to the end. She

28

intervened when she noticed a neighbor, friend, or coworker in need. But she wasn't generally the sort to join vigilante groups or to challenge legal boundaries in order to make a statement. *Maybe I just haven't been presented with a strong enough reason to challenge boundaries,* she thought.

\*\*\*

*Looks like the bitch is gone somewhere.* He didn't see evidence that the gardener was there, either, so he decided to pull into the driveway and leave another message. He stopped in front of the large house and set the parking brake. Without turning off the key, he stepped out of the driver's side door, scanned the property with his deep-set eyes, and thought to himself, *It's mine. All mine. Soon. Very soon.* He then looked down at the object in his hand, raised it over his right shoulder, and threw it with all his might toward the house. Upon hearing the crack and clatter of glass breaking, he glanced around and then quickly slipped back into the vehicle. He started to leave, when something caught his eye. *What's that in the upstairs window?* he wondered. *A cat! A grey-and-white cat. Now there's an opportunity I didn't expect to come by.* He opened the truck door and started to step out, but changed his mind. *No, not now, next time. Yes, that'll be the next cat to disappear,* he thought, a sinister smile playing on his lips.

\*\*\*

"That was a filling breakfast," Savannah remarked while helping her aunt settle into the passenger seat of Margaret's Jeep Liberty. "Where are we going now?"

"Toward the old dump," Margaret responded without inflection. "Do you remember how to get there?"

"Sure," Savannah said as she slid into the driver's seat. "That's where Dad used to take me scavenging. Brianna and I found all sorts of neat things out there."

Margaret wrinkled up her nose. "What kind of things?"

"Everything you can imagine—hair barrettes, pencils, wheels off toy cars, marbles, sun glasses—I used to love finding sun glasses cause I was always losing mine." She glanced over at her aunt, saying, "Once I found a pipe like the one old Mr. Forster used to smoke."

"You remember Grandpa's pipe? You were pretty young when he passed," Margaret calculated.

"I was eleven when he died. And that pipe of his used to fascinate me—that, and the fact that he was always looking for his eyeglasses. He'd say, 'Hey, Skiddle, have you seen my specs?' Remember how he called me Skiddle and Brianna was Doodlebug? The funny thing is, his glasses were always right there on top of his head."

The two women laughed.

Savannah glanced over at her aunt, hesitated for a moment and then started, "Auntie, about his death, did they ever determine…?"

# Chapter 2

"Here. Turn right here—we're going up on that knoll," Margaret said with the giddiness of a teenager on her way to a weekend party.

"Oh, those houses down there are new," Savannah remarked.

"Yes. Now stop up there near that brush."

Savannah looked around at their rather barren surroundings and asked, "Why are you whispering? There's no one up here."

"Just pull over," Margaret instructed. "I think we have a good enough view." She leaned forward and reached under her seat. "Where are those things?"

"What things? What are we doing out here?" Savannah wanted to know.

"Is there a pair of binoculars under your seat?"

Savannah felt around under her seat and pulled out a fairly large pair of Bushnells. A puzzled look on her face, she cocked her head slightly and asked, "What are we going to do with these? Spy on people?" She chuckled as she handed them over to her aunt.

"We sure are." Margaret held the glasses up to her eyes and began scanning the area. After a few seconds, she put them down and reached over to the console, pushing the window buttons for the driver's and passenger's side windows until they were all the way down. "Go ahead and shut off the engine, would you, Vannie?" She then turned toward her niece and said, "We believe that someone is coming out to these new tract areas and picking up cats. Not strays or ferals, but people's pets."

Savannah's expression changed to one of concern. "Oh, that's what Max mentioned this morning. That's awful. What are they doing with them?"

31

"We don't know," she said staring out across the terrain. "The cats are just disappearing without a trace."

Savannah looked around. "Maybe it's coyotes—this is kind of a wilderness area."

"We don't think so. There are quite a few cats missing now and no one has seen a coyote near here recently. Anyway, the cats seem to be going missing during the day—early morning and late in the afternoon. All these cats stay in at night." She looked over at her niece before continuing, "We're having an emergency meeting of the HCA tomorrow morning at my house. We hope some of the residents have something new to report that will help us figure out what's going on."

"HCA?" Savannah queried.

"Hammond Cat Alliance," Margaret explained, as she raised the glasses to her eyes again.

"You've formed an alliance for cats? That's cool." Savannah smiled. She then took on a more somber demeanor. "So you think someone is taking the cats?" She thought for a moment and then suggested, "Could be some deranged professor out at the college collecting cats for the science lab. I knew a few odd ones at vet school."

Margaret let the binoculars drop to her lap. "Who knows? There are a lot of theories out there—witchcraft rituals, cat haters in the neighborhood..." She gazed out over the housing tract and shook her head slowly from side to side.

"Are the police involved?"

Margaret turned quickly toward her niece. "Pshaw, Vannie. You know as well as I do that, while the police may respond to a stolen-dog call, the only thing they're apt to help with when it comes to a cat is getting it out of a tree. And then they call the fire

32

department."

"Really?" Savannah asked with interest. "Cats are being stolen and the cops won't do anything?"

Margaret put the binoculars back up to her eyes and scanned the streets below. "We're not sure they're being stolen, yet. That's why we have surveillance going on at all hours of the day. Even if we do find out that someone's stealing the cats and who's doing it, we still may have to take things into our own hands."

Savannah looked confused. "Why?" she asked. Before Margaret could answer, her niece straightened up and stared into the rearview mirror. "Oh, Auntie, we have company. The sheriff's here."

"Drats!" Margaret said as she quickly stuffed the Bushnells under her seat. She watched through the right side mirror as the deputy walked up to her open window.

"Good morning, ladies," he greeted. "Well, Maggie, I thought this was your car. Haven't seen you since the dance last month." He nodded toward Savannah. "Hello Miss." Turning his attention back to Margaret, he said, "What are you doing out here? Is everything okay?"

She smiled at the officer. "Yeah, Jim, we're just enjoying the scenery. You see, my niece here, Savannah, used to live in Hammond. Her dad ran Jordan's Farm Equipment for years. I'm showing her some of the new tracts. Things haven't changed much over time, but enough so as a hometown girl would notice."

He looked out over the valley of homes, rubbed his chin and, attempting to make eye contact with Margaret, said, "That's where the cats have come up missing, isn't it?"

She squirmed a little in her seat and looked

away. "Now, Jim, you know we've gotta get to the bottom of this. Someone may be hurting cats. There *is* a law against cruelty to animals, you know."

"Sure I know, and I like cats as much as the next guy, but it isn't our job to investigate situations like this—not until we have some real evidence. This should be turned over to the animal humane league. Do you know what I mean, Maggie?" he asked. She nodded and looked down. The deputy continued, "We don't know what we're dealing with here and I don't want you or any other members of your group to get hurt."

He stared at his feet for a few moments and then said, "Are you aware that there's a cat hoarder over west of the interstate?"

Margaret's demeanor gained energy. "No, I didn't. What's her name?"

"Oh, I think you can get that information on your own—just ask at the nearest pet supply store."

She then looked up at him apprehensively and asked, "There isn't any dog fighting going on, is there?"

"Not anymore," he said with a hint of satisfaction. He then rapped on the door frame twice, saying, "Well, be safe, ladies. Nice to meet you, Savannah." He started to turn away and then changed his mind. "Maggie, I understand you broke your foot. Sorry to hear about that. I guess we won't see you at the dance this weekend."

"Oh don't be surprised. How else will I snag my niece a beau if I don't take her out dancing?" she said, obviously amused at the idea.

"Auntie Marg!" Savannah scolded.

Jim laughed and then his tone turned serious. "Maggie, I heard there might have been foul play with your injury. Is that right?"

Margaret glanced quickly in her niece's

direction and then looked down at the floorboards. "Oh that's just one of those rumors. I'm sure it was strictly an accident."

The deputy stared over at Margaret for a few moments and then said, "Well, you call me if anything else suspicious happens. Will you do that?"

"Sure will. See you at the dance, Jim. Thanks," Margaret said as he walked away.

Once she saw the deputy enter his car, Savannah turned toward her aunt and looked intently at her. "Suspicious? Foul play? Auntie, what's going on?"

"We'll talk about it later, Vannie," she said, speaking rapidly now. "Come one, girl, let's head over to the strip mall on the other side of the interstate."

\*\*\*

The two women found a clerk stacking forty-pound bags of kitty litter on a shelf in the back of Wayne's Pet Supply. Leaning on her crutches, her casted foot bent up behind her, Margaret said, "Hello. I'm looking for a friend of mine—only I can't recall her name—you know how it is when you get older and rattled," she feigned to the twenty-something employee. "She has cats—lots of them—and she told me she lives out this direction; I just can't remember the street name."

Savannah shot a slightly disgusted look at Margaret, thinking, *Auntie, you can do better than that. You aren't anywhere near old enough to be that confused.*

The slender young man thought for a second before picking up another bag of litter. He plopped it on the stack, then looked over at Margaret. "Do you mean Ms. Lipton? Comes in here all the time. She has lots of cats." He tugged on the top of the bag to straighten it.

"She must have twenty or thirty of them. She lives over on Birch. I make deliveries to her house sometimes." He removed one glove and wiped his brow with the back of his hand. "Can't exactly tell you the number, but it's East Birch."

"East Birch," Margaret repeated while watching him put the glove back on.

"Yes," he said, reaching for another bag. He then remembered something and straightened up to face Margaret. "Oh, and she has a couple of flags flying with cats on them. She really likes cats." He grabbed the next bag and stacked it, saying, "But you know that since she's a friend."

"Yes, we met at a cat writers' convention," Margaret lied.

"Well, if you see her, would you tell her the cat food she likes is on sale? I know she'll want to stock up."

"Oh, is that right? How about if I buy some and take it to her? She'll like that, won't she?" Margaret asked.

"Sure, I guess. It's this feed over here," he said walking down the aisle toward a large display of cat food. "She buys the fifty-pound bags."

"Can you load two twenty-five-pound bags in the car—Savannah would you open the back? I'll go pay up front. Thank you…" Margaret looked at the young man's name tag. "Jason. Thanks a lot, Jason."

\*\*\*

Margaret pointed up the street. "It must be the two-story up there on the left. I see flags. And, oh, there are cats on the porch. Hmmm, she lets them out? That's kind of unusual for a hoarder. But they come in all sizes, shapes

36

and flavors, I guess."

"So how do you expect to get in, Auntie?" Savannah wondered.

"You just watch me. I can talk my way in. Maybe I'll pretend to be an employee of the pet store. How about that?"

"I mean, how are you going to get up those steep stairs on your crutches? And what employee of a pet store is going to deliver something in your condition?" she said with a smirk.

Margaret snapped her fingers. "Drats. Didn't think of that. Oh wait. Maybe that's her over by the side of the house. Looks like she's trying to lure cats out from under the porch." In a burst of excitement, Margaret promptly opened the car door, set the tips of her crutches on the ground, and edged forward until she was standing on her good foot. Savannah was already there to give her a hand. Margaret was doing pretty well on the crutches, but getting out of a car or up from furniture was strenuous for her. Besides, she had the extra nuisance of a new cast on her foot and the uneven terrain in this yard.

As soon as she was standing, Margaret called out, "Hello there! Hello! Are you Ms. Lipton?"

The diminutive woman stood and peered around the corner of the house. "Yes," she said softly.

"I'm Margaret and this is Savannah from the Hammond Cat Alliance. We heard that you were feeding a lot of cats and we wanted to help with that. We brought a couple of bags of food."

"Well, how nice of you," the woman said, an inquisitive look on her face. "You're from where? How did you find out about my cats?"

"Hammond Cat Alliance. We're all about helping cats. And it looks like that's what you're doing here. Look at that beauty!" Margaret nodded toward a striking calico shorthair on the top step of the porch. "Absolutely regal. And isn't he handsome?" She pointed a crutch in the direction of three cats sunning themselves on the wide porch. You obviously take good care of them," Margaret said generously. *Unless these cats are in good shape when you steal them,* she thought to herself.

"How nice of you to say that. Not everyone likes cats, you know. I have neighbors who complain about them," she said shaking her head in disbelief. And then she perked up and asked, "Would you like to come in and see the others? I can fix us a cup of tea."

Margaret smiled. "That would be lovely, Ms. Lipton. But I don't think I can manage those stairs on these things." She nodded toward the crutches. "… unless you have another way in."

"It's Dora," she offered. "Yes, come around this way. We can go in on the ground floor. We should see most of the cats in that area, anyway." Margaret noticed that the woman didn't seem as feeble as she did upon first acknowledging them. Perhaps she was eager to have human company. Or maybe she just enjoyed showing off her cats.

Savannah walked to the back of the car and took out one bag of cat food. She called after Dora, "Where do you want this?"

"We'd better bring it in the house and put it in the pantry. Any bag of food left out is fair game for naughty cats, if you know what I mean," she said with a chuckle. Dora motioned for the women to walk ahead of her and then she edged over to the far side of the front yard and began clapping her hands together gently, saying, "Come on kitties—time to go inside. Boomer, Lily, Bramble, Smokey—treat time."

38

As if they understood every word she said, all four of the porch cats scurried down from their sunny perch and scampered along the pathway. After pushing through a kitty door flap at the left of the ground-floor door, the foursome disappeared into the house.

"Wow, that's impressive," Savannah said as they walked through the door into the kitchen. "Are all of your cats that obedient?"

"Oh my, no!" Dora laughed as she rushed to place a plastic cover over the kitty door. She then walked across the kitchen toward another door which led to the rest of the downstairs area. "Some of the others will want to make your acquaintance, I'm sure. It's okay if they come in, isn't it?" she asked before turning the knob.

"Of course," the two women said in unison.

"Where do you want this?" Savannah asked, referring to the bag of cat food she held in her arms.

"In here, dear." Dora, who now seemed more wiry and agile than fragile and frail, motioned toward the pantry. She then rushed over to the kitchen table and pulled out a chair. "Please sit down...Margaret, is it?"

"Yes, thank you," Margaret said as she eased into the straight-back chair.

Savannah looked around in the oversized pantry. "Gosh, you do have a lot of cat supplies on hand, don't you?"

"I try to keep stocked up. I never know when I'll be receiving more fur kids," she said with a laugh. "And I take advantage of sales and coupons."

"So how do you get the cats? Where do they come from?" Margaret blurted, eager to nail the culprit in the catnapping.

As Dora filled the teakettle with water and set it on the stove, she explained, "Well, some are strays.

Some are remnants of cat-hoarder situations. You know how it is." She turned to face her guests. "Once people know you can't turn a cat away, they tend to take advantage of you. In fact, I'm afraid I'll have to say no to some cats in the near future. I hear there's a hoarder not too far away from here. Animal control has been monitoring the situation, and it doesn't look good. It appears that they'll soon be placing the healthier cats when they close this couple down and my space and energy are so limited."

"Do you often let the cats out in front?" Savannah asked as she joined her aunt at the table.

"No. Only those four you saw outside just now can come out with me while I garden or enjoy lemonade on the porch." She pushed her dark-rimmed glasses up on her nose with an index finger. "I was hoping they would help me catch a sweet little girl who found her way under my porch. I've been trying to lure her out so I can check her over and decide what to do with her. She was just about to walk toward the saucer of milk when…"

"Oh we scared her back in? I'm sorry." Margaret grimaced. "Maybe we can help you draw her out before we leave."

"Don't worry about it," Dora said, waving a hand in the air. "I spend my life working with cats and they each have a way of their own. I think I was put on this planet to learn patience, because it sure takes a big dose of it when you live with cats." She looked over at her guests and asked, "Do you ladies have cats?"

"Yes," Margaret said. "Both of us have rescue cats. But there was a time when I had eleven cats. I just couldn't stop bringing them home or letting them stay when they showed up on my property. Know what I mean?"

40

"I sure do." Dora reached over, took three teabags out of a porcelain container, and dropped them into the pot of hot water.

"So do you have anyone helping you with your cats?" Margaret wondered.

"Oh yes. I couldn't manage them alone. A couple of my friends volunteer here nearly every day and I have a dear child who works with me three afternoons a week." She glanced up at the kitchen clock while wiping her hands on her blue paisley apron. "In fact, Charlotte should be arriving just about any time."

Margaret looked around the room. "Well, you would never know you have multiple cats in here. How many are there?"

"Hmmmm, the number changes," Dora said as she considered how to respond.

*Depending on how many you steal in any given week?* Margaret imagined.

"If I'm talking to the police or a snoopy neighbor, it may be eight or nine, tops. But between us cat people, I sometimes peak at twenty-five. A more realistic number is probably around a dozen to fifteen. I turn them over if I can. I don't keep all of those that come to me."

"So you are running a cat-rescue facility, then?" Savannah asked.

"Well, yes! Sort of. I do some fostering for other facilities in the area. I board cats. I've even been known to have a kitty daycare." Dora smiled as she poured the hot tea into matching china cups with saucers. "Sugar and milk, right there." She nodded toward a creamer and matching sugar bowl in the middle of the table and then set the tea pot on a hot pad. She lifted saran wrap off of a plate and said, "These are snickerdoodles. I made them yesterday. They're pretty good. Not all of my culinary creations come out so good anymore. I'm out of practice."

"You say you run a kitty daycare?" Savannah asked with obvious interest while moving a feather toy back and forth across the floor for a little black cat with round yellow eyes. "Cats come here for play dates?"

"You might say that. People sometimes feel bad leaving their cats alone all day while they're at work. They may be too tired at night to give their cats the play workout they should be getting when they've been cooped up all day. So they bring kitty here where they have stimulation, activity, and company. Charlotte loves to play with the cats, and the owners get a better night's sleep when some of their more rambunctious kitties have played all day." Dora laughed.

Savannah noticed a kitty bed in pink and black cat-paw print fabric in a corner of the room. A tabby was curled up inside. "That is an absolutely adorable little bed."

"Oh, I make those and sell them at bazaars and flea markets. My grandson is getting me set up to sell them on the Internet. I also make kitty toys, like these kickers," she said as she picked up a tightly stuffed fabric toy. She tossed it in the direction of a half-grown tuxedo cat and he grabbed it, wrapped his paws around it and began kicking it with his back paws.

Everyone laughed.

Just then a dark long-haired tabby strolled over to Savannah and began sniffing her shoes. "Oh, that's Tuffy," Dora said. "His sister Taffy is the tabby in the bed over there. They're boarders. The kitty up on the pedestal," she said motioning toward a large wooden cat tree, "is Spunky. He's one of mine. He's sixteen now—doesn't look it, does he? And Golden Boy is the pretty yellow fellow under the table in the corner.

There's Ruthie." She pointed to a striking white cat. "Notice her odd eyes—one green and one blue."

"They are wonderful," Margaret said. "Beautiful and so well-cared for."

"I just love cats. I need a little money to supplement my income in order to care for my own cats, so I offer these kitty items and services which means I get to know even more cats." Her eyes danced as she spoke. "I work with the local shelter to find homes for those that are adoptable. That's satisfying and also sad." She lowered her head and said rather solemnly, "I get attached, you know."

Margaret sat silent for a few moments observing Dora carefully, and then she asked, "Are you aware that someone has been stealing cats from people's yards over in the new tracts near the old dump?"

"What? I didn't know about that," Dora said. "I don't get out much. Right out of their yards?" And then she frowned. "There isn't any dog-fighting going on is there?"

"It doesn't seem as though there is," Margaret said.

"Some sort of witchcraft rituals?" she offered.

"Gosh, we hope not. You haven't had any problems over here, have you?"

Dora shook her head slowly. "Not that I know of." She looked up at Margaret. "I think I would have heard something at the shelter if there was a problem here."

Savannah stood up and walked toward the door. "I'll bring that other bag of kibbles in."

Margaret took that as a cue. She reached for her crutches and put them in position to raise herself up off the chair. "You'd think this would get easier. But my muscles just get sorer and sorer—right here, mostly."

43

She indicated across her abdomen. "And in this one poor leg that has to take all the weight." She looked over at Dora and said, "If I'd known I was going to break my foot, I would have lost some pounds, that's for sure."

"Oh Auntie, you look great," Savannah said. "Just stay there for a moment. I'll be right back to help you up."

"Oh, so you're related?" Dora asked after watching Savannah close the door behind her.

"Yes, Savannah's my niece," Margaret explained. "She's here from Los Angeles helping me get around."

Dora tilted her head a little and smiled at Margaret. "How nice." And then she said, "You ladies have been so kind."

"Dora, it's been a pleasure. Thank you so much for introducing us to your kitties. They are really wonderful. And the snickerdoodles…yummy."

"You're welcome; I enjoyed the company. Come by any time you're in the area."

"I'd like that." Margaret reached into her pocket and pulled out a card. "Here's my number, in case you hear anything about the catnapping." And then she said, "Do you think you could give me directions to the hoarder you mentioned?"

"Sure," Dora said while walking over to a small desk and reaching in for a pencil and paper. She had just finished explaining her crude diagram to Margaret when they heard a soft voice call out.

"Hello."

The two women turned toward the door. "Oh hello, Charlotte. Come in. This is Ms…" Dora picked up Margaret's card and looked down at it before continuing, "Ms. Forster. You passed her niece on the

44

way in, I presume."

"Yeth, Mith Lipton. I thaw her outthide. Hello, Mith. Forthter," she said as she walked over to her and held out her hand.

Margaret extended a hand for a weak handshake. "So you help Ms. Lipton with the cats?"

"I love the cath and Mith Lipton leth me help and payth me," she said.

Margaret observed the hint of Down's in the girl's face and structure. "That's nice, Charlotte. I love cats, too."

Dora put her arm around the girl and squeezed her shoulders. "She's a wonderful help. And she has learned to ride the bus here by herself..."

Before she could finish, Charlotte chimed in, "Buth number five. Get off at Oak and walk two blockth."

Dora smiled at the girl. "And she doesn't miss a thing when it comes to caring for the cats. She knows exactly who's who, their favorite toys, where they prefer sleeping, what they like to eat, who needs to get up in the sink for a fresh-water drink. And boy can she clean."

"How old are you, Charlotte?" Margaret asked.

"Almoth fifteen," she announced proudly, while pushing back a wispy red curl from her face.

"Savannah, this is Charlotte," Dora said after Savannah had put the second bag of food in the pantry and walked up to the others.

"Oh, hello Charlotte," she said while shaking hands with the girl. "So you help take care of the cats?"

"Yeth," Charlotte said quietly. "Thith ith my job."

"Cool." Savannah smiled.

"Where do you live that you have to take the

bus here?" Margaret asked.

"Eatht Heighth Mobile Park, Thpathe 42," she said, looking over at Dora for confirmation.

Dora nodded.

"Oh, that's near where I live," Margaret said. "…on the other side of East Heights on Cranberry. I walk up there a lot—when I'm not on crutches."

"I like to walk. And I like cath. Do you have cath?"

"I sure do. Maybe you could come over and meet my cat sometime." Margaret smiled.

"Okay!" Charlotte said, looking to Dora for validation.

Margaret nodded. "Very nice meeting you both. We really need to be going. I hope to see you again. Hugs to all of the kitties," she said, as she turned toward the door.

"Oh, watch it," Dora said with a chuckle. "Charlotte takes everything quite literally, I'm sure she will be doing a lot of hugging today."

Charlotte's smile broadened at the thought.

***

"Well, what a nice lady," Savannah said while starting the car and swiveling in her seat to see if she was clear to back out of the driveway.

"Yes she is," Margaret agreed. "Turn left here, would you?"

"Left? But we came in from that direction," she said nodding toward the right.

"I know, Vannie, but I want to check something out. Left!"

After using Dora's map to direct Savannah, Margaret said, "That's gotta be it! Stop here. She

46

scrutinized the nondescript stucco house which was badly in need of paint and situated in the middle of a dry weed patch.

"What is this place?" Savannah asked, turning up her nose at the sight.

"It's where the cat hoarder lives," Margaret explained. "I think this is where Jim sent us and we happened upon Dora by mistake."

Savannah smiled. "It was a pleasant mistake, don't you think?"

"Sure was. Now let's go check these people out."

"Hellllooooo," Margaret called, knocking hard on the front door. "Is anyone here?" She could see a couple of cats in the window through shredded sheers and thrashed mini-blinds.

"What?" a thin, balding man asked rather abruptly upon opening the door a crack.

"Hello," Margaret said. "I'm with the Hammond Cat Alliance and just wanted to stop by and see if you need anything for your cats."

"Like what?" he asked brusquely, while using one foot to hold back an array of curious cats.

"Oh, help with the cats—food, litter…we just want to make sure the cats are getting everything they need."

"Why wouldn't they? And what business is it of yours, anyway?"

"Who is it, George?" a female voice screeched from inside.

When he turned to address her, Margaret could see an obese woman sitting in an over-sized recliner drinking what appeared to be a giant-sized soda from a convenience store. There were cats of all colors, sizes, and shapes in the room; several lounging on the many pieces of furniture.

"Some women want to know if we need anything for the cats," he reported.

"Hell no. We don't need nothing from no busybody women. Our cats are jus' fine."

"You heard her," he said as he pushed the door to close it.

"Wait!" Margaret shouted. She lifted one crutch and set the tip of it between the door and the door frame. "That cat behind you is sneezing. Its eyes are runny. Is it seeing a vet?"

"Yeah, we're gonna take him next week when our money comes in. What's it to you?" He pushed the door against Margaret's crutch.

"You're going to have a whole lot of sick cats if you don't isolate him," Margaret blurted. "My niece here is a vet," she said. "Isn't that so, Vannie?"

"Well…yes," Savannah said hesitantly, "if what the cat has is contagious."

"It could be deadly," Margaret insisted. "The cat needs to be seen now and he needs to be separated from the other cats."

"What's going on? Who are you people?" the woman demanded as she waddled over to the door and pulled it open wide. "Shoo! Shoo!" she said, waving a sheet of newspaper in the direction of several cats that had followed her. "You git out again and I'm gonna leave you out there!" she screeched.

As the cats skittered back into the room, the woman turned to Margaret and Savannah and said, "Now listen up. We take care of the cats when the money comes in. When there's no money, there's no extras for anyone—us or the cats."

"So how do you get the money?" Margaret insisted.

The woman looked Margaret up and down, smirked a little, and said, "The Internet. We operate on donations through the Internet and we do jus' fine, thank you very much." She glared at the two women who were standing on her porch for a few seconds and then said, "Now George is calling the police. Either you keep harassing us and git arrested or you git the hell outta here now and mind your own business."

*Holy cow, we're going to be arrested,* Savannah thought. She tugged on the back of her aunt's blouse and said, "Come on Auntie, there's nothing we can do here. Let's go."

"Yeah, good idea," the woman said before slamming the door hard. As Margaret and Savannah turned and started to walk away, they heard the woman screech, "Get the fuck outta the way, you mangy flea bag!"

"Oh my gosh," Savannah whispered loudly. "Those people are scary. I'm afraid for those cats. Something is way wrong here. Did you smell that stench and see all the trash in that room?"

Once in the car, Margaret spoke up, "Vannie, there sure is something wrong here. I believe this is a case of Internet fraud at the expense of innocent cats."

"What do you mean?" Savannah asked as she drove the car away from the curb.

"Well, I'm pretty sure they have a website where they exploit the cats by showing their photos and telling sad stories about how they are ill or have no food to eat. People donate money to help the kitties without knowing that it's actually a scam. There are cats in need and there are certainly legitimate organizations using the Internet to help cats, but I'll bet my bottom dollar the money these people are collecting isn't going toward the cats' care. Did you see that giant TV in that room?"

"And the classy new car in the driveway," Savannah added. "Oh my gosh, what a terrible situation. We have to report them, Auntie."

"From what Dora says, the authorities know about them and are planning to close them down," Margaret said. "I just hope it's sooner rather than later. Just to be sure they follow through, I'm going to make a few calls when we get home."

The two rode quietly for a few minutes when Margaret spoke up. "Where do you suppose they got all those cats? Do you think hoarders go out and steal cats? I guess they might if they're running a scam and they're not taking proper care of the cats," she reasoned.

Savannah thought for a moment before saying, "Yeah, if they run out of cats, they would certainly need more to photograph." She shook her head. "Gosh, that's just sick!"

Suddenly, Margaret lurched forward in her seat. "What time is it? Uh-oh, it's after two," she said, looking at the clock embedded in the dashboard. "We need to get over to the vet's office."

"Okay," Savannah said. "How are you doing with that foot? You haven't been keeping it up much today."

"Haven't had a chance. But I rest it on my purse as we drive. Actually, it's pretty good. I don't feel so vulnerable since I got the cast."

"But you don't want that foot to swell inside the cast, lady!"

Margaret waved her hand in the air. "Oh, you sound just like some kind of nagging doctor."

"If you didn't want a nagging doctor here this week, you should have invited my mother or how about Uncle Ray?"

50

"Okay, you got me. I'll take the nagging doctor any day," Margaret acquiesced.

\*\*\*

"Turn right at the next stop sign," Margaret instructed. "It's that building on the left." And then she faced Savannah and said, "Now, when you see this vet, I don't want your eyes popping out of your head."

"What? What's wrong with him?" Savannah wanted to know.

"Oh, you'll see," she responded in a teasing tone.

Savannah parked the car, glanced over at her aunt and let out a shallow sigh. *Now what?* she wondered. *Indeed, hanging out with Aunt Marg is already proving to be anything but an ordinary vacation.*

She had gladly taken time off when she heard that her aunt needed help. She felt as though she had dug herself into a rut. *Ruts are for retired people*, she thought. So she wasn't exactly thrilled with the way her life was going. She was working too much, spending too much time volunteering at the shelter. And, although she hadn't admitted it out loud, the residue from her breakup with Travis a few months earlier was still affecting her. She needed a distraction—but now she wondered if she was swimming against the tide.

Margaret's voice brought Savannah back to the here and now. "Would you get that little carrier out of the back, Vannie? Thanks."

"Hello, Scarlett."

The freckle-faced brunette of twenty-five looked up and then rushed from behind the counter in the veterinarian's office. "What happened to you, Ms.

Forster?" She put her hand on Margaret's back and walked her toward the closest chair. "Here, sit down." She then moved a small table over for her to rest her casted foot on. "Are you all right?"

"Sure—just broke a bone in my foot. My niece is here to help me out for a while. Vannie, this is Scarlett. Scarlett, Savannah. We came to pick up the neuters you did for Max Sheridan."

"Right on, Ms. Forster. Dr. Ivey will be with you in a moment."

"Thank you," Margaret said while motioning for Savannah to sit down beside her. As Savannah lowered herself into one of the molded chairs, she set a small plastic and wire pet carrier on the floor at her feet. They were the only ones in the waiting room.

"Hi Maggie." It was a man's voice. Savannah looked up. Her face began to burn and she was sure her heart skipped a beat. Walking toward her was one of the most gorgeous men she'd seen in quite a long time. Frighteningly gorgeous—run-away-now-or-get-your-heart-broken gorgeous. *As if he isn't already a 10.5 on the appealing man scale, he's holding two adorable black-and-white kittens in his hands,* Savannah thought, as she took in the yummy scene before her.

The veterinarian's eyes were on his tiny patients as he approached the two women. "They're ready to go," he said. "They both did just fine. Have you met them, yet? This is Tommy." He rubbed the larger kitten's cheek with his thumb. He looked up at Margaret while saying, "And this little guy is Tonka." But something else caught his eye. "Oh, hello," he said, nodding toward Savannah. "I'm Michael Ivey." He stared at her for a moment and then offered an apology: "I'd shake your hand, but…" He smiled down at the two rather docile kittens, still groggy from the

52

anesthesia.

When Savannah didn't speak right away, Margaret interjected, "Dr. Mike, this is my niece, Savannah. She and her family lived in Hammond for many years—in fact, their home still stands just a few blocks from here."

"Oh? Here on a little vacation? How long do you plan to stay?"

"Hi," Savannah managed as she diverted her gaze from his piercing stare. She rested her eyes on his shoulders—a safe zone. Or maybe not. *Even through his lab coat, I can tell he's buff...and look at that tan. Holy cow, is he an Olympic swimmer?* she wondered? *Certainly not a gymnast—too dang masculine.* "For as long as my aunt needs me," she finally managed.

"Cool," he said, his light-blue eyes intently studying her face.

*I wish I'd worn makeup today. Who would have thought I'd meet such a steaming hot man in my travels with Aunt Marg? Of course, that's part of Auntie's charm. You never know what's going to happen next or who you're going to meet.* She took a chance and glanced up at Michael Ivey's face again.

Noticing the obvious sparks between the two and her niece's sudden lack of total consciousness, Margaret smiled and said, "Savannah is a veterinarian, too."

"Oh really?" He eyed her with even more interest. "Where do you practice?"

*Embarrassing...* Savannah thought. *I wish Auntie would stop telling people that.* "I'm working as a vet tech right now in a large hospital just outside Los Angeles," she said, trying not to sound like a failure. She didn't actually consider herself a failure. After the situation with Travis, she had to take a time-out.

Opening a practice when she was still so emotionally whacked, would be a mistake. Or was this a cop-out? She hoped to work out the logistics of it while she was away from LA and Travis.

"Do you want me to carry these kittens to your car?" Michael Ivey was saying.

"Oh, I'm sorry. We have a carrier. Here it is." Savannah picked it up, set it on a nearby table strewn with magazines, and opened the little wire door.

"In you go, guys," the veterinarian crooned. "You know the drill, right, Savannah? Keep them quiet, watch for swelling or redness…"

"Sure," she said with a nod. "I guess we'll tell Max when we deliver the kittens to him, right Auntie?"

"That's the plan. Shall we go?"

Michael Ivey held Margaret's crutches while she lifted herself up out of the chair. "See you tomorrow, then. The meeting's at 7?"

"Yes, donuts and coffee," she called over her shoulder as she headed for the door, which Scarlett held open for them.

As Savannah approached the open door with the carrier, she couldn't help herself. She had to take another look at him. She turned before exiting the lobby with every intention of saying a casual, "Nice to meet you." But when she looked at him, his gentle, but penetrating stare rendered her speechless and she continued walking out the door, catching the jamb with her shoulder. *How embarrassing,* she thought. She hurried toward the car before he could see the blush she felt raging to the surface.

\*\*\*

She'd driven several blocks before Savannah realized

54

her aunt was speaking to her. When she finally focused on her words, she heard Margaret saying, "I thought we could take a tour of Max's place today, but I'm kind of tired. I hope you don't mind just dropping the kittens off and heading home. We can come back tomorrow. Maybe you'd like to spend time socializing some of the kittens. It's important that they interact with people as often as possible, you know. There's a greater chance they'll make good pets."

"Huh? Yes…a…I would. Definitely." *What's going on?* She wondered. *I've met good-looking men before. Lots of them. There was that professor—Jerry Barnes—at college. What an Adonis. The man who comes into the clinic with those three bulldogs. He's handsome, indeed. And what about Travis? He's certainly a nine-and-a-half on any woman's hunk-a-meter. Which is an important reminder,* Savannah thought, *that looks aren't everything.* In fact, she'd learned over the years that some of the best-looking men (and, for that matter, women) she'd met were terribly flawed. *So what's wrong with Michael Ivey?* she wondered.

Savannah looked over at her aunt. "I'm glad you want to rest. The way you were going, I was afraid I'd be the first one to cry 'uncle.' You sure are the Energizer Bunny. Do we need anything while we're out?"

"How about we go later to get the donuts for the meeting," Margaret said, sounding rather weary.

"And food for Rags," Savannah added. "I only brought enough of his food for a few days."

"Speaking of the klepto…" Margaret laughed, "I wonder how he's doing there in that big house on his own. Doesn't he usually go outside to burn off some of his energy?"

"Yes, at home. I thought I'd give him a few days

here. If he's adamant about going out, I may take him outside for short spurts during the day. He's pretty good about staying close if I watch him. Otherwise, well, you know, he's off burglarizing the neighborhood." She thought for a moment and then reasoned, "You don't have traffic out here, so that's not a concern. But, from the sounds of it, you get 'vermin' as you call them— you know—possums, wild boar, and…alligators," she said, grinning over at her aunt.

"And coyotes and owls, not to mention catnappers," Margaret interjected.

After handing the kittens over to one of Max's volunteers, Savannah drove the short distance to Margaret's house and pulled in as close as she could get to the porch for her aunt's convenience. She parked the car and then walked around to the passenger door to give Margaret a hand. As she held the crutches steady, she looked out across the rolling green landscape off in the distance. "This really is a beautiful area."

"Yes, it is," Margaret replied—standing in place for a moment, a crutch under each arm. "I love it out here," she said with a smile. And then her demeanor changed suddenly. "I just hope I can hold onto this place."

"Why can't you, Auntie?" Savannah wanted to know. This was the first time she'd heard her aunt make such a statement. As far as she or Margaret's siblings knew, her aunt was set for life—unless she'd done something stupid with her money, again.

When Savannah's grandparents died, they'd left each of their four children a pretty substantial inheritance. The other Brannon heirs invested their money, most of which came from the property and stock the senior Brannons had acquired while operating a successful lumber mill for many years on the outskirts
56

of Hammond. Aunt Margaret was between husbands when the elder Brannons were killed in a car accident and she was bent on having fun with her inheritance. She became overly spendy and overly generous. She also bought a house, which her siblings were happy to see; they figured she would always have a place to live. However, unbeknownst to anyone in the family, she soon ran out of money and began borrowing against the house until her mortgage was too much for her to handle. She ended up losing her home.

She didn't want to get a job; Margaret was not one who could stand too much regimentation. So she went in search of another option. *Enter Tom Forster,* Savannah thought to herself. This union seemed to be the answer to her aunt's prayers. *Ole Tom didn't do too bad for himself, either.* She smiled at the thought.

Savannah's family moved to Southern California shortly after the couple was married, but the sisters, and, on occasion, their brother, devised many reasons over the years to get together in their suburban home in Los Angeles, at the Forster ranch or somewhere in between. A favorite rendezvous place for Savannah was Big Sur. Her parents often did a house swap with friends who lived there. One summer, when she had experienced a particularly bad breakup with a special teen heartthrob, she spent a lot of time on a secluded beach near their vacation home, healing. Aside with being a healing place for her growing pains, this spot held many happy memories for Savannah. She still stopped there often when taking Highway One through Big Sur. In fact, her plan was to spend a few days in that area when she headed back to the big city sometime next week.

Savannah had already formed a positive opinion of Tom Forster by the time the couple moved into his family home to care for his aging grandfather. She liked Uncle Tom because he treated her, Brianna and their cousins like people, unlike some other adults did. Maybe that's because he had a child-like nature. He was always the one to instigate a game or activity when boredom began to set in. He even had a way of making chores fun. Savannah thought he would have made a good father, but neither he nor her aunt ever had any children.

"Auntie, you haven't been refinancing this place, have you?" Savannah asked, as if it was any of her business. *Well, she opened the subject,* Savannah reasoned.

"Um, no," she answered while working her way carefully along the pathway toward the expansive porch.

*As if she would tell me.* Savannah thought. *As if I really want to know…*

"Let me help you, Señora."

The women looked up and saw Margaret's gardener/handyman Antonio hurrying toward them. "Hola, Antonio," Margaret said. "Gracias, but I'm almost there. I'm just thankful that Granddaddy Forster built this porch with deep steps. Much easier to navigate with crutches." She exaggerated a pout and an attitude. "I just wish they'd given me a walking cast. I'm not supposed to use this foot at all—walking with crutches would be so much easier if I didn't have to hold this foot up all the time."

"I build you a ramp, Señora Maggie."

"That's sweet, Antonio, but I'm not going to need one quite at this point in my life. Maybe in another twenty or thirty years," she said laughing out loud.

"Oh, Señora, in those many years, my Juan will be here with you. Mama Esperanza and me—we will

58

be gone. Tired and gone. Our son, Juan can build your ramp," he said in all seriousness.

"Pshaww!" Margaret said as she reached the front door with her eager aides. "You and Esperanza are youngsters. You'll be growing things and she'll be cooking things for many years to come."

Savannah unlocked the door and Margaret started to hobble in, obviously feeling the stress and strain of the day. Suddenly, she stopped and turned toward Antonio. "Señor, are there any greens in the garden for a nice salad this evening? We have some of Helena's enchiladas left—a green salad would be nice."

"Si, Señora," Antonio said with enthusiasm. "I bring lettuce, cucumber, onion. Okay?"

"Perfect. Thank you, Antonio."

He started to turn, but spun back around and said, "I work behine house…back here..." He pointed toward the back of the house. "…cutting grass, cutting roses, making piles…" He motioned as if raking. Then he smiled. "Gato watch."

"What? Oh, the cat," Margaret said with a chuckle. "That's Rags, the señorita's gato."

"He want out—hit glass," Antonio explained while moving his hands in a clawing motion in front of him.

"Poor Rags," Savannah said. She turned to her aunt, "Let me get you settled and then I'll go check on the cat."

"Oh, here he is. He heard us come in. Hi Ragsdale. What trouble have you been into today, pray tell?"

Savannah cringed. "I'm afraid to look."

Savannah followed her aunt into her bedroom to see if she needed help getting situated for a nap. She filled Margaret's water pitcher and then walked over to the bed where Layla had been sleeping. "Here, Layla, sweetie. You move over and give Mommy some room," Savannah said matter-of-factly as she scooted the little fur ball off to the side.

"Isn't she just the most adaptable little thing?" Margaret cooed. And then she quieted her voice saying, "I almost wonder if she has a little brain damage from when she was a kitten. We don't know how long the kittens were without their mother or what their birthing was like. But she is, without a doubt, the most accommodating, sweet cat I've ever known. Nothing bothers her. She's so easy-going…almost like she's… brain damaged," she said the last words using a hushed tone.

"She is a doll. I hope my wild animal doesn't influence her in all the wrong ways," Savannah said, as she gathered up Rags in her arms and left the room. "Let's check your food and water supply, buddy, and maybe make a grocery list." She released the cat onto the floor in front of her. His forward motion uninterrupted, he continued to trot toward the kitchen. "You must be hungry, boy," she said, noticing that the bowl of kibbles she'd set out for the cats was nearly empty. Their water bowl was half empty. Upon closer examination, Savannah discovered that the bowl was sitting in a puddle. She grabbed a handful of paper towels and began soaking up the water. "Did you go swimming in here, or what?" After refilling the water bowl, she opened a small can of cat food. About then, she spotted Layla peering from around the corner. "Uh-oh, someone else is hungry. You know the sound of a can opening, don't you, girl?"

She gave both cats a dollop of savory salmon cat food on small paper plates and then searched for the foil to cover the can. *Oh, plastic cat-food-can lids, even better. Now to find a pen and paper. Probably near the phone,* she reasoned. She walked the length of the spacious farmhouse kitchen to near the side door where the phone was attached to the wall. A small table stood under the phone and, indeed, there was a pad and a jar of pencils and pens of all kinds on the table top.

"Finished eating already, Rags?" she asked as she noticed him nosing around under the little table. She started to turn toward the refrigerator to examine its innards, when something caught her eye—something shiny. *Glass! There's broken glass on the floor.* "Rags, no," she said as she dropped the pad and pen on the table and lifted the cat up off the floor. "We don't need you getting glass in your paws. Let's get you out of here. You, too, Layla." She scooped up the petite tangerine cat with her free hand and carried them to the closest bathroom. "You both stay here while I clean up the mess." She placed them on the plush plum-colored bath mat and, much to their dismay, she left, closing the door behind her. *Thank heavens the bathrooms don't have those lever door handles. This is one room Rags can't escape from,* she thought as she turned to walk away.

*Now what did Rags break?* she wondered, as she rushed over to where she'd seen the broken glass. *It looks like the glass came from an ordinary window,* she thought. *At least it's not a priceless vase that had been in the Forster family for a thousand years,* she mused. *But how did he break a window?* was her next question. *And which window?*

She pulled the red-checkered café curtains back from the large window next to the door. It was intact. Then she looked at the window on the kitchen door. *Broken. By what? How?* She stood in place, scanning the room. *What's this?* she wondered, as she stepped toward the counter top. *A rock. A rock with a piece of paper attached with silver tape.*

She picked up the palm-sized stone and peeled the paper from around it, knowing full well that if this was a crime scene under the direction of CSI: Miami, she was tampering with evidence. She imagined herself now the number-one suspect and could visualize Eric or Calleigh (no, Eric—for sure, Eric) cuffing her and taking her in for questioning.

*Stop being silly,* she scolded herself.

She unfolded the paper and turned it over. "GET OUT" it read in large black letters.

*Hmmm,* she thought. *I never did get a chance to ask Auntie about the note I found earlier. And now here's another one. What could this mean? Is someone out to hurt my aunt?* Savannah felt a knot in the pit of her stomach. *Is she in danger? Are we all in danger?*

"Meooowwwww. Meooowwww."

*Oh gosh, what are those cats up to? I'd better get this mess cleaned up so I can let them out before they disturb Auntie. Then I'll talk to Antonio. Maybe he saw something…or someone.*

"There you go, kitties," Savannah soothed as she opened the bathroom door and let the two hostages out. Rags bounded over the top of Layla and jaunted off to parts unknown. Layla stopped as if composing herself and gave her tail one quick wave before stepping confidently out of the room. "Okay Princess Layla, your royal high felineness," she said while smiling and shaking her head from side to side.

After watching the cats disappear into the dining room toward the living room, Savannah opened the side kitchen door and stepped out onto the porch in search of the gardener. She walked around to the south side of the house and spotted him working in a raised garden bed. She yelled out, "Antonio, can you come here for a minute? I want to show you something."

"Si, Señorita." He dropped his spade in the soft dirt and rushed over to where Savannah stood.

"Antonio, did you see anyone here today while you were working?"

He thought for a moment, then shook his head slowly. "No, Señorita. No one."
"Something wrong?"

"There's a broken window. I wonder if you can fix it."

The slight Mexican man frowned. "I see no broke window. Where is broke window?"

"Right here." Savannah led him up onto the wrap-around porch and pointed at the gaping hole in the window of the kitchen door. I must speak to Señora Margaret first, to see if she wants to talk to the police."

"La policia?" he said, looking puzzled and a tad frightened. "Bad man broke window in Señora Maggie's casa?"

"It looks that way. Someone threw a rock through the window."

Antonio gasped and took a step back. "Madre Mary! Who want to hurt the Señora?"

She looked down at the gardener. "Maybe someone just wants to scare her and make her leave this house. Do you know who that might be?"

He shook his head slowly. "I see no one, Señorita. I in back of house working all day."

"I know, Antonio. That's okay," she said, hoping to calm him. She, herself, certainly wasn't feeling calm inside. She started to walk through the door and then stopped. "Oh, Antonio, can you cover the hole with a piece of wood or canvas, please? We don't want the cats getting out." *Or anything or anyone to get in,* she thought.

\*\*\*

Two hours later, Savannah looked up from the magazine she was reading and noticed her aunt hobbling into the living room on her crutches. "Are you feeling more rested?" she asked.

Margaret lowered herself into her favorite chair. "Yeah, I'm still a little tired—not used to these things," she said, nodding toward the crutches. "And we did cover quite a bit of ground today." Layla was stretched in the middle of the ottoman, as usual. "Scootch, Sweetie," Margaret cooed as she shifted the relaxed cat over a few inches to make room for her foot. She then lifted her leg using both hands and rested it next to the purring feline. "Ahhhh," she said as she leaned back in the chair. "I could get used to a cat's lifestyle—sleep, eat, lounge, sleep, eat, nap... And then there's all that petting," she said with a twinkle in her eye.

Savannah laughed. "I doubt that, Auntie. You're too much of an on-the-go-lady. By the way," Savannah cleared her throat before saying, "something arrived for you today."

"By UPS?"

"No." Savannah winced slightly. "You could say it came by air."

"What are you talking about?" Margaret insisted, leaning slightly forward.

"Someone hurled a rock through your kitchen window."

Margaret pressed her lips together—a look of disgust on her face. After a few moments of silence, she

64

said, "Well, damn."

"And there was a note on it."

"A note?" the older woman said flatly.

"Yes, like the one I found in your lingerie drawer this morning. It said, 'Get Out!' in big black letters."

Margaret stared down at her hands as they lay in her lap.

"What's going on, Auntie?" Savannah asked quietly with a hint of tenderness in her voice. "Who wants you out? Does this have to do with the cat situation?"

"Oh no, I don't think so. But I can't be sure," she said with some hesitation. Margaret looked over at her niece and then began to speak. "The notes started coming a few weeks ago. What do they mean? I don't know. I haven't heard of any big-time investors interested in this land—if I had, I might just sell for the right price, actually. They wouldn't have to badger me," she quipped. "I've spoken rather discreetly with others around here. As far as I can discover, no one else is getting any messages like this."

Savannah studied her aunt for a moment and then asked, "How did the other note arrive—also by rock?"

"No. I came in from a meeting one evening and found it on my bed. I must have shoved it into my lingerie drawer that night in case I needed it at some point as evidence for the sheriff. And when Helena moved my stuff down to the ground floor bedroom after I broke my damn foot, I guess she unknowingly transferred the note."

"How did someone get in?" Savannah asked.

"I don't know. Maybe Helena inadvertently left a door unlocked that day when she finished here. Or maybe someone came in while she was cleaning. It's a big house, if she was vacuuming downstairs, someone could slip right in and run upstairs to my bedroom."

"Did you question Helena?" Savannah asked.

"A little. I didn't want to startle the woman for no good reason."

Savannah looked at her aunt for a solid minute without speaking—not quite knowing what to say or what to think. Finally she asked, "Have there been other notes or threats?"

It was obvious that Margaret was uncomfortable talking about this. She wanted, instead, to focus on the upcoming meeting and the work they were trying to do on behalf of the community's cat population. She also knew that she owed some sort of explanation to her guest. After all, if she was in danger, so was Savannah for as long as she stayed under her roof. Finally, she took a deep breath and, with some effort, she said, "Someone left a dead cat on my porch. I'm sure it was road kill, but…"

"But what?" Savannah prodded.

"They had stabbed the body with an old knife and pinned it to my front door." Margaret rested an elbow on the arm of the chair and cradled her forehead in her hand murmuring, "It was an ugly thing to come home to." She sat back, looked over at Savannah and continued, "Thankfully, Max was with me that evening and he, bless his heart, took care of things. Don't you know, though, that made me all the more concerned that someone might harm Layla? She's such a dear. It would just be horrible…" She choked up at the thought.

Savannah leaned her head on the back of the sofa and stared up at the ceiling. "It doesn't appear that you've told any of this to the sheriff, have you?" she asked.

"Not yet. Too much other stuff going on. I'm just trying to be careful. I want to understand what this is all about."

Savannah sat upright. "Yeah, I saw how careful you can be today, Auntie—nearly getting arrested for spying. And then badgering those cat hoarders." Savannah grinned over at her aunt. Then her demeanor became more serious. "Now, tell me, do you think the person behind these threats has anything to do with you breaking your foot?"

Margaret sat silent for a few moments considering the question. "I don't think so. I stupidly caught the toe of my sandal under a loose slab of concrete and, when I fell, a bone in my foot snapped. It all happened so fast. It was right out here in back," she said, motioning with her hand. "In fact, the next day, Antonio fixed those uneven stepping stones." Her brown eyes darted around the room for a moment before she added, "That's when he found the hole."

Savannah sat forward, stared intently at her aunt and asked, "What hole?"

"Somehow, I guess the ground where the original cesspool was had given way. A board across there rotted or something. I'm not sure. I didn't see a hole. Antonio told me about it, later. He said that it's lucky I didn't fall in. The only thing stopping me was the fact that I fell before I got to it. From what Antonio said, you couldn't see the hole. He found it when he set a crowbar or some other tool on the grass covering the old cesspool and the ground gave a little. It's just fortunate that he noticed it." Margaret bit her bottom lip and stared off into space. Finally, she continued, "He said the thing was deep, Savannah—maybe eight feet. And we often walk out there. It's near the tomato garden. It's truly a wonder that we didn't fall into it before. I mean, we've had parties out there—kids running around and all…" She suddenly felt a chill and shivered a little.

"Auntie," Savannah practically yelled, "did it ever occur to you that someone knew that old cesspool was there, came on your property, and booby-trapped it?"

# Chapter 3

"What are you doing up so early?" Savannah asked while walking slowly into the kitchen rubbing her eyes, and yawning. "It's not even light out."

Margaret leaned against the sink counter, measuring coffee into the pot. "Oh, I woke up and decided to get an early start. We have a big day ahead of us."

"Here, let me do that," Savannah said. "You sit. Get that foot up."

"I'm okay. I'll sit during the meeting. My foot was up all night."

Savannah put on her sternest look. "Remember, I'm not here as a guest. You don't want the swelling to return. I'm sure the doctor warned you about that, right?"

Margaret looked away from her niece and busied herself at the counter while muttering, "You sound like some kind of doctor, girl."

"I am some kind of doctor. Remember? I deal with fractures all the time," Savannah reminded her.

"Yes, but I'm not a duck or a pig or a cow." She laughed as she opened a drawer and pulled out a handful of paper napkins.

"Not that much different when it comes to a break, Auntie. I'm here to help, remember?"

"Yes, I remember." Margaret turned to face her niece, looking into her still sleepy green eyes. In a more serious, sincere tone, she added, "I really appreciate you being here."

Savannah sensed that her spunky, capable aunt was referring to something more than just the helping aspect of her visit. *She really is spooked,* she thought. *And that makes me nervous.*

Margaret turned back toward the counter and the task at hand. "There definitely are things I need help with. People will be arriving shortly. I had my shower, such as it was. By the way," she said, looking over at Savannah, who was now standing along the counter not far from Margaret, "I'm so glad you found that old shower chair upstairs. Using that hand-held gizmo, I can just sit there, hold my foot outside the shower curtain, and feel as though I'm having a real shower. Works slick." She looked down at her cast. "I'm running out of clothes I can wear with this thing, though."

"Well, not much goes with purple. Why a purple cast, anyway, was that all they had?"

"Heck no. I *chose* purple. If I must put up with this thing, I might as well have one in a color I like. Anyway, I have plenty of clothes that go with purple. The problem is dressing over the cast. I have to wear wide-leg sweats, shorts, or skirts—something that will fit over this bulky thing. I seem to wear mostly jeans, normally."

"Well, I'll do some laundry this afternoon and I'll go out and get you more sweats, if you want." She pulled playfully at the side seam of the pair her aunt wore. "…something not quite so baggy. Auntie, You have a nice figure for…"

Margaret quickly twisted toward her niece, an index finger raised in her direction. "Don't you dare say it, Savannah," she scolded.

"Say what?"

Margaret glared at her and said in an exaggerated mocking tone, "You have a nice figure *for your age*. I either have a nice figure or I don't—age has nothing to do with it. I hate when people qualify comments like that," she spat.

70

"Whoa, Auntie. Where did that come from? You are a good-looking fifty-seven-year old—right? Fifty-seven?"

"Who told you that?" she teased.

Savannah tossed her head and said flippantly, "I did the math."

"Well, you should mind your own business," Margaret said with a grin. And then she looked hard at her niece and added, "Just be glad you got the tall, svelte genes from your dad's side of the family and not these short, plump ones."

"Plump?" Savannah laughed out loud. "You're not plump—but you are curvy. I don't have nice curves like you, my mom, and Brianna."

"But look at you—you have a tight butt—men like tight butts, slim hips, a nice bosom… Oh Savannah, you are lovely." She stopped and looked somewhat askance at her niece while studying the faded blue pjs She wore. "However, not so much at the moment. I mean, is that what you wore when you slept with Trevor?"

"Travis," she corrected.

"So you admit you were sleeping together," Margaret teased.

"No…I mean…Auntieeee…" Savannah whined. And then she abruptly changed the subject. "Now, sit and let me get you a glass of juice. I'll put the donuts on platters. I see you have cups and napkins out already."

"Okay, Vannie. I'll take your professional advice and sit for now. Then you go get ready. I want you to be here for the meeting. I think you should know about what's been going on."

Savannah walked around the table and pulled out a chair for her aunt, stepping over Rags, who was sprawled in the middle of the kitchen floor. "I wouldn't miss it." *What else would I be doing?* she thought. *Of course, I'm interested in the situation with the cats. Plus, I heard Michael Ivey say he would be here. I wouldn't mind another chance to look at him.* She was a little surprised at the tingle she felt inside when she brought the local vet to mind.

***

"Max, come on in. Looks like the cats let you off duty early this morning," Margaret said with a wide smile.

"I just got the necessities taken care of—you know that the morning routine is just the tip of the iceberg."

"I know," she said shaking her head slowly from side to side. She motioned toward the refreshment table Savannah had set to her specifications in the dining room and added, "Go pour yourself a cup of coffee."

The doorbell rang as Savannah entered the room. She was wearing jeans, a blue and white striped tee, and a blue light-weight cardigan sweater. Her hair was still wet from her shower and pulled back in a tight knot. She had taken the time to put on makeup this morning. She didn't want to be caught without it again. She stopped Margaret as she started to head for the door. "Auntie, please sit down and get comfortable. I can greet your guests."

Savannah watched her aunt lower herself into her chintz flower-print overstuffed chair and then she positioned the matching ottoman for her to rest her foot on. Once Margaret was seated, Savannah turned toward the door, which Max had already opened to let a batch of guests in.

After several minutes—during which people arrived, issued appropriate greetings and chose their

72

refreshments—Margaret scanned the room and motioned for a tall, slim, bleached-blond woman wearing jeans and a black tee shirt with a rhinestone cat on the front to start the meeting.

"Meow! Meow!" Almost everyone stopped what they were doing and turned in the direction of the sound as the woman squeezed a stuffed *talking* cat. "Let's get started," she said in a raised voice, because a few people on the other side of the refreshment table were still chatting out loud. "Some of us have to get to work in a little while." She squeezed the chenille cat two more times as the last of the stragglers complied.

"Meow?"

"What's that?" she asked as everyone turned toward the hallway adjacent to the large room.

"Awwww," one older woman said when she saw Rags walking cautiously into the room, "he came in here to check out the cat he heard."

Everyone chuckled and some of the women clucked and wriggled their fingers near the floor in an attempt to capture Rags's attention. By then, however, he had spotted the stuffed cat and was on a mission to examine it. As he came closer to the woman holding the toy, he slowed his pace and began sniffing the air while staring intently at the little feline intruder. When he was close enough, he reached up and put his paws on the woman's knees, still sniffing in the direction of the toy. She moved it closer to him and his next antic filled the room with laughter.

He took the stuffed cat in his mouth, jumped down and, walking like an emperor penguin, carried it off toward the hallway.

"Rags. No. Bring that back," Savannah scolded as she jumped up from her hard-back chair to retrieve the cat and his new friend.

"Oh, that's okay, let him play with Meowster. We'll get it when I'm ready to go," the blond woman said.

"But what if…" Savannah attempted to protest.

"There are more where that one came from. Just let him go. That was priceless—what a way to start the meeting." She was still laughing, as were several others in the room. "Well wasn't that a treat?" she said before getting down to business. "As most of you know, I'm Ida Stone. I run the Tabby Haven Foster Cat program in Haley. I'm also the president of the Hammond Cat Alliance. To my left is…" She paused.

"Oh, I'm Betty Gilbert," a woman in her early forties responded. She sported a long dark ponytail and a heavy set of bangs. She looked as if she had been active out in the sun most of her life. She was fit and her skin tan and leathery. She nodded toward the large man sitting next to her. "My husband, Gil, and I are on the HCA board and we volunteer at the Hammond Cat and Kitten Rescue." They both wore jeans, sport shoes and Western shirts in two different blue-and-green plaid patterns. Betty's was open down the front revealing a bright yellow designer tee. "We also help with a small cat colony out in the industrial area," she said. "Oh, and we train horses and give riding lessons."

Gil Gilbert motioned to the person sitting to his left to go ahead, indicating that his wife had sufficiently introduced him.

"Michael Ivey. I'm the vet in these here parts," he said with a chuckle. Savannah noticed that he was wearing jeans and a tee that molded perfectly to his body. Strands of his straight dark-brown hair hung over one brow. She allowed her eyes to linger even after Margaret took the floor. When his gaze met hers, however, she quickly looked away. *Darn,* she thought

74

to herself, *am I blushing? Oh no, I hope he doesn't notice.*

"This is our hostess, Margaret," Ida said, motioning toward her. "I want to thank you for putting up with us this early in the morning."

"Sure. My pleasure."

Ida gave her an expectant look.

"Oh yes, I'm a sometimes foster mommy to kittens. I'd like you to know that the cat you just saw walking away with our spokes-cat is *not* one of my prodigies."

Everyone laughed.

"I also volunteer at Max Sheridan's cat rescue facility."

"Oh Margaret, you are so modest," Ida said. "She is the founder of this organization and the past president and will take on and has taken on just about any task we ask of her."

Margaret waved her hand in the direction of the compliment as if she would rather not have the attention. But many people in the room knew that wasn't the case. Margaret loved the attention.

"Next," Ida prompted.

"I'm Max Sheridan. I rescue feral and stray cats, and with our wonderful volunteers," he nodded toward Margaret, "we do our best to find forever homes for them. I keep those that are unadoptable or place them in suitable colonies in the tri counties. Some, of course, wind up as barn cats—whatever works for the particular cat…"

"I'm Hildy Barnett," a plump woman with long graying hair clipped back in a ponytail said, by way of introduction. "I breed Himalayans."

The woman sitting next to her looked around the room and said, "They are absolutely yummy Himmies."

She smiled and then realized everyone was waiting for her to introduce herself. "Oh yes, I'm Karen Waxton and I raise Brits—uh British shorthairs." She was striking, with light-brown curls soft around her face, lovely skin and large blue eyes accentuated by plenty of eye makeup.

"And you, hon? Are you a relative of Margaret's?" Ida asked.

"Yes, I'm Savannah. I'm here taking care of my aunt."

"You have your job cut out for you if you hope to keep that gal down," Betty remarked.

There were chuckles all around.

"And the cat burglar is yours?" Ida asked.

"Yes, that's Ragsdale."

"He has a beautiful coat. What's his background?" someone asked from across the room.

"He's a rescue."

A few people applauded quietly and made comments, "Good for you."

"We love rescues…"

"Well, welcome to Hammond, Savannah," Ida said warmly. She then looked at the woman to Savannah's left and asked, "And you are?"

While everyone else in the room focused on the woman sitting next to Savannah, Michael's eyes lingered on the tall blond. *What a fascinating woman—and a veterinarian, at that! She's beautiful. I can't keep my eyes off her.*

Savannah looked toward Hammond's veterinarian and caught him staring at her. *Gosh he's a hunk,* she thought as she lowered her eyes and blushed a little. At least she was pretty sure she blushed. She felt like she was virtually glowing.

"Anna Robles," the stout Hispanic woman

next to Savannah said. "My cat is gone like others in our neighborhood. Gina, Kitty and Clarice came to the meeting last time. We need help finding our cats." She hesitated for a moment and then choked up, saying, "We miss our Rascal."

A fragile-looking elderly woman in a housedress, her white hair in tight curls close to her head said, "It's just awful to think that someone is picking up our family cats and running off with them… to do what? I can't imagine why. One of the missing cats is on medication, for heaven sakes!" She looked around the room. "Can't the sheriff do something?" she asked. She then put her hand up to her mouth for a split second, lowered it into her lap and said, "Oh, I'm Kitty Wilson. Our Brillo is gone, too." She hesitated, and wiped a tear from the corner of her eye. "Just gone," she said choking up.

"You shouldn't let your cats out, you know," Karen Waxton said in her naturally husky voice. "They're vulnerable to all sorts of dangers. You're lucky they weren't picked off by coyotes or owls."

"We know that," the woman to Kitty's left said while smoothing a strand of her light-brown hair behind one ear. "We all take precautions with our cats. Some of them are so unhappy as inside cats that we can't keep them in."

"I have three inside cats," Kitty interjected. "Brillo just wouldn't stand being cooped up all day and night. We were in the process of building him an outdoor run when someone snatched him."

"How do you know someone took him and that it wasn't a coyote?" Gil asked.

"Gina saw him!" Kitty said, obviously excited. "Tell them, Gina."

A thin pregnant woman in her early thirties

77

cleared her throat before speaking. "I'm Regina. Yes, I saw a kid—he looked young—come right up on my walkway not ten feet from my porch and pick up one of my cats. Right in my yard! I yelled at him through the window and a neighbor heard me. He was watering his lawn. When he saw what was happening—that this kid was running past him with Patches in his arms—he turned the hose on him. Thankfully, this freaked out Patches. She started clawing the guy and he let go. Patches ran under the first shrub she saw and then went up a tree. The kid ran off around the corner. We don't know where he went or who he was. We finally coaxed Patches down and into the house at around dusk, and she even agreed to stay in for a few days after that," she said, smiling slightly.

She lifted her long black hair off her neck and shoulders, tying it back with a band that she slipped off her wrist. Addressing Karen Waxton, she continued, "I work at home and have two children running in and out. I try to keep the cats inside or at least in the backyard as much as possible. But, cats do have minds of their own. And with small kids…" her voice faded. And then she said, "Now our old boy Buster's missing."

Regina continued, "I live in the same neighborhood as Kitty, Clarice, and Anna. And we're not the only ones who are missing cats. But no one we've spoken to has seen a coyote or an owl—well, you wouldn't see an owl in the daylight and most of these cats come in at night."

"I think we'd be seeing herds of coyotes, due to the number of cats that have come up missing just in our tract over the last six weeks," Clarice said. "How many is it now, Anna? Eight? Just in Ravenwood. Cats are starting to disappear from a newer development near us now. I think they've had four or five go missing

78

from over there."

Regina interjected, "Another neighbor we talked to said he saw an old dark-colored pickup truck driving slowly up and down his street—two streets over. He said that he watched as a blond boy—around thirteen or fourteen—got out of the truck and approached some children who were playing with a cat across the street on their front lawn. The man picked up his cell phone ready to call the sheriff—he thought the kid was after one of the children. When this guy approached the children, the cat got spooked and ran off. One of the little girls must have gotten scratched because she screamed. The kid hurried back to the truck and they took off."

"Okay, this item is on our agenda," Ida announced in an attempt to get everyone's attention. Then she turned to the four women and said, "Thank you for updating us on the situation. We will be talking more about it. Let's finish introductions so we can get on with the meeting. Looks like we have just a few more. Would you two ladies introduce yourselves?"

"Sure," a heavy woman dressed in a faded smock dress and Croc clogs said, as she squirmed in the wing-back chair she was seated in. "I'm Olivia Hershner. I have Cat's Cradle Rescue and Boarding over in Mason."

"Barbara?" Ida acknowledged the woman sitting next to Olivia.

"I'm Barbara Rinaldi," the sturdy thick-bodied woman with a boyish haircut said. "My husband Howard and I manage several cat colonies throughout the tri counties."

"Okay, thank you," Ida said. And then motioning toward an olive-skinned man wearing a plaid beret, she said, with a smile, "Rudy?"

"I'm Rudy Silva, private investigator."

"Oooooh,"

"Coooool,"

"All right."

"Right on!"

Comments were being repeated in unison.

"Thanks Rudy," Ida said. "For everyone's information, Rudy is here at my request. It is true that the sheriff can't do much to help us with the cat-disappearing problem, based on what we know so far. So we're hoping that we can get enough incriminating information to make a case that the sheriff's office *will* pursue. We need to know something about who's taking the cats and where. However, there's a long-standing belief that cats can't be owned. This could put us at a real disadvantage when it comes to protecting our pets." She looked down at the notepad in her lap and then continued, "It's rather frightening to think that if someone wants one of our cats, they can take it and the authorities would or could do nothing."

Ida paused for a moment, crossed her legs, and continued, "Do any of you remember the scandal with Natalie Wood's sister's Siamese cat? You folks over forty might. For the rest of you, Lana's cat was stolen out of her apartment. I think she even knew or suspected who took it. But the police said that even if they found the cat, there was nothing they could do because a cat is an independent agent." She looked over at Rudy Silva before saying, "And this was a registered cat."

She continued, "But it seems that the laws now are vague and adapted for various situations and regions. With the advent of micro-chipping, the laws may have or will have to change." She took a deep breath before going on, "Here, in this county, the people

80

at the sheriff's office seem to have more pressing things to worry about than missing cats. However, Rudy believes that if we work together to gather some facts and maybe even get a license number or photo of the suspected catnapper, they might be able to help us find out where the cats are being taken and why. Rudy, do you want to speak to that?"

The stout sixty-five-year-old, who looked to be around fifty, shared his understanding of laws involving cats. "As Ms. Stone explained, there are no hard-and-fast laws involving cat ownership, and this is complicated by the attitude of and pressure on the particular police force or sheriff's office and even the individual officers." While he cautioned members of the group against doing anything that would put them in danger or get them in trouble with the law—such as trespassing—he encouraged them to be vigilant. He outlined the safe zone in so doing: "Create a neighborhood-watch system, and be diligent in keeping watch. Encourage your cats to stay indoors or at least in your view at all times, and report anything suspicious to the authorities."

He looked around the room and then said in a serious I-mean-business tone, "Leave the surveillance work to me or the sheriff. Don't approach anyone on your own. Your job is to keep your animals safe and report anything suspicious." He reached into his shirt pocket. "Here, I'll pass around my card."

Savannah glanced over at her aunt who looked a tad sheepish. After all, what the two of them had done the day before could be considered spying and trespassing, no doubt—not to mention giving false information in order to locate someone while having ulterior motives, and badgering private citizens. She heaved a sigh when imagining what escapades were ahead.

"Why would someone take cats?" Kitty asked. "Some of them are beautiful, but others that have gone missing are—well—rather ordinary-looking. No offense, ladies."

"Oh no, I agree," Clarice said. "Our Samantha, while we love her to pieces, is just a run-of-the-mill short-haired tortie. No show cat, by any means with that crooked tail. In fact, here are some pictures of Sam and some of the other missing cats." She fumbled around in her purse and pulled out an envelope, saying, "I'll pass them around."

Once the photos reached Margaret, she looked at each of them and then asked, "Can we keep these?"

"Um…" Clarice glanced over at the other ladies from Ravenwood before saying, "We want them back at some point."

"Do you have a scanner? Can you make copies?" Betty asked.

Savannah stood up. "I can do it, Auntie." She took the envelope from her aunt and started toward the hallway.

"I'll help."

Savannah looked over just as Michael Ivey stood up and began walking toward her. She felt her heart flutter and she began to stutter, "Um…well sure…I guess. The office is in here." As she walked through the door of the study, her sweater caught on the lever handle and stopped her forward motion. Michael promptly walked right into her and then quickly apologized.

"No, I'm sorry," she said as she untangled herself. *When did I become such a klutz?* she wondered.

*Gosh she smells good,* he noticed.

"I think this is the copy machine," she said as

82

she switched it on.

"Looks kind of like the one I have in my office."

"So do you make copies? You know how to do all of this office stuff?"

"Not really," he admitted.

"Then why did you volunteer to help?" she asked, looking at him suspiciously, a playful smile dancing at her lips.

"Truth?" he teased.

"Yes, I guess so. Unless you think I'd rather hear a lie."

*Quick-witted,* he thought. *I like that. I hope she doesn't think I'm being too forward.* "To get a chance to talk to you."

Savannah tore herself away from his alluring smile and faced the copy machine in hopes that he wouldn't see her turning crimson.

"You have to wait for it to warm up, don't you?" he asked.

"Yes, I suppose. She turned toward him and asked, "So what do you want to talk about?" Savannah was certain she saw *him* blushing now. She smiled.

He put his hands in his front jeans pockets and looked down. Savannah noticed several straight strands of his hair falling oh-so-attractively over his right eyebrow. He pushed them back with one hand, cleared his throat, and said, "How would you like to help me with a case? One of my techs came down sick last night and the other is out of town on a family emergency. I have a cat with what appears to be a foreign object in her stomach and I want to get to it before it goes any farther."

"Oh, poor cat."

"And she's a stray, so there's no one to ask all the vital questions of. I can do the surgery anytime you're available, if you are able to…uh…or would like to…assist me with it."

"Um, sure, I guess I could. I'll check with my aunt."

Michael looked over at the copy machine, pointed and said, "The green light's on. I think it's ready to go."

"Oh, uh…copies," Savannah stammered. "Yes. It looks like it's ready."

After only a few minutes, Savannah and Michael returned, and this didn't go unnoticed by everyone. *Well, well.* Margaret thought. *It looks like those two are taking things to the next level all by themselves. Am I a matchmaker or what? And I wasn't even trying.* She wondered if the smugness she felt on the inside was showing on the outside.

Ida was aware of the couple's return, as well. She said, "Oh great, Georgia. Thanks."

"It's Savannah," she corrected with a smile.

"Oh, I'm sorry. A little memory-association glitch."

A few guests chuckled.

"It happens more than you might think," Savannah said quietly. "I'm sometimes called Atlanta or Sequoia."

She glanced up and her eyes met Michael's once again. *Am I staring at him or is he staring at me?* she wondered. *Is it a coincidence that every time I look in his direction, he's looking back?*

"Here are your originals." Savannah returned the envelope to Clarice. "And here are three copies of the best shots of each cat," she said while handing them to her aunt.

"Good. I would like to have a set of these," Margaret said. "And Betty and Gil, you should have a
84

set, and how about you, Rudy? Will you be involved in the recovery effort to the point where you'll need these?"

The man shifted in his chair, seemingly not sure how to respond. Just what did these people expect him to do? It seemed to him that the options were pretty limited when it came to locating missing cats. *But then, it depends on what's happening to them,* he reasoned. "Sure, I'll take those pictures. Why not?"

Max cleared his throat. "Madam President, may I respond to Ms. Wilson's question?"

"Certainly, Max. Please go ahead."

He straightened his posture, ran his hand through his curly salt and pepper hair and looked over at Kitty. "I'd like to address your question about why people might take cats. I've been doing some research." He frowned and looked around the room. "This isn't easy to hear. It isn't a pretty picture. But these are some of the reasons why people might steal cats." He hesitated for a moment when he noticed a grimace on some of the women's faces. "As unpleasant as the subject might be, I think it's important for you all to know what you might be up against. You can't fight something you don't understand. And you won't find your cats or be able to stop the catnapping if you're barking up the wrong tree." He chuckled and offered a quick apology for his choice of clichés.

He cleared his throat and continued, "You mentioned people taking pretty cats." He nodded toward Kitty. "Yes, that's one reason why someone would take a cat—because they like its looks. Some cats go missing because someone thinks they're stray. I once kept a mother cat and her litter and raised them even though I knew where they lived. I didn't go on the property and take the cats, of course. But when the mother cat brought her kittens to me one day, I figured she needed a safe haven from the chaos I'd witnessed on the property down the street. This was her third or fourth litter and, in my book, when someone doesn't have their cats spayed and neutered and lets them breed indiscriminately, it's an issue of neglect. No one ever came looking for her and her kittens, so I just played dumb. I got her spayed, found good homes for her and two of the kittens and I still have Big Boy at my place."

Several people nodded and smiled.

Olivia gave a thumbs up.

"In bad economic times, people will take cats rather than pay the adoption fees at the shelters. Heck, someone walked out of the animal shelter over in Haley with a kitten in their pocket just last week. They want pets, but they don't want to pay for them. Or maybe they don't qualify—the landlord won't authorize a pet, for example.

"Children have been known to pick up cats they find in their neighborhoods—in particular kittens. How many of you have kids who have brought home kittens?"

There were a few knowing looks and nodding heads along with hushed conversation.

"Did you do a full search for its owner?" Max asked, as he scanned the room with his dark-brown eyes under heavy brows. "Yes, typically a parent will believe their child when he or she tells them, 'someone gave me the kitten,' or 'it's lost,' and they agree to adopt the poor kitty. Or you might do minimal checking—depending on how cute the kitten is." He smiled over at the ladies from Ravenwood.

Then, in a more serious tone, he said, "Sometimes kids can get rowdy and they'll grab a nice cat they see in the neighborhood and harm it.

86

The cat might get frightened, and run so far he can't find his way back home. I know of cats who have run away from home when the owners brought in a dog or another cat. And sometimes a good Samaritan will feed a cat that appears to be a stray and the cat decides to stay."

Again, there was quiet conversation among the group and Max noticed a few women nodding.

"We've talked a little about predators—coyotes, owls, and, in some areas, wolves. But there are also dogs that chase or kill cats. We don't have strict leash laws here, as most of you know."

A loud rumble of voices reverberated throughout the room.

"The subject of today's meeting, however, is people stealing cats. So that's where we're going to focus. By the way, Ms. Waxton is right when she says a cat is safer kept inside, and healthier, too. They live longer."

"Just seems unnatural," Anna said under her breath.

"There are compromises," Max reminded her. "As Ms. Wilson mentioned, you can create wonderful safe areas for your cats who absolutely must be outdoors. I realize there are some cats that you just can't litter train—especially when you're dealing with ferals. That's why I removed all the carpeting in my house and replaced it with tile flooring. But I also have outdoor enclosures for my rescue cats and my own cats. Come over to my place sometime and see the overhead runs and wire enclosures I had built for them. Mine is fairly elaborate, but you can do something similar for quite a bit less money."

Max swept the room with his gaze and said, "The invitation to come see my outdoor cat run is open to all of you. My place is right next door." He then leaned forward in his straight-back chair and crossed one arm over his lap. "Now to the bad stuff. People use cats to train fighting dogs," he said trying to avoid eye contact with anyone.

"What?" Clarice gasped. "How's that?"

Max hesitated and then looked down and quietly said, "Just use your imagination."

Kitty gasped and whispered something in Clarice's ear.

"Oh God," Clarice said shaking her head in disbelief.

Max continued. He was speaking more quickly now. "Cats are used in science labs. Professors and students have been known to pick up what they believe are strays for experimentation. I think most of you know that cats are used to test makeup, skin products and the like. While, of course, there are more legal ways to obtain cats for this sort of testing, there's evidently a black-market element in the works, as well. There are always people who will do any slimy thing for a few dollars."

He paused, shifted in his chair and then continued, "In some cultures, they eat cats. I don't think we have that faction here in our community. But when I was in the restaurant business in Chicago, health-department reps used to come in with all sorts of stories about finding cat carcasses inside the freezers in Asian restaurants."

Max took a deep breath and continued, "People take cats to use as mousers. There are misguided cat hoarders who are so against cats being given outdoor privileges that they'll pick up those they find wandering around in neighborhoods. Then they raise them in horrendously filthy and unhealthy conditions."

88

He hesitated and Betty spoke: "I just read the other day that there are people using cat pelts for clothing and other items. Can you imagine? Just makes me ill."

The women from Ravenwood sat silent. Kitty dabbed at her eyes with a tissue and Clarice patted Kitty's knee.

"Not a pretty picture, indeed," Ida said quietly. And then she asked, "So Max, what is your opinion— why do you think so many cats are disappearing from this one neighborhood?"

He shook his head slowly back and forth before saying, "I've never heard of so many cats going missing at one time like this. Outdoor cats get hit by cars, they get poisoned or accidently locked in neighbors' sheds— there are all kinds of dangers for cats. But why so many are going missing from one area all at once, that's a puzzle. I have to say, it indicates to me that it's more than coincidental. I'm inclined to go along with the general consensus—that someone, for whatever reason, is picking them up and hauling them off somewhere." He swallowed hard, looked down at his hands and said, "Let's hope we can find out who very soon."

Silence loomed large in the room. "After a few moments, Anna pointed toward the hallway. "Oh look at that. Isn't she gorgeous?!"

As if on cue, Layla strolled cautiously into the room.

"What a treat," Betty said. "We needed to see this lovely creature after hearing all of that dismal rhetoric."

"Beautiful baby."

"Such a cutie."

"Look at those eyes…"

There were smiles all around.

"This is Layla," Margaret said with pride in her voice. "She is the sweetest thing ever and she was a throw-away. She was in pretty bad shape when we found her at around four-weeks old." Margaret reached down and ran her hand over Layla's back and along her tail as the cat rubbed against her leg. Layla then jumped up on the ottoman, head-butted Margaret's purple cast and curled up with a plop next to her foot.

"Ahhh, thank you, Layla, for making that grand entrance. Breathtaking and what timing," Ida said.

Margaret stroked Layla's pale tangerine fur. "I have to tell you, this is more of a gift than you know. This girl is just about as shy as they come. She isn't around people all that much, other than me, Max, and now Savannah. She does not like noise or commotion and she stays clear of strangers. For her to come into a room full of people like she just did is an absolute first. So call it what you will—I think she knew we needed her presence," Margaret said—her voice cracking a little.

A brief silence was replaced by hushed tones as everyone pondered and quietly marveled at the gift.

After a few moments, Betty asked, "And what about the big guy? Rags—where's he?"

"Oh, he's probably hiding the stuffed cat in hopes that he can keep it," Savannah said with a chuckle.

Michael glanced over at her. *Nice laugh,* he thought. *What a lovely, lovely woman.*

Again, their eyes met. This time, they locked for an instant. *Gosh, he's gorgeous,* she thought before quickly looking away. She shivered a little at the thought of spending time with him later in the day.

"Well folks, I think we have a better idea of what we can and can't do with regard to the main
90

issue at hand. Ladies," Ida addressed the Ravenwood residents, "our hearts go out to you. And we are with you in your to attempt discover what's happening to your beloved cats and to have them returned safe and whole."

She then glanced around the room. "I know some of you have to get to work—most of us have litter boxes to clean," she laughed quietly. And then she took on a more serious tone, "I understand that we still have the issue of—well, I might as well say it—the conflict among us. What do you say we table that discussion for today and focus on the missing cat situation? Are you all onboard with this?"

"Yes."

"Yeah."

"Definitely."

"Can I see a show of hands? Is there anyone opposed?" She glanced over at the board members. "Thank you—no one is opposed. Okay, as some of you know, Margaret agreed to head up a committee to work on the missing-cat problem. Margaret, do you have anything to say before we adjourn?"

"Yes," she said. "First of all, I want to say, I love it. Look at us working together. See—we can do it."

A rumble of comments and a smattering of smiles rippled through the crowd.

"I'd like to propose," Margaret continued, "that we do more investigation. And as Mr. Silva suggests, be really diligent in the neighborhoods where the catnapping is taking place—keep a closer eye on things for now. Can you four ladies meet with representatives from the other tract or tracts involved and spread the word that we are going to help; but they all need to be proactive?"

The foursome looked at one another and then

turned back to Margaret, nodding in agreement.

"Then I'm willing to head the investigation. I'll work with Mr. Silva, and we'll put our ears to the ground and see what we can learn and what direction we need to go in order to stop the catnapping and, hopefully, retrieve your cats. That's our goal, right Alliance members?"

"Here, here!"

"Absolutely."

"Amen."

"Who wants to be on my committee? Betty and Gil, I'd sure like to be able to count on you. And Max, of course."

"Sure thing," Gil said.

Betty nodded.

Max nodded, as well.

"Anyone else?" Margaret asked.

"You can call on me anytime—I can do work or computer research from home—phone calls—that sort of thing," Hildy offered.

"Well thank you, Hildy. That would be great. That's probably enough involvement at this point until we know who and what we're dealing with."

"Thank you Margaret," Ida said. "If there's nothing else, let's adjourn the meeting. I see that there are a few donuts left."

"And hot coffee and tea," Margaret added.

\*\*\*

"I thought the meeting went well," Max said over his shoulder as he led Savannah, who was pushing Margaret in her wheelchair, toward the cat pens on his property.

"It sounds like you two have your work cut out

for you—trying to figure out what happened to those cats," Savannah said, a hint of reserve in her voice.

"You two?" Margaret craned her neck to look at her niece. "You're part of the team now, my dear. In fact, you're my legs, remember?"

"Oh," Savannah said, cringing slightly.

"You know you can't come here without expecting some kind of adventure. Right Max?"

"Not if you hang around with your aunt for very long." He turned toward them and stopped. "Savannah, you wouldn't believe some of the things she's gotten me into." He shook his head as if in disbelief.

"What?" Margaret insisted—a challenging tone to her voice.

"Well, there was the time you confronted that motorcycle-gang leader who was riding around on his bike with a cat strapped to the back in a cage. Remember?" Before Margaret could respond, he said, "And what about that day you kidnapped me and made me help you round up all those cats left after they condemned that apartment building over on Simpson Street and evicted everyone?" Obviously addressing Savannah now, he explained, "I don't think anyone took their cats with them. That was one hard job and on the hottest day of the year, too," he lamented.

"Oh you loved it," Margaret said. "What else do you have to do all day? You would lead a mighty boring life if it wasn't for me."

"Boring, you say? Well, there's gotta be a happy medium between what you consider boring and your brand of excitement, lady. You almost got us arrested when you tried to raid that rescue-cat facility over in Mallory." He leaned toward Margaret, placing his hands on the armrests of the wheelchair. "Do you remember that? Huh?" he asked while trying to make eye-contact with her. Margaret's grin widened as Max's theatrics accelerated. "A little too much excitement for me," he said as he stood up and ran his hand through his hair. "Savannah, you should have been there. I mean there were broken windows, yeowling cats, people yelling at us from the upstairs bedrooms and, oh yes, sirens and police cars."

Margaret huffed, "How do you even know those sirens were from police cars coming to that spot? We were long gone before any *imaginary* police cars showed up. I did get the photos I wanted for evidence, didn't I? And we had that place shut down. Right, Mr. Boring?"

By then Savannah was laughing hysterically. "You two are like a couple of senior delinquents," she said between chortles. "And you act like a married couple."

She couldn't help but notice the look between the two of them. *Well,* Savannah thought to herself, *more than just friends, I'd say. Good for Auntie. He's a nice gentleman.*

*A married couple, indeed,* Margaret thought. She admitted that she loved Max and she certainly enjoyed their occasional (becoming more frequent) rendezvous. She considered Max a great friend and a wonderful lover. She thought about Savannah's offhanded question her first morning there. *Yes, he is the one I wear my sexy underwear for. And I've never known a man who could make me feel so sexy. I guess it'll be a while before we can be together again what with my cast and Savannah's visit. Ohhhh, maybe we could sneak around.* Margaret smiled at the thought. *Yes, I'm sure if I put my mind to it, I can arrange for an encounter of the passionate kind, even if it is a quick romp in the cattery when no one's looking.* Margaret
94

especially enjoyed the thrill of a risky romantic adventure.

Max opened the outside gate. "Come on in, at your own risk. I think the chair will fit in here. The other gate opens inward, so no problem."

Savannah steered the chair into the large enclosure and then stopped to look around and try to take it all in.

"It used to be a commercial greenhouse," Max explained. "It converted rather nicely into a cattery, don't you think?"

"It's great!" Savannah said as she noticed numerous spacious cat pens, each adorned with cat trees in various forms, styles and colors; toys; litter boxes; and, of course, water and kibbles bowls. Savannah noticed that most of the cats in the wire enclosures looked healthy. She stopped and peered into a long narrow pen. "What's wrong with this one?"

"He was found out in the warehouse district, quite undernourished. He looks a lot better, now, doesn't he, Maggie?"

"Oh yes. He was really gaunt when we brought him in. Max has done wonders with him."

He gave Margaret a sideways glance and said, "Don't let your aunt fool you. She's here practically every day. She's the main reason why so many of these cats make it." Looking over at Savannah, he continued, "Maggie has a way with their psyche. She makes them feel loved and this helps them gain back the confidence they may have lost when they were abandoned or even abused." He walked ahead to an enclosure off to the side away from the others. "Take this little guy, for example. He was lit on fire—probably by a group of kids who hadn't been taught about the humane treatment of animals. He lost an eye, as you can see, part of an ear, and the fur on his tail will probably never grow back. He's scarred physically and certainly emotionally. But Maggie and some of the other volunteers have helped him begin to trust again. My sense is that he was a stray; he may have been part of the colony over in the barranca behind the old prison. When they closed that facility and moved to the new one out on the interstate, it appears that they left a lot of cats they may have been using as mousers around the place. Anyway, Gus is doing well under the circumstances."

Savannah squatted down, reached her hand through a space alongside the wire gate and scratched the little cat under the chin. "What a brave boy you are, Gus. You hang in there," she cooed. Gus purred up a storm.

She felt something bump her from behind. She pivoted enough to see a long-legged grey cat vying for her attention.

"That's Chester," Max said. "He's our greeter. He's one of our best public relations cats."

"Where's Sammy?" she asked, remembering him telling her about the cat on only two legs.

"He's in the house. I have my own cats separate from the rescue and cattery cats. I bring some of them out regularly to influence our hard-core ferals or I might take a feral inside to get them used to a household situation," he explained. "You'll have a chance to meet Sammy and the others."

Suddenly, Savannah spotted cats lounging in a grassy area outside a large window. "Oh, that's your outside pen?"

Max smiled. "Yes, want a tour?"

She walked over to get a better look through the window. "Sure do."

96

Her aunt rolled up next to her. "This you gotta see, Vannie. It's Max's answer for cats who *must* be outside."

"And those who can benefit from a little exercise and fresh air," he added.

Savannah looked around. "How do they get out there?"

Max pointed to the left of the window just below the ceiling. "You see that tube? They come up this ramp and go out through the opening. Those cats, like Chester, that are free to roam in this common space, have access to the out-of-doors just about any time during the day." Max looked around the large room. "I guess most of the others are outside as we speak. Oh, I see Brandi and, I think that's Katrina napping in the bunk-room."

Savannah glanced over. To the right of the double-gate entrance was another sizable area outfitted with kitty hammocks and beds, cat trees with private sleeping areas, padded square and cylindrical enclosures with places inside to sleep, and even bunk beds. She then turned her attention back to the tube. "A magic tunnel, kind of like Alice in Wonderland," Savannah said with a hint of excitement and anticipation. "Wow! I love it!" She strained to see the full extent of the passageway through the window.

"Max, take Vannie out and show it to her," Margaret suggested. "I'll spend a little time with Gus. Here, help me get inside. I'll just sit on his cat tree."

After they got Margaret settled in Gus's enclosure, Savannah followed Max out through the double gates and they walked alongside the wire-and-plywood tube that meandered throughout his property about seven feet above the ground.

"Look at that drop-down area. This is so cool."

Savannah watched as two cats lounged on a perch in a large wire pen, and a third leaped after a butterfly fluttering around the landscape.

"All cat-friendly plants," Max said. "There's nothing poisonous and many that attract butterflies. There are three of these drop-down areas, as you call them."

"It's absolutely wonderful. Look how contented the cats are—there's one sleeping up in the tube enjoying the sunshine. This is fabulous! Max, you are a genius."

He shook his head. "Oh, it wasn't actually my idea. I heard about it at a cat show and added some special touches."

"Well, it's still wonderful. So all of the cats that are not in the enclosures can come out here at anytime?"

"Not really. At night, I close them in the bunk-room area you saw over near the isolation booths."

"Isolation—that would be for the newcomers?" Savannah asked.

"Yes. We have all incoming cats and kittens checked out for leukemia, upper respiratory diseases, fleas, and so forth before introducing them to the current residents. We're regular clients at Michael Ivey's clinic," he explained.

Savannah's heart felt like it turned a somersault as she remembered the vision of Michael standing there holding the two kittens in his hands. She gave her head a little shake in an attempt to bring herself back to the present. "How much turnover do you have?" she asked as they stopped to watch three more cats lounging in an even larger wire enclosure under the shade of a California sycamore tree.

"I placed forty cats and kittens last year."

"Impressive," Savannah said.

Max picked a long blade of grass and stuck it through the wire in hopes of enticing one of the cats to play. "Well, I'm not breaking any records and I'm not interested in doing so. There are facility operators in this and surrounding counties who boast about placing closer to 100 cats and kittens in a year. That's well and good, as long as the kitty homes are stable and permanent. I'm a small operation. I'm more interested in rehabilitation—which is your aunt's specialty, as I said. We do a lot more socializing here than most facilities take the time to do. And I don't know for sure, but I think we have a higher percentage of successful adoptions."

Savannah looked over at Max and asked, "How did you get started?"

He put the blade of grass between his lips and thought for a minute about how to respond. Finally, he dropped the weed and said, "Like I told you yesterday, I've been fond of cats ever since I was a kid. After college, I had the opportunity to go to culinary school and I became a chef."

"Wow! Ever have your own Food Network show?"

Max laughed out loud. "No. Wrong era, I'm afraid. I'd probably have a show focusing on making cat and dog food, if I were to do it today. Let's see, I could call it, 'The Culinary Cat,' or 'Furry Feasting.'"

"How about 'Feeding Your Feline?'" Savannah suggested.

"Or 'The Doggy Bag.'"

They both laughed. And then, abruptly changing the subject, Max said, "I'm thirsty, how about you?"

"Yes. I could use some water. But I'd love to hear the rest of your story, Max. Sounds fascinating."

"Okay, let's rescue your aunt from Gus or vice versa and we'll go inside for some refreshment."

\*\*\*

*No one home—good.* The man steered his dark-colored pickup into the driveway. He stopped in front of the house and looked up at the second-story window where he'd seen the grey-and-white cat. *Not there. That's okay,* he thought, as he plotted his next move. He sneered. *I'll find him. He'll want this fresh fish I brought just for him.* He opened the wire door of the plastic carrier on the seat next to him, slid out the driver's side and left the door ajar. He'd had enough experience with cats lately to know that he had to act quickly once he got his hands on the animal. He slipped on a pair of tan leather gloves for added protection.

*What's that?* he wondered. *Looks like someone's coming. Shit.* He yanked off the gloves, tossed them on the floorboard of the truck, jumping in after them as fast as he could. He turned the key, pulled hard on the steering wheel, and headed out the exit of the circular drive and onto the road, hitting 40 mph within seconds.

"Who is that?" Esperanza asked. "He hurries!"

Antonio removed his hat and scratched his head. "I don't know. Mucho trees. Did you see him?"

"No. Just a dark car and dirt—dust," she said as she stopped her Toyota in front of the Forster house."

Antonio stepped out of the car and immediately bent down. When he stood back up, he was examining something he held in his hand. "It's a glove," he told his wife. "Not my glove. Not Señora Maggie's glove. Maybe that man's glove," he said, staring off in the direction of the highway.

He shook his head and dropped his hand to his

side. He then walked up to the car window to tell his wife goodbye. "Come back and get me for dinner."

She nodded and watched him deposit the tan leather glove on the porch and then head out to the backyard.

Before she could drive away, he called after her, "Look. Gato watch." He pointed to a window on the second story.

Esperanza looked up at the cat, smiled, and then waved goodbye to her husband.

\*\*\*

"Welcome to my cat house," Max said as the trio entered his kitchen.

Margaret looked around. "No pussy-foot stampede today?"

"Must be nap time. Let's get our lemonade before they notice we're here."

"Can I help?" Savannah asked.

"Yes, thanks. There are glasses in the cupboard on the left. And I think Helena left some cookies in that plastic container."

"Helena works for you, too?" Savannah wondered.

"Yes. Your aunt and I share a lot—same neighborhood, same housekeeper, same love of cats." He looked over at Margaret as if making a private statement.

"Yum, cookies," she said in an attempt to ignore his intent. "Are they the oatmeal raisin she brought me last week?"

"I ate those. These are chocolate-something."

Once the lemonade was poured, a few cookies were placed on a small plate and everyone was seated,

Savannah addressed Margaret, "Max was telling me how he came to start this wonderful rescue operation." She looked over at Max and said, "I'd like to hear the rest of the story."

He shot a look toward Margaret. "You've heard this before—don't want to bore you."

"I never tire of hearing about your interesting life, Max. Please, go on."

"Okay," he said with a sigh. "Where were we?"

"You were going to start a cooking show called 'The Culinary Cat,'" Savannah said, her eyes twinkling with amusement.

"Say what?" Margaret asked, a surprised look on her face.

Max slapped at the air. "She's joking." He then squinted his eyes and cocked his head slightly as if he were trying to remember. "Oh, so I was a private chef for a while. I also worked for some pretty classy joints in various cities throughout the West and in Chicago. I was quite enamored with the whole cooking scene for a while. And then I wasn't." He paused. "By the time I decided to do something else, my marriage had ended and my son had finished college and started working in the technology industry in Baltimore. I had only me to think about—me and my cat, at the time."

"So you've always had cats?" Savannah asked.

"Pretty much, I'd say. I can't recall any long periods that I went without a cat. But by the time I gave up my love of cooking…"

"Whoa, back up there, cowboy," Margaret interrupted. "You didn't give it up." She then turned to Savannah and said, "He is an absolutely marvelous cook."

"Well, no, I didn't give it up altogether," Max agreed. "But, let's say I gave up my obsession with it. I was able and ready to leave that career behind. Now, I wanted to focus on another love of mine—cats. I guess I was lonely after my divorce and with my son so far away. All I had left was the family cat. I really liked that little guy and became rather interested in knowing more about cats. I was living in Chicago at the time and heard there was a cat show in town. The idea intrigued me and so I went to the show. That's when I fell madly in love with the British shorthair. Long story short," he said, "I became a breeder."

He took a generous swig of lemonade and then tapped an ice cube that floated to the top of the glass a couple of times. Max wasn't all that proud of some decisions he'd made in his lifetime. And breeding cats was one of them. It wasn't easy for him to talk about it.

"Brits are lovely cats," Savannah said. "Those I've known have made really nice companions. I just love their chubby cheeks and those great round eyes. Hard to resist."

"And those I saw at the show that day were so calm, unlike some of the more nervous breeds. I just felt good in their presence. I bought one that day, as a matter of fact. Phoebe and I (with our tag-along, Elmer—a mutt of a cat) moved to the suburbs and began planning our breeding program. I joined all of the appropriate associations, attended meetings, did tons of research and, a few months later, I opened my cattery. I sold my little teddy bear kittens to people all over the world. They were especially popular overseas. About six years later, I qualified to become a cat-show judge."

"You were quite embedded in the industry, weren't you?" Savannah mused.

Max chuckled. "Oh yes. I think your aunt will tell you that I don't do anything halfway. Right, Maggie?"

Margaret contemplated the question and had to agree that when he was passionate about something, he gave it his all. That's why she felt so much pressure from him at times when he pursued the question of marriage so fervently. She loved Max. There was no denying it. But marriage? She wasn't ready for it at this point in her life—maybe never. She liked things just the way they were. "That's right, Max. You can become obsessed…or possessed," she added with an impish laugh.

"Aw, Auntie, is that fair? Maybe it takes one to know one," Savannah said, a wide grin. Before Margaret could react, Savannah turned to Max and asked, "So what disturbed this lovely lifestyle?"

"In a word, Ellie. He looked down at his glass of lemonade as if in deep contemplation.

"Oh, a female!"

"Yes, Savannah, you might say that," Max said thoughtfully. "The cattery wasn't supporting me, you see. Besides, it could be confining. So I took a job as a restaurant chef in downtown Chicago. I'd always been aware of cats hanging around the garbage cans in the alleys behind the restaurants in the city. I felt sorry for them. I saved scraps for them and all. But now—maybe it was because I had become so focused on cats—I began seeing these alley cats as if I were seeing them for the first time. The same cats came night after night. Some were aggressive, some frightened. Some of them would come initially looking pretty good—only a little gaunt. Then they might show up one night missing an eye or an ear. Some were diseased. Abscesses got seriously out of control. And kittens. There seemed to always be pregnant females. Some would bring kittens with them to the garbage bins when they were old enough. Some had obviously lost their kittens."

Max reached out and petted a big yellow cat that had wandered in on quiet paws. He looked down at him for a second and then continued, "This began bothering me more and more. One night I heard a commotion in the alley." He took a deep breath. "I went out just in time to see some kids, who were old enough to know better, tormenting one of the cats. Before I could stop them, they had done some serious damage." Max couldn't hide the anger he felt inside. It showed like a beacon on his face. He virtually growled through gritted teeth, "I came unglued!"

Savannah sat in silence, swallowing a flow of emotion. Margaret appeared to be holding her breath.

"My heart absolutely broke for this cat. I was pretty sure she was with kittens at the time. I lost it. I rushed those kids—would have beaten them to a pulp if I'd been fast enough to catch them. I even called the authorities, but there was nothing they could do. The kids were long gone. I had a good description and a policeman did actually come out and listen to me. But I knew that was probably the end of it." Max paused and took a deep breath. "That wasn't the end of it for me, though," he said defiantly. "That night, I went out and looked for the little cat." He choked up a little as he said, "I found her. She had crawled away and hid under some old boxes. She was unconscious."

Savannah cringed and closed her eyes in an attempt to erase the image. It didn't help.

Max said, his tone steady and sure, "I put the assistant chef in charge, left the restaurant and took the cat to the nearest all-night vet clinic. I knew about the place because one of my Brits had a problem delivering one night and I had taken her there. Anyway, the little cat was in bad shape. There were some broken bones and she lost her kittens. But

105

I could tell that she was tough. I don't know if it was her determination I saw or my own reflecting in her. But I had a feeling that she was something special and I asked the vet to do everything he could to save her.

"Actually, I guess that's when I came to realize that all cats are special and deserve every chance we can give them. I think that's what I was put in that position to learn. This little cat represented something more to me than one stray I could help. She represented a shift in my very being."

"Ooooo, goose bumps," Savannah said with a shiver. By then a tabby had joined them in the kitchen and had agreed to sit on her lap. She found this especially comforting while hearing Max's gripping story.

"The little cat recovered and I took her home. She was an ugly duckling next to my beautiful Brits," he said, laughing out loud. "And she didn't know how to behave. I'm not sure she'd ever been a household pet before. But I suspect she did know people at some point in her short life. She had a lot to learn, and so did I. This little girl turned out to be one of the most interesting and charming cats I'd ever owned. Present company excepted Grizzy and Big Boy," he said, acknowledging the two cats that had just wandered in. "And you, too, Gretchen; I see you hiding around the corner there."

He continued, "Truly, there was something about her—and to think that someone could just throw her away like that and that someone could abuse her. I still get choked up when I think about my little Ellie." He paused. "Yes, I named her Ellie, for the restaurant where I worked—Ellison's. I never wanted to forget the cats in that alley. To me, she represented all ferals, strays and abused cats everywhere."

106

He took a ragged breath. "This was a definite turning point in my life. Ellie is the reason why I quit breeding and judging and why I shifted my whole focus to those cats who are already here and that nobody wants. Ellie and the others in the alley are the reason why I'm here today. She even made a vegetarian out of me." He straightened his posture, tilted his head a little and said, "I'll bet you don't know many vegetarian chefs."

Savannah shook her head. "How's that, Max?"

"Well, one night I was holding Ellie in my arms…it took a while and a lot of patience, but she finally gave in and decided that she rather liked being massaged and stroked. So anyway, I was holding her like a baby, looking down into her face, and I realized at that moment that I could never eat animal meat again."

The only sound in the kitchen for the next several minutes came from the cats. There was a mixture of purring, chirping, and a quiet and occasional mew. Finally Savannah looked over at Max and asked, "So what brought you here?"

He leaned back in his chair, and said, "Well, I got my Brits spayed and neutered—even the kittens. I sold them all and Ellie, Elmer, and I moved out here to start a new life. Sure, there are plenty of cats to save in Chicago, but I was ready for a change. I didn't know where we would end up. I started scouring the Internet in search of ideas and opportunities. When this nursery came up for sale, I thought it would make a great cat facility and I put in a bid. I've been here for nearly three years."

"Dare I ask…about Ellie?" Savannah said quietly and hesitantly, a lump in her throat.

Max reached out toward a young cat that had stretched up, placed her front paws on his leg and began

107

kneading enthusiastically. "Easy, girl," he said with a grimace. "You have needles in those paws of yours." He lifted the cat into his lap, ruffled the fur on her head and then continued his story. "Well, I guess Ellie's work on earth was finished. She was only about eight when her kidneys began to fail. Despite the fact that she lived like a queen the last few years of her life, her rough beginnings must have caught up with her. She died in my arms the day I opened this facility."

Savannah could no longer hold back the tears. She picked up a napkin from a stack in the middle of the table and dabbed at her eyes. Margaret sat with her head down, obviously touched by the story even though she'd heard it a time or two or three.

"And you named the place after her," Savannah said, her voice cracking.

"Yes, this is El's Cat Rescue Shelter."

Savannah looked down at the napkin she was picking at with her fingers.

"He's a unique cat person, that's for sure," Margaret said, looking at him with fondness. "And he has what many don't—a head for business as well as a heart for cats. That's an unusual combination, you know?"

Savannah nodded her head. "Yes, I've seen that in the veterinary field." She turned to Max and asked, "Do you rely on donations?"

"Yes, we have a few fundraisers throughout the year," he said. "The dance coming up is a fundraiser sponsored by all of the local cat-rescue places. This is a first—a start toward our working together rather than trying to each run our own shows separately. Maggie and I believe that we can accomplish more together than when there are so many different agendas. Many heads working together are better than individual heads working apart." He looked up at Margaret and said, "If I could only convince your aunt that two hearts are better than one."

Savannah looked over in time to see her aunt's face tinge pink. *Cool*, she thought. *Very cool.*

\*\*\*

"That was a friggin' good score this morning, Alex ole buddy!" the taller boy said to the smaller one as they walked home from school together that afternoon.

"Yeah, four easy ones. That's friggin' ten bucks each!" He turned toward his friend and asked, "Whatcha gonna do with your take, Cody?"

"Maybe buy cigarettes and beer," he said with a big grin.

"Friggin' cool," Alex said. "But who's gonna get it for ya?"

"I'm thinkin' that old guy we work for might."

"He's friggin' creepy."

"Yeah, I know, Alex. I'm kinda scared every time we hafta get in that old rattletrap with him. Don't you wonder where he's gonna take us and what he's gonna do?"

"You watch too many scary movies, dude!"

"Oh yeah? Ever notice that big knife he carries on his belt?" Cody asked.

"I can't even look at that guy. He creeps me out. He has a knife?"

"Yeah. When he picks us up today, let's ask him if he'll buy the stuff and we'll get wasted on the weekend." He grabbed his friend's shirt and pulled him around to face him. "Hey, we can spend the night in that old barn behind my house," he said, obviously excited at the thought. "No one ever goes in there and my ole man won't know nothin'."

"Hey Cody, your old man drinks beer and smokes cigarettes. Maybe we can get some from him."

"Naw, I tried that once. Got caught. I think he keeps track of his stuff now. Doesn't trust me for some reason." He looked over at Alex and the two of them laughed.

"Okay then, we'll ask the old fart. You ask him, okay?"

"Yeah, whatever." And then he added, "Do you think he'd let us drink the beer up at his place?"

"The creepy guy? You want to party at that place? Are you crazy?" he asked punching Cody in the arm. "Who knows what he might do to us up there in the hills. Naw, I don't trust that guy at all." Alex then turned to his friend and said, "He really creeped me out the time we saw that fat bitch bending over to pick up her newspaper in that short thing she was wearing. Do you remember how he acted and what he said?"

"Yeah, that was weird, man," Cody recalled. "I wouldn't be surprised if he went back there after dropping us off." Then he pushed Alex playfully and said, "He's been in prison, you know."

"Really? For what?"

"He didn't exactly say. But that day you couldn't go with us, he told me stuff about prison. He's about as bad a dude as I've ever met," Cody said. "It's friggin' crazy that we're even working for him. Why are we doin' it, anyway?"

"Money!" Alex thought for a minute and then added with a devilish grin, "You gotta say it's kinda a kick—this work that we do."

Both boys laughed and Alex jumped in the air to slap Cody's hand for a jubilant high five.

***

As Savannah pulled up in front of her aunt's house after the short drive from Max's place, Margaret's cell phone rang. She fumbled around in her purse. "Darn, I can never find that thing." Finally, "Hello? Oh Ms. Lipton…uh, Dora. Yes, I remember you, how are you? Yes, what's up?"

Savannah watched as her aunt's face changed from pensive to curious to dubious and then she seemed downright ecstatic. "Really?!!?" she said, as she glanced over at her niece—her eyes flashing with excitement.

"Sure, I know the area." She listened intently. After several seconds, she asked, "Are you sure?" and then, "Well, I'll see what I can find out. Thank you very much for calling," Margaret said into the phone as she gave Savannah a knowing look.

"By the way, Ms. Lipton… Okay Dora… are you aware of the benefit we're having Saturday night here in Hammond? Proceeds are to be split among all the cat-rescue organizations in the Alliance, if you can imagine that!"

"Yes, I know," Margaret continued, "little cooperation among them. That's so true. Anyway, I'd like to invite you to come out for the dance and I think I can pull some strings to have you collect some of the donations. You are a licensed business, aren't you?"

She listened for a few seconds and then said, "Oh, well, maybe you'll qualify for a cut next time. I'll send you a flyer. Do you have email? Oh. Okay, got it—DoraCat37@yahoo.com. Try to come and meet some of the people who love cats as much as you do. I think we could probably help each other do a better job of keeping cats safe. And bring Charlotte. Okay, Ms…I

111

mean Dora. Thank you again."

"Zowie!" Margaret said as she slammed the phone down on her lap and gazed, as if stunned, out the car window.

"What?" Savannah wanted to know.

Margaret turned in her seat toward Savannah. "Do you remember that sweet girl we met at Dora's house?"

"Charlotte, yes," Savannah recalled with a smile. "She has a place name, too."

"Well, evidently she's more savvy than some people think and she overheard something she thought was important. Some kids at her school were talking about their escapades which involved *grabbing cats*." Margaret emphasized the last two words by speaking them slowly and clearly, and watched for her niece's reaction.

"What? Someone is bragging about it?"

"Yes," she blurted. "According to Dora, Charlotte overheard a couple of boys say that they were being paid for this cool job of finding and grabbing cats and delivering them to a ranch up in the foothills." Margaret became more animated—her voice more shrill. "Savannah," she said reaching out and placing her hand on her niece's arm, "evidently, one boy was showing off the scratches he got while struggling with a fierce cat."

"Oh, probably Patches—Gina's cat!" Savannah said.

"Yes!" Margaret was having trouble containing her excitement. She was speaking faster now. "Oh my gosh, girl. We've cracked the case! We know where the cats are being taken. Charlotte didn't get the boys' names, but Dora was pretty sure the information she got will be helpful to us. And it is! I know the place where
112

they're taking the cats. It belongs to Russell Bray."

"Oh my gosh," Savannah said reaching for the door handle.

"Wait!" Margaret almost shouted.

Savannah looked over at her aunt, wondering what she was thinking now. She wasn't completely surprised to hear her say, "Let's go up there and see what we can find out."

Savannah thought about it. She then looked over at her aunt and shook her head. "No, Auntie. It's nearly 3:15 and we've run around a lot again today. I think you should rest that foot. Let's go in and get you comfy in your chair with your foot up and I'll fix us something to eat. We can talk about how to approach this situation. Okay?"

Margaret relaxed against the car seat. "Of course, you're right Vannie. Sorry for jumping the gun. I am kinda tired." She reached over and opened the car door. "Roll the windows back up, will you? Don't want vermin in my car."

"Oh yes," Savannah said with a chuckle, "possums, alligators…wild boar…"

"Ha ha," Margaret said. "You just wait until you wake up and step out of bed on a snake or have a mouse run across your toes."

"I'm not squeamish, Auntie," Savannah said as she exited the car. She walked around to help Margaret and continued, "I sure didn't like hearing the possibilities Max talked about this morning, though— all those awful things people do to cats. It's great to see so many people on the cats' side. Refreshing." As she stood there watching Margaret get situated on her crutches, she said, "I'm so glad I came, Auntie."

"So am I, honey. So am I."

"What's this?" Margaret asked no one in

particular.

"What?" Savannah stared over in the direction her aunt faced. "Looks like a glove. Maybe it's Antonio's," she suggested.

"A leather glove?" Margaret said. "Gardeners don't wear leather gloves, do they?"

"Maybe if they're stacking wood or something." Savannah picked up the glove and took a closer look while her aunt stepped up on the porch. "It has little poke-holes in it—like pin holes. That's strange," she said. "Once you get settled, I'll go out and ask Antonio if the glove is his." And then she called after her aunt, "What do you want me to do with it?" she asked.

"Just leave it there where we found it."

\*\*\*

A few minutes later, an old-model, dark-colored pickup truck stopped at the end of the driveway in front of the Forster house.

"Can't you just drive in and get it?" Cody begged.

"No, I can't. Now git out and run up there and git it like I said."

"Run all that ways? Are you crazy? That's about a mile," Cody said.

"No it ain't no mile. Now go on. Git that glove and hurry," the driver said as he continued to nervously glance around in all directions.

Cody started to climb out of the truck, when the driver grabbed his sweatshirt and pulled the boy toward him. "And don't let nobody see you, do you hear me?"

"Yeah, I hear ya. Now let go, old man."

After a few minutes, the boy returned. "Here's your stupid glove, now let's git outta

114

here," he said as he dove through the passenger side door and into the old truck."

*\*\**

"No Señorita. It is no my glove. I find it on the ground after the stranger drives away."

"Stranger?" Savannah asked. "What stranger? Did you see what he looked like?"

"No, he drive fast—lots of dirt behine him," he said making a swooping motion with his arms.

"What kind of car?"

Antonio hesitated, rubbed his chin.

"Was it a big car? Small one…" Savannah prompted.

"Truck," Antonio said with a grin. "Peek-up truck."

"What color?"

Antonio looked down and shook his head from side to side. "Dark, verde, maybe?"

"Dark green?"

"Si."

"Okay Antonio. Thank you. I'll tell Ms. Maggie."

Savannah walked around to the front of the house to examine the glove again. But when she reached the railing where she'd left it, she discovered that it was gone. Brow furrowed, she glanced around the area. Suddenly, she heard what sounded like a car revving up. She looked in the direction of the sound in time to see an older dark-colored pickup truck taking off quickly from the end of the driveway. *Hmmm, that's strange,* she thought.

"Meow."

She looked behind her and saw Rags walking

toward her on the porch. "Uh-oh. Sorry buddy. I guess I left the door unlocked again. Come on, let me get you something to eat," she said as she scooped him up and carried him back into the house.

\*\*\*

"Well, good morning, sunshine," Margaret greeted her niece. "And what time did you get home last night?"

"Gosh, around midnight, I guess," she said trying to hold her telling grin down to a minimum.

Margaret dropped her magazine in the rack next to her chair, fixed her stare on Savannah and asked, "And when did you actually come in and go to bed?"

She smiled sheepishly. "Um, sometime this morning."

"That was quite gallant of Michael to pick you up," Margaret said.

"Well, he had a call out this way and wasn't sure I knew how to get to his clinic…"

"So how did it go, Vannie?"

Savannah virtually threw herself into the soft cushions of the loveseat in a swoon and gushed, "Oh, Auntie, I had the best time."

"I mean how did the surgery on the cat go?" her aunt said, trying to maintain a straight face.

"Oh…" Savannah said. She cleared her throat and toned down her obvious exuberance. "Surgery went fine. Cat's resting comfortably. She had swallowed something plastic and it wasn't moving through. Poor thing. She'll be okay." She laid her head back on the sofa for a few moments and then said, "Michael is a wonderful vet. I loved working with him."

"I can see that," Margaret said with a grin. "Soooooo, tell me the rest."

116

"What rest?" Savannah feigned innocence.

"You can't fool me, Vannie. You two don't just spew sparks when you're together; it's more like a lightning bolt or an exploding transformer."

Savannah began to laugh uncontrollably. "Lightning?" she said between chortles. "Exploding transformers? Funny." And then she suddenly stopped, looked over at her aunt and said, "I think I'm hysterical. Why am I hysterical? I'm not that kind of silly girl."

Margaret shook her head. "You look like a girl in love, kiddo."

Savannah tilted her head. "But I've only known him a few days."

"Doesn't matter. Ever heard of love at first sight?"

"Yeah, but I didn't believe it," Savannah said somberly.

"Well, believe it, girl. I think that's what's happening here. Now go get dressed. We have an important mission to accomplish today."

"Oh, okay—will there be coffee?" Savannah asked.

"Yeah, yeah. We'll take some travel mugs. Now get going before the love bug gets the best of you."

Savannah headed up the stairs toward her room, thoughts of Michael Ivey running through her head. *I've never had such a lovely evening hanging out at a vet clinic,* she thought. She was still stunned at how fast the evening went. By the time they decided that the patient could be left alone after surgery, four hours had passed. Then Michael drove her home and they sat on the porch swing and talked until nearly three in the morning. *Just talking,* she smiled to herself as she pulled the blankets up on her bed and headed into the bathroom for a quick shower. *...and a little cuddling. Gosh, he sure makes me* *feel good.*

"Savannah, no dawdling now."

"Okay, Auntie."

* * *

"Have you talked to anyone about what Dora told you yesterday?" Savannah asked as she drove out toward the foothills under her aunt's direction.

"Nope. Want to see what I can see, first."

"Don't you think we should call Rudy?"

Margaret frowned. "Who?"

"Rudy Silva...the man in the beret who was..."

"Ohhhhh, him," she said pressing her lips together and gazing out the side window. She looked over at Savannah. "I thought we should check it out first and then we can give him a call."

Savannah glanced over at her aunt. *She doesn't have any intentions of calling him,* she thought. After a few minutes, she broke the silence, "You said you know this place. What do you know about Mr. Bray?"

Margaret thought for a few seconds. "Not much...that he bought the property a few years ago and he runs horses. He's a widower with a couple of boys who aren't interested in ranch life. He hires people to help him out there. Helena's sister used to work for him. She said he was a bear to work for—expected a lot and didn't treat people very well. She said he is just an unhappy, angry man. His main ranch hand is like his clone, only this guy also leans toward being a bit of a psycho. I haven't met either one of them. But Helena's sister, Martha, didn't stay long—couldn't handle the *energy* on the ranch, whatever that means. Too much testosterone, maybe?" She thought for a moment and then said, "Or maybe she meant negativity. Some
118

people can feel it like it's real."

"Well, I can. Can't you, Auntie? Aren't there just some people you find hard to be around and you can't quite put your finger on why? It's just that being near them sort of makes you feel uncomfortable, somehow."

It didn't take Margaret long to respond. "Actually, yes. There was this one relative of Tom's who gave me the creeps. He was a kid when I first met him. He had a way of looking at you that made your skin crawl. I wondered why they let him socialize with the other family members. I always thought he should be locked up or something. I felt evil vibes coming from him. In fact, he did wind up in an institution after having some sort of breakdown. He has spent time in jail, too. I haven't thought about young Joe Forster in a long time."

"That sounds like an extreme case. But yes, that's what I'm talking about. You do know what it feels like, then."

"Here," Margaret said quickly, "turn right here."

Savannah took a look ahead. "Yikes! Are you sure your car can make it? The road looks pretty rutted and steep."

"Sure it can. Why do you ask?" Margaret frowned.

"Well, it is a Jeep, but not the four-wheel type. Isn't the Liberty kind of a foo-foo step-sister to the real Jeep?"

"Heck no, this isn't a foo-foo step-sister to any car. I love my car and she can do everything I ask her to." She motioned toward the dirt road. "Just drive."

"Okay, but I'm not carrying you back if we get stuck."

"We won't get stuck. I've done this before."

"You've been up here before?" Savannah asked.

"Sure—years ago. Didn't you ever come up here to neck?"

"Neck?" Savannah said with a giggle. "Do you mean make out?"

Margaret waved her hand in the air. "Whatever." She then asked, "Well, didn't you?"

"Not in the cars my boyfriends drove."

Margaret was right. The car climbed the rutted road just fine. Once they reached the crest, she said in a hushed tone, "Stop here."

The women sat in silence for a few minutes while Margaret assessed the situation at the ranch house below. "Well, I'll be…things are starting to make sense."

"What do you mean?"

"Well, my dear niece, if this guy is paying kids to bring in cats, he's probably using them as mousers for that big barn over there where he keeps hay and grain for the horses." Margaret explained with a bit of flourish.

"But so many cats…why does he need so many?"

Margaret hissed, "Coyotes, owls—you name it—live off of those cats. They must not be able to keep them long enough to get a good handle on the rodent problem out here. This joker doesn't know what he's doing and I'm not sure he cares."

"So what are we going to do?" Savannah asked, fearing the response.

"We'll investigate to find out if he has some of the missing cats."

Savannah looked over at her aunt. "How do we get close enough to look for the cats without being seen?"

120

"I'll suggest that we set up a reconnaissance mission out here. We already have our force—just wish I could get more involved—damn it, anyway!" Margaret scowled as she looked down at her cast.

*This woman certainly doesn't lack passion,* Savannah thought.

"We'll get night goggles, camouflage clothing— the whole shebang," Margaret announced with glee. "We'll send two or four people in at a time to survey the situation—get videos of any suspicious activity. And we're going to take the evidence we collect to the sheriff's department and animal regulations. Hand me those binoculars under your seat," Margaret directed.

"I can't find them. I think they're under *your* seat, Auntie."

Margaret reached down. "Oh, here they are." She lifted them up and then handed them to her niece. "You have better eyes. I want you to look. See if you can spot any cats."

Savannah put the binoculars up to her eyes, adjusted them, and started searching as quickly as she could. *I'm not sure I want to see evidence,* she thought. *I'd just like to hang out at a safer location.* "Wait, there's a cat—two cats. Awww, poor things. They look scared. One has a bloody ear. Damn him!! Shit!" she yelled forcing a hushed tone. "He's out there beating on a horse. A very skinny horse. What's wrong with that idiot?"

"Yes, that's another story. I've heard that he doesn't handle his horses very well. Helena's sister thinks there's something shady going on with them, but she doesn't know what it is. We're not too far from a range of government-managed mustangs. He might be plucking some from there—to do what with, I don't know. Do any of the cats look like these in the pictures we got from Clarice yesterday?" Margaret asked.

Savannah studied the snapshots again. "Well, there's a white one—I think. It's pretty dirty. Could be this one," she said, pointing at one of the pictures her aunt had dug out of her purse. "I see a tortie or calico off in the distance. She's frightened by the commotion with that poor horse. She just went under the porch. I don't know if it's the tortie in the photo or not. Maybe if we get some pictures or video of these cats and examine them…"

"Yes. Good idea," Margaret said. "I don't suppose there's anything we can do up here today. We know where it is. We know he has cats here and he is our number-one suspect since he's our only suspect. Let's go back to town and talk to some of the Alliance members about this."

"Egads," Savannah said as she slowly turned the car around and began to head down the rutted road, "going down may be worse than coming up—if that's possible."

K-Whack! Whomp!

"OW! Oh my God!!" Margaret howled, slapping her hand against her right temple.

"What was that?" Savannah gasped. She looked over at her aunt, who was staring at a bloody hand.

"Something hit me—my God, have I been shot?"

# Chapter 4

Savannah stopped the car and hit the door lock, which she found had automatically been engaged. "Roll up your window! Roll up your window!" she yelled before noticing that her aunt was bent forward as if trying to duck out of sight.

Remembering that the window controls were in the console between the seats, she began pushing buttons until the passenger-side window was securely closed. As she watched the window slide up, she thought she saw something move. She turned just in time to catch a glimpse of what appeared to be a person clambering up the steep bank. The figure disappeared over the peak into a stand of trees. *Red plaid. It looks like he's wearing red plaid, like a lumberjack shirt,* she thought.

"Let's get out of here. Hurry!" Margaret whispered as she fumbled around in the console compartment. She finally removed a wad of napkins and held them to her head as Savannah put the car in gear and continued as fast as she dared down the rutted dirt road.

"Are you okay?" Savannah asked, her voice shrill and shaky.

"I think so," her aunt replied. She pulled down the sun visor, lifted the mirror cover and began to examine her wound. "Gads, it's kinda messy, Vannie. And it hurts like heck."

"Do you think you need stitches?"

"I don't know. Hard to tell."

"I'm taking you to the emergency room," Savannah insisted.

Margaret produced a strained laugh and said, "We don't have an emergency room, remember?"

"Where can we go to get you looked at? To your doctor's office?"

"Naw, just drive me to Dr. Ivey's. He can evaluate whether I need treatment or not."

Savannah hesitated and then she said, "But Auntie, he's your vet!"

"Yes," Margaret confessed looking sheepishly at her niece. "Dr. Ivey is the first responder for some of us who don't want to drive to the nearest urgent-care facility in Straley, which, as you know, is thirty miles away."

*What was that—did my heart skip a beat?* Savannah wondered. *I felt a bit giddy there for a second at the thought of seeing Michael again.*

\*\*\*

"Ms. Forster. Oh my gosh, you're bleeding. What happened?" the petite receptionist asked as she came from behind the counter to help Margaret to a chair in the waiting room.

"I'm not sure, actually. I think I'm okay. Something came through the window of the car and hit me in the head."

"You were in the car?" Scarlett asked. "Did it break a window?"

"No," Savannah offered. "We had rolled our windows down to let in some air. I think my aunt had her window all the way down. If she hadn't, she may not have been hit."

"Or the window might have been broken by whatever hit her and you'd have glass all over," Scarlett responded. She then turned to Margaret and asked, "What did hit you, Ms. Forster? A bullet?"

"I don't know," Margaret said rather

124

breathlessly. She looked up at the receptionist. "Anyway, Scarlett, I'd like to see Dr. Ivey."

"Sure, right away." She pivoted quickly, her pert ponytail swinging behind her.

Savannah suddenly thought of something. "I'll be right back," she said as she headed toward the door.

When she returned, Michael Ivey was leaning over her aunt, examining her head wound. "Hmm. Now, you know I can't treat you," he said in all seriousness. He stood and continued looking down at Margaret, saying, "But it's almost lunch time and the last morning patient just left. I sent Scarlett to lunch and told her to close the office for an hour. Come on back to my house and we'll have some iced tea."

He helped Margaret to her feet, reached down to retrieve the crutches, and waited until she was stable. "Well, hello," he said, having just noticed Savannah standing there. "Nice to see you again." *How trite,* he thought, but he felt compelled to say something to her, lest he look awkward just staring into her beautiful face.

Savannah felt her cheeks warming up.

"I'm ready," Margaret said. "You can turn loose of my crutches any time."

"Oh. Uh… sure. Um," he stuttered. "Follow me, ladies."

As the trio walked through the spacious veterinary clinic, Michael slipped off his lab coat stopping to hang it on a hook just inside one of the rooms. He winked at Savannah. "Now I'm not officially in veterinary mode." And then he led his guests out the back door, down a ramp and toward a charming log house tucked behind the clinic.

"How convenient that you live on the premises," Savannah observed.

Michael slowed his pace and then matched her

stride saying, "Yes, it is convenient—sometimes almost too much so, if you know what I mean."

Savannah remained silent, hoping he wasn't implying that she and her aunt were taking advantage of his availability.

When Michael pushed open the unlocked door to his home, the trio was enthusiastically greeted by an inquisitive nose.

"Hi Lexie," Margaret crooned as she hobbled through the door.

"What a cutie." Savannah couldn't help but succumb to the charms of the dog. "An afghan mix?"

"That's my best guess," Michael said. "Someone brought her to me in pretty bad shape a year or so ago. No one claimed her. She took to Walter right away, so I've kept her with me ever since."

"There's Walter," Margaret said as the veterinarian led his guests into the kitchen. He pulled a chair out from the small table and Margaret sat at his invitation. "How's the big guy?" she murmured, while holding her crutches in one hand and wriggling the fingers of her other hand in hopes of encouraging the black fur ball to play. She turned to Savannah. "This is one of the smartest cats you'll ever meet."

"Oh, he'll do anything for a treat," Michael said with a laugh.

"So how did you acquire this handsome fellow?" Savannah asked—knowing full well the temptation and opportunity for anyone who works with animals to bring them home—and knowing that most of those who were brought home had a story behind them.

Michael looked over at the cat and said, "He and his siblings were living under the porch of a house that was scheduled for demolition. Thankfully, one caring worker on that crew spotted the kittens and a local cat-

126

rescue group ended up with them. They brought them in for their routine round of vaccines, spay/neuter and this one had some health issues. I kept him so I could treat him and ended up—as you can see—keeping him. He's doing quite well, under the circumstances. He's going on five years old."

Savannah knelt down next to the cat and he began chirping and rubbing against her hand.

"Lexie," Michael said in a warning tone as the dog walked toward Savannah. "Don't you bother Walter." But it was too late. The dog had intercepted the petting session by pushing her head between Savannah's hand and the cat. Walter didn't give up a good thing that easily, however. He jumped at the dog, wrapping his paws around her face. She pushed him down with one of her paws and began licking him. He grabbed her muzzle with all fours and kicked his back legs against her chin. This caused Lexie to jump back and the dance was on. As if they were performing for the attentive group, all of whom were now laughing at the animals' antics, they stepped up their activity and added a little hide-and-seek, peek-a-boo, and missile attack.

"They do love to be on stage," the veterinarian said as his two pets ran off to play chase. He sat down in front of Margaret and peered at her wound. After dabbing at it with an antiseptic pad, he asked, "Well, Maggie, do you know what hit you?"

"No—maybe a rock falling from the bank as we drove by," Margaret suggested.

"Where were you when this happened, for heaven sakes?"

"Um, I was just showing Vannie around."

The doctor remained silent waiting to hear the rest of the story; however, Margaret wasn't sure how much to tell him. They had, after all, probably been trespassing. Finally, he said, "This is kind of nasty for a random rock to have fallen into your window. It looks to me like it hit you with some force behind it."

"Like from a slingshot?" Savannah asked, opening her hand to reveal a small sharp-edged rock. "I found this on the floor mat in the car."

The veterinarian looked more closely at the rock and then asked, "Did you see any children with slingshots while you were driving out in the boonies?"

"No," Savannah responded. "But I did see something." She wondered why she felt safe talking about it with this man. "I saw a figure running from the spot where Aunt Marg was hit."

"You did, Vannie? You didn't tell me that," Margaret said, her voice raised a few octaves.

"There was a lot going on. I just wanted to get us out of there and get you some help," she explained.

"I think that person—probably a man—wearing a red plaid lumberjack shirt may have shot at the car with a slingshot and just happened to get one through the open window." Savannah shook her head when considering how much worse it could have been. "He could have put your eye out, Auntie."

"Good sleuthing, Savannah," Michael said, looking at her with obvious interest.

She began to fidget and felt her face get hot again.

The veterinarian reached into a small first-aid kit, chose a round bandage and placed it on Margaret's wound, saying, "Now stay out of the line of fire." He then looked at her and asked, "You *are* going to report this to the police, aren't you?"

Savannah spoke up, "Absolutely."

But Margaret cancelled her out with, "Oh, I

don't think so."

"What? Auntie, someone may have done this on purpose."

"Or it was a random act by some nincompoop."

"Either way, it should be reported," Savannah insisted.

"Oh, let's discuss it later, Vannie. I have my reasons for not wanting to involve the sheriff at this point," Margaret said as she heaved herself up onto her crutches and headed for the door.

"Thank you for the treatment, Michael," she said over her shoulder.

"What treatment?" he asked. "You know I only treat animals."

"Meow," Margaret joked.

# Chapter 5

"Auntie, look!" Savannah's posture had become rigid, her voice shrill. She pointed toward the opposite side of the street as they slowed down for a stop sign.

"What? What?"

"It's a man wearing a red plaid shirt!" she exclaimed.

Margaret took a quick look and sat back in her seat. "So it is," she said without emotion.

Savannah looked directly at her aunt, saying with some fervor, "Remember, I told you I saw someone in the bushes wearing one of those?"

"I remember," she said. "If you'll pay attention, you'll see plenty of shirts like that. It's what men wear here. In fact, the man you just pointed out—well, he's our undertaker, probably just returning from a little fishing trip up the river."

"Oh," Savannah said as she relaxed into her seat. "Do you know if he owns a slingshot?" she asked in jest. "By the way, how does that bump feel? Still hurt?"

"Yeah a little," she said, reaching up and touching the bandage. "I think there's some swelling. I hope this doesn't blacken my eye."

"Oh, I hope not," Savannah said with a frown. "Now, don't mess with it. Do you have something at home for pain?"

"Sure, Motrin, Advil, Excedrin—take your pick."

"Well, let's get you home. You really ought to rest, what with a new fracture and a near concussion…" Savannah said.

"Now who's exaggerating?" Margaret harrumphed.

130

*\*\**

"So, can you get everything together by tomorrow night?" Savannah heard her aunt asking someone on the phone as she walked into the living room with two tall glasses of iced tea.

Margaret motioned for Savannah to set a glass on the table next to her and to sit down on the embossed-satin settee across from her. "Yes, it is risky," she said into the phone. "If you're seen moving around the place, you'll have to climb out of there quickly, back to the road for your get-away."

Savannah smiled a little at her aunt's terminology and the obvious thrill she was getting from planning the undercover escapade—a downright illegal escapade. But if the effort saves some of the stolen cats from harm or death, maybe it will be worth it. They certainly didn't have the blessings of the authorities, but there was nothing the sheriff could do without evidence. Someone had to get evidence, and that's what this vigilante group hoped to accomplish.

"You have descriptions and photos of some of the missing cats. This could help. It would be even better if you saw someone bringing a load of cats to the Bray place tomorrow night." Savannah watched as Margaret gave a little shiver of excitement at the thought. "I guess that would be too much to expect, though. Just do what you can do—see what you can see. We'll look forward to your report. Good bye, Betty; and thanks."

"You really are sending people out there—even women?" Savannah asked. "Did you tell Betty what happened to you today?"

Margaret reached up and touched the bandage

131

on the side of her head. "I'm sure it's swelling. Doesn't hurt too much, though." She looked over at Savannah, hesitated and then responded to her question, "No, I didn't tell them about the accident. They're not going to be driving their car up that hill—makes too much noise and they may be seen if they use their headlights. There's no way they can make that drive at night without headlights. So they'll park below and walk in using night goggles to see. We borrowed some from this guy who photographs birds in their burrows at night. I guess a rock could fall off the hill and hit someone like it did me," Margaret continued. "But it's doubtful."

"Fall off the hill?" Savannah nearly shouted. "That rock did *not* fall off the hill. It was hurled or shot. As Michael said, there was too much force behind it to have simply fallen," she stated with emphasis, hoping her aunt would take the accident (or assault) more seriously.

"What's he got now?" Margaret asked, straining to get a better look at the large grey-and-white cat, who had just walked into the room.

Savannah glanced over in time to see him pick something up in his mouth and head for the stairs. "Rags, wait," she called after him. "What do you have there?"

Rags stopped and turned toward her briefly before rushing up the stairway and disappearing.

"Well, I'll be. This is a first," Savannah said as she descended the staircase.

"What was it, Vannie? What did he steal this time?"

"A cookie," she said scrunching up her face in a frown.

"A cookie?"

"Yeah, one of those oatmeal cookies Helena left

for us. There was only one left and I put it in a plastic bag earlier."

"He doesn't eat stuff like that, does he?"

"Nope. I guess maybe he's working on his earthquake survival kit," she said with a laugh. Suddenly, she jumped a little, reached into her jeans pocket and pulled out her cell phone. She looked at it and then said, "It's Travis. I'd better take it. I'll be in my room."

***

"Vannie," the old intercom crackled with static.

Savannah jumped to her feet and walked briskly over to the receiver on the wall. Rags was already there stretching toward the speaker as if he were looking for Aunt Margaret in there. "Yes?" she responded.

"Can you come down?"

"Sure. Be right there." And then she thought to ask, "Where are you?" There were intercoms in six or seven of the eleven rooms, including two of the bathrooms.

"Living room," Margaret replied.

"What's up, Auntie?" Savannah asked, as she bounded down the last step and entered the room. She noticed that her aunt was standing using her crutches, windbreaker in hand. "Are we going somewhere?"

"Yes, if you don't mind," she said as if she were slightly distracted by her thoughts. "A woman called about her missing cat and I'd like to go talk to her. She sounds so distraught; poor thing."

"Sure," Savannah said without hesitation. "Your chair's still in the car. Let me get my purse."

"So what did Travis want? Are you at liberty to talk?" Margaret asked after they'd traveled a mile or so in silence.

"Oh yes. No problem," Savannah said. "He just wanted to make sure we're good, whatever that means."

Margaret waved her hand in the air. "I know what that means. He wants you to tell him it's okay for him to screw around—that he no longer has a reason to feel guilty."

Savannah responded quickly. "How do you know so much about relationships?" And then she grinned and glanced over at her aunt. "It sounds like your silky undies get quite a workout, huh?"

"Watch that fresh mouth of yours, Vannie," Margaret teased. "Well, isn't that what he wanted? Permission to do what he's been doing (or he's been wanting to do) without having to worry about you freaking out or getting all possessive?"

"Pretty much," Savannah said softly while pursing her lips.

"So how do you feel about it?"

Savannah thought for a few minutes and then said, "Relieved. Sad, but actually relieved. It's over. It's been over for a while. It just took me stepping back to be able to see the truth."

"Good for you, Vannie. I'm glad you're ready to move on. Oh, here we are, turn right. It's 230 Oriole. She couldn't even give me directions, she was so upset. I looked it up on my computer. I think we turn right on Robin—oh yes, there it is, Oriole. That must be her sitting on the porch over there."

As Savannah and Margaret approached the porch, a striking petite woman with black hair highlighted with natural silver streaks stood to greet them.

"Hello Mrs. Minsky. I'm Margaret and this is my niece, Savannah. I'm so sorry to hear about your kitty," she said expressing genuine concern.

"Call me Edie. So nice of you to come over," she said, dabbing at her red swollen eyes with a tissue she had pulled from the pocket of her green denim slacks. "I'm sorry," she said as she blew her nose into the crumpled tissue, "I just can't stop blubbering. I love Sally so much and I'm so worried about her. She's never been away from me and she needs me more than ever now, you know. As I told you on the phone, she's ill. Dr. Ivey and I have been working hard to keep her comfortable and happy." She took a breath while twirling the tissue around in her hands. "I'm not one of those who will keep a cat who's suffering alive for my sake. I know I will lose her someday, but…" She began choking up.

Savannah walked up the steps, put her arms around the woman, and held her for a few moments while she collected herself. When Savannah stepped back, Edie took a ragged breath, opened the front screen door and invited her guests inside.

"Can you make it up these two steps, Auntie? Here, let me help steady the crutches."

Edie held the door open. Once they had entered the spacious living room, she motioned for the two women to be seated. Margaret plopped down on a plush rose-colored loveseat, her loose-fitting cotton blouse momentarily ballooning in the updraft. Savannah took the crutches and leaned them against the wall next to the front door and then settled on a satin-print chair.

"Can I get you some tea?" Edie offered.

"No thank you," Margaret said. "Just tell us what happened, Edie. How did they get their hands on Sally? She doesn't go outside, does she?"

"Oh no. Never." She hesitated. "I made a horrible mistake. It was all my fault," she said between sobs. "I feel just horrible."

Savannah walked over to the distraught woman. She stood behind Edie with her hands on her shoulders in an attempt to sooth her. When Edie began to relax, Savannah knelt in front of her. She reached up and pushed a strand of her salt and pepper hair away from her face and said in a soft voice, "I know this is just awful for you. Maybe we can help. Just tell us what happened."

Edie sat up straight, took a few deep breaths, looked at Savannah through striking grey eyes, and began telling her story. "I was taking her to see Dr. Ivey. We'd started a new treatment a few weeks ago and he wanted to see her today and do a blood count." She swallowed hard and straightened the collar on her green-and-white striped blouse. "I put her in the carrier and took her out to the car, talking to her all the way, as I always do." Her face lit up in denial of her sixty-three years as she said, "I believe she understands what I say—maybe she tunes into my thoughts. But, I'm telling you, she responds to my words in ways that you cannot believe."

Savannah smiled and nodded as she moved over to an ottoman off to Edie's left and perched on the edge of it.

"Anyway," she continued, "I put her carrier in the front seat of the car when I remembered I'd forgotten my notes. I'd promised Dr. Ivey I would write down a sort of diary of Sally's days and her routine to help us determine if the new treatment was helping." She paused for a few seconds, as if struggling to collect her thoughts. "The phone rang while I was in the house and I picked it up to see who it was. I was also waiting to hear from my own doctor on some tests. It was one of those dang telemarketers. Well, when I came back

136

out no more than two minutes later," she said in a strained voice, "the car door was still open and Sally and the carrier were gone. Just gone."

Margaret leaned forward and asked, "Did you see anyone?"

"No." She lowered her head and shook it slowly. "No one. I didn't see anyone." She then raised up and looked at Margaret thoughtfully. "Oh, someone drove by in an old truck—looked like teenage boys. I think I've seen them in the neighborhood before. They just happened to be driving by, I'm sure. I didn't pay any attention to them, really."

"What kind of truck—what color?" Savannah asked.

"Like I said, I didn't notice."

"It might be important if you could remember."

Suddenly, the front door opened. Edie's face lit up and she walked toward the woman who entered with outstretched arms. "Oh Gina, thank you for coming. Who's with the children?" she asked as she stepped back from their warm embrace.

"Brent came home early. I'm so sorry about Sally, Mom," she said looking her directly in the eyes. "This must be just awful for you. Do you have any idea what happened?"

"Well, someone took her. They took her right out of my car!" She started to cry again, both of her hands over her face as she leaned into her daughter. Gina rubbed her mother's back for a few moments. Finally, Edie stood up straight, blotted her face with a tissue, took a deep breath and said, "I'm sorry. Where are my manners? Gina, you know Ms. Forster and her niece…"

"Oh, yes. Hello Ms. Forster. Nice to see you both again." She acknowledged each of them with a nod. "This is really sad, isn't it?" she said as she led her mother over to a Victorian flower-print sofa. "To think that someone would take her right out of the car like that. Did you see who did it?" she asked her mother. "I'm sorry I couldn't talk long enough to get the details when you called. The kids were…well, you know how it is."

"She saw a truck go by with teenagers in it," Margaret said. "I wonder if these were the same teens you saw in your neighborhood."

"What would teenage boys want with my Sally?" Edie asked. "Oh my gosh, I'm so scared for her. She needs her medicine and her fluid treatment. She must be terrified."

"Is there anything we can do for you, Edie?" Margaret asked. "Did you call Dr. Ivey?"

She brought her hands up to her mouth. "Oh my goodness, no. I plum forgot. I called Gina first and she gave me your number."

"Okay. I'll call him and tell him you can't keep your appointment," Margaret said.

Savannah jumped up. "Here, I'll do it, Auntie. I think it would be a good idea to find out just what her condition is. What's his number?"

Edie and Gina looked up expectantly as Savannah returned from the front porch after making the call on her cell phone.

"He asked me to convey to you how very sorry he is. He sounds crushed and angry at the same time. He said this is about the sixth client he's heard from this week with missing cats. He is completely at a loss as to what's happening," Savannah reported.

"Sally?" Edie said weakly as she stood and walked over to the front window.

Savannah hesitated. She then joined the

distressed woman, took her hand and looked her in the eyes. "He said we can only hope to find her before…"

Edie turned to face Savannah. "Before what?" she insisted.

Savannah took a breath and continued, "He believes she will be okay without her treatment for as many as four days."

Gina shook her head. "Surely we'll find the cats by then."

"Four days away from me…she just won't understand. She's my constant companion," Edie said as tears ran down her cheeks.

"We're working on finding the cats as we speak, Edie. I promise. We have a lead and we have a plan in the works. We *will* find her," Margaret said.

"Can I get you a glass of water—or I could make some tea…" Savannah offered. "I'd be happy to."

"Yes, a glass of water for my mom…that would be nice. Thank you," Gina said. "Kitchen is right in there. Here, Mom, let's sit down."

When Savannah returned with a tray of tall glasses and a pitcher of ice water, she noticed that the trio was sitting on the sofa looking through a photo album featuring Sally since she was a kitten. "Tell us how she came to you," Savannah said after she had served the water and pulled a chair closer.

Edie smiled through her tears. "I had never owned a cat. Gina and my other daughter Donna had a few cats growing up. I never did make up to them— they just sort of came and went. I was a fairly young widow. Once the girls were grown, I began dating a man—had been dating him for more years than I care to reveal. I wasn't all that happy then and I'd read somewhere that owning a pet could have a positive impact on your mood—make you smile more—even make you healthier. My older daughter and her husband had a cat then and I'd become quite fond of him."

She grinned rather sheepishly when she said, "Stanley hated cats. He actually told me that he would never come to my house again if I got one. So adopting a cat was sort of my round-about way of breaking it off with him."

Everyone laughed.

"So where did you find Sally?" Margaret asked.

"About ten years ago, I began the hunt for just the right kitten. I stopped at farm houses and houses in town each time I saw a sign for kittens available. But there was never any chemistry between me and all the litters of kittens I saw. Then, one day, I stopped at a pet store with my grandson. Jeremy loved to go see the bunnies, fish, birds, hamsters. Sometimes they had cats and dogs. Well, this day, we walked in and there was sweet Sally and her brother in a cage waiting for adoption. They were about eight-weeks-old. As you saw in the photos, she has pastel shades of grey and gold patches with lots of white. She was timid and stayed close to her yellow-and-white brother." Edie looked off into space for a moment before continuing. "Oh, how I wish I had taken them both. I hope he found a good home," she lamented.

She smiled a little at the memories of her kitten. "Sally was not cuddly or even very friendly. She didn't like to be held and never jumped on my bed or sat in my lap. She was a loner. I remember cupping my hands around her tiny face, looking into her big green eyes and promising I would always love her and care for her—that we were a team and I would be her mommy. I got Sally in July or August and my relationship with Stanley ended in the fall. I made a good decision.

Edie smiled. "I'm now dating a wonderful man;

he loves cats. He has been nothing but kind to Sally and worries about her as much as I do. He tries to do everything he thinks she wants—an open door to the screened-in porch, her blanket fluffed to make her bed more comfortable, the bathtub water turned on so she can lick from the spigot…"

Edie ran her fingers softly over a photo of the cat. "Sally has changed since she has grown older. She now jumps on my desk and lap. She follows me like a puppy and she wants to be close to us. She even travels with us in our motor home." Her face lit up when she announced, "She has been to twelve states so far."

"It sounds as though she is a special kitty," Margaret said. "What a personality. Look at her sleeping with her head on your foot. How cute is that?"

"And this one," Savannah said, "where she's watching you embroider."

"Oh yes," Edie said with some enthusiasm, "she loves to watch me do needlework."

"Mother, tell them about the wrinkles in her sheets," Gina prompted

"Oh, she is so cute," Edie said with a smile. "I keep sheets on this chair for her and on the bed. She likes sleeping on the sheets, but she doesn't like wrinkles." She laughed. "She will sit there and stare at us without blinking when she wants us to smooth out the wrinkles. No kidding. Talk about a spoiled kitty," Edie said. And then her demeanor changed. She suddenly felt the pain of her loss and the fear of not knowing where Sally was and what was happening to her.

Margaret looked over at Edie. "We must go now. Can I take this picture of her with me? I promise to bring it back. I just want to show it to members of our surveillance team."

"Yes, by all means." Edie stood to usher her guests out. "Thank you so much for taking all this time with me."

Margaret steadied herself on her crutches. "Sure, Edie. Now call me if you think of anything that might help us figure out who is taking the cats, will you?"

# Chapter 6

Margaret woke with a start. She hadn't been asleep long—the events of the past few days were wearing on her and she was excited about the prospect of recovering the cats. Why else would she have so much trouble falling asleep? Even the double dose of Motrin, while it took the throb out of her head wound, didn't help bring sleep. Her mind couldn't release the worry about the missing cats. But she had other things on her mind, as well—thoughts her niece had brought up— fears she had refused to acknowledge. *Who did uncover the old cesspool in my backyard? Who knew it was there? Was it uncovered on purpose—to hurt me…kill me? Oh, I don't have time to think about that.* Margaret shivered as if to chase away the unwelcome thoughts. *There are cats' lives at stake. I must focus on the cats.*

She turned on her bedside lamp, swung her right leg over the side of the bed, and reached for her water decanter. She filled her glass and took a swig, while glancing at the bedroom door. Still closed. Rags would not be visiting her tonight. There was another presence in the room, though. Layla was curled up in her cozy leopard-print bed. The little cat lifted her head and peered at Margaret through squinty eyes, yawned, stretched out her front paws and then lay back down and went to sleep.

*I wish it was that easy for me,* Margaret thought, as she lay back down in her own bed.

Briiiinnnnngggg, Briiinnnnnggggg.

*The phone? At this hour? What time is it?* she wondered as she glanced at the clock. *4:15!*

"Hello," she croaked. Clearing her throat, she tried again, "Hello."

"Maggie, it's Betty. I know I woke you—so

sorry, just couldn't wait to tell you that it was a rough night, but we made progress. I think the committee will be pleased with our report. Maggie, we identified a couple of the cats that were taken. That's the good news. Gil got close enough to get some video. But are you aware that they're dealing in horses?"

"Yes and no. I know they have horses that don't look all that healthy. But I haven't figured out what their gig is."

"While we were watching, a stock truck came onto the property and two men loaded up as many horses as they could cram in—I'm telling you, some of those horses were in bad shape. There were a few good-looking ones, but some were having trouble making it into the truck, they were so weak. While they were being loaded, Bray and a man who came in the stock truck stood side by side, making notes. Once the horses were loaded, the two of them seemed to be doing some figuring and then money changed hands. The other man pulled out what looked to be a wad of bills and counted out some in Bray's hand. We used the night-vision equipment you borrowed for us and saw a couple of horses that looked like BLM mustangs. We think they may be stealing horses to sell to slaughter houses."

"Oh, that's awful. Something we should look into. What kind of truck was it—did it have a logo?"

"It looked as if it had a logo, actually, but it was covered by one of those magnetic signs, which was blank. Well, we pretty much had the information we needed by then, so we decided to hoof it back to the car and follow the truck."

"You didn't!" Margaret hissed. "You followed it?"

"Sure did, girl. We figured we had some criminals on our hands and we wanted to see what they
144

were up to. We're on our way back to the city now."

"Betty, where did the stock truck go? What happened?"

"They pulled off the road about 150 miles out of town. Private property, so we decided not to follow them in. We think they're headed for a slaughter house across the border. Hopefully, with this information, now the authorities will investigate."

"Is it illegal to sell horses to a slaughter house?" Margaret asked.

"No, unless the horses they're selling are stolen. If we can prove they're stealing horses, we could put them out of business."

"Did you get pictures?" Margaret asked.

"Yes, quite a bit of video."

"Well, I'll be! Those creeps really are into some shady dealings. Now if we can find out where they're getting those horses…some look like mustangs from the BLM ranges, you say?"

"Oh yes. I know a couple of people who have adopted some of them when authorities do the round-ups. I couldn't make out whether or not they had the freeze brand, though."

"Freeze brand?"

"The mustangs get a freeze brand when they're gathered from the range lands for the adoption program."

"My head is swimming, Betty. And I'll bet you are exhausted. Sounds like you and Gil did an all-nighter. Go home; rest. We can talk later. Can you meet me at animal control this afternoon with this information? We'll let them decide whether or not to alert the authorities. And Betty…thank you so much for all that you do for our pets. You and Gil have gone beyond the call of duty."

"It's my passion, too, Maggie. Someone has to stand up for those creatures that don't have a voice. See you later."

Margaret knew it was no use trying to go back to sleep, what with visions of horse rustlers, catnappers, and someone who wanted to scare or hurt...or even kill her going through her head. She leaned back against the headboard and looked over at Layla who was out of bed now, walking slowly toward her. The little cat hopped up on the bed, climbed over onto Margaret's outstretched legs, and sat there staring into her favorite person's eyes. Layla was unusual in that way—she'd look Margaret straight in the eye and stare as if she could read what her owner was thinking—as if she were picking up information clairvoyantly. And Margaret wasn't too sure she couldn't key into her thoughts. Which was okay with her most of the time. She loved peering into those perfectly round green eyes. They seemed all-knowing and loving at the same time. Comforting.

The only thing she enjoyed more was cuddling and snuggling with the little cat. "You are such a dear, Laylee. I just love you to pieces," she whispered into her fur as she held her close. Layla purred, seemingly in response.

\*\*\*

"Good morning, Auntie," Savannah said as she sauntered into the kitchen where her aunt stood rinsing out a few dishes. She wrapped her arms around Margaret in a bear hug and asked, "Did you sleep well?"

"Well, aren't we chipper? What made you so happy?" Margaret asked, pivoting on one foot to take a
146

strength. I have a few things I'd like to do today."

"Oh, what?" Savannah asked as she pulled the skillet out from under the cabinet and retrieved the eggs and ham from the fridge.

"We need to get you something to wear to the dance, for one thing."

"Dance?" Savannah looked puzzled.

"Remember, we have that benefit dance tomorrow night. Everyone will be there. I think I'll wear my lace and silk skirt with my purple sweater. I'd better practice up on my wheelchair dancing," Margaret said with a giggle. "Did you bring something you can wear? If not, we'll look through my closet. I still have some skinny clothes that might work for you."

"Cool. So what day is this? Friday? What's on the agenda? Anything interesting?" Savannah asked with a big grin on her face.

"Well, let's hope not too much so. But yes, I'm sure it will be an interesting day," Margaret said thoughtfully. "I want to do a little sleuthing. Are you with me?"

Much too happy to disagree with anything or anyone, Savannah said, "Sure, Auntie. Lead the way."

"I want to get my filthy car washed, number one. I'd like to do some checking at local feed stores to find out if any horses are missing…"

Savannah turned toward her aunt. "Horses?"

"Yes, I'm told that old man Bray might be stealing horses and running them possibly to a horse slaughter house in Canada. I want to ask some questions at a few trucking companies. I did some checking online and discovered that the closest horse-meat-packing plant is in British Columbia. That's over a thousand miles, round-trip. I presume these yoyos are selling the horses outright. They probably aren't doing

48

closer look at her niece.

"I'm always happy," Savannah replied while pulling a kitchen chair out for her aunt.

"Pshaw!" Margaret said as she plopped down in the chair. Suddenly, she looked up at Savannah. "Oh wait—you went out last night. I heard your little Honda putting down the driveway around nine. Did you go over to the clinic?" She smiled in anticipation Savannah's response.

"Yes." Savannah tried to maintain a calm in h voice. "Yes, I did. Now, do you want scrambled egg and ham for breakfast or yogurt and granola? We als have some fresh fruit."

"Vannie," her aunt said in a teasing voice, "y were with Michael again last night, weren't you?"

She cleared her throat nervously. "Yes, we wanted to discuss one of his cases."

"So it was business, huh?" Margaret looked over at her niece suspiciously. "Monkey business, i you ask me."

*Observant gal, this one,* Savannah thought. *Should I tell her what has me feeling rather giddy What would she think if I told her we spent most o night at Michael's house talking and how we were engaged that we completely lost track of time. An kiss… My knees are still weak just thinking about kiss—so unexpected—so right.*

"Hello…" Margaret said. "Earth to Savan

"What? Oh, sorry." Savannah felt a little flushed. "I guess my mind wandered. What did y say?"

"Oh my. You've got it bad, don't you? I she hesitated in an attempt to get Savannah's ful attention, "let's have scrambled eggs and some ( ham that Helena brought over. We're going to n

closer look at her niece.

"I'm always happy," Savannah replied while pulling a kitchen chair out for her aunt.

"Pshaw!" Margaret said as she plopped down in the chair. Suddenly, she looked up at Savannah. "Oh wait—you went out last night. I heard your little Honda putting down the driveway around nine. Did you go over to the clinic?" She smiled in anticipation of Savannah's response.

"Yes." Savannah tried to maintain a calm in her voice. "Yes, I did. Now, do you want scrambled eggs and ham for breakfast or yogurt and granola? We also have some fresh fruit."

"Vannie," her aunt said in a teasing voice, "you were with Michael again last night, weren't you?"

She cleared her throat nervously. "Yes, we wanted to discuss one of his cases."

"So it was business, huh?" Margaret looked over at her niece suspiciously. "Monkey business, if you ask me."

*Observant gal, this one,* Savannah thought. *Should I tell her what has me feeling rather giddy? What would she think if I told her we spent most of the night at Michael's house talking and how we were so engaged that we completely lost track of time. And the kiss... My knees are still weak just thinking about the kiss—so unexpected—so right.*

"Hello..." Margaret said. "Earth to Savannah."

"What? Oh, sorry." Savannah felt a little flushed. "I guess my mind wandered. What did you say?"

"Oh my. You've got it bad, don't you? I said," she hesitated in an attempt to get Savannah's full attention, "let's have scrambled eggs and some of that ham that Helena brought over. We're going to need our

147

strength. I have a few things I'd like to do today."

"Oh, what?" Savannah asked as she pulled the skillet out from under the cabinet and retrieved the eggs and ham from the fridge.

"We need to get you something to wear to the dance, for one thing."

"Dance?" Savannah looked puzzled.

"Remember, we have that benefit dance tomorrow night. Everyone will be there. I think I'll wear my lace and silk skirt with my purple sweater. I'd better practice up on my wheelchair dancing," Margaret said with a giggle. "Did you bring something you can wear? If not, we'll look through my closet. I still have some skinny clothes that might work for you."

"Cool. So what day is this? Friday? What's on the agenda? Anything interesting?" Savannah asked with a big grin on her face.

"Well, let's hope not too much so. But yes, I'm sure it will be an interesting day," Margaret said thoughtfully. "I want to do a little sleuthing. Are you with me?"

Much too happy to disagree with anything or anyone, Savannah said, "Sure, Auntie. Lead the way."

"I want to get my filthy car washed, number one. I'd like to do some checking at local feed stores to find out if any horses are missing…"

Savannah turned toward her aunt. "Horses?"

"Yes, I'm told that old man Bray might be stealing horses and running them possibly to a horse slaughter house in Canada. I want to ask some questions at a few trucking companies. I did some checking online and discovered that the closest horse-meat-packing plant is in British Columbia. That's over a thousand miles, round-trip. I presume these yoyos are selling the horses outright. They probably aren't doing

the hauling themselves. They're just bringing in horses for a kill-buy agent."

"Or we could save energy for the dance and make some calls," Savannah suggested.

Margaret stared at her niece for a few seconds. "I'll think about that," she said, having no intention of using the phone to run down the information she was after. "I'd also like to give Max a hand if we have time. I haven't been much help these last several days."

Savannah smiled. "I'd like that." She set a bowl of fruit in front of Margaret. "Here, Auntie. Eat up. Sounds like we're going to need some energy."

\*\*\*

Margaret peered over her glasses when Savannah entered the living room dressed and ready for their day. "You look nice. New jeans? What's the occasion?"

"Can't a girl get cleaned up once in a while?"

"And makeup. You're wearing makeup. Vannie, you are lovely au naturel, but you are a knockout with the subtle way you wear makeup. I like that blouse on you, too—shows off your svelte figure. That's a nice shade of mauve for you. Good job."

"You look fresh yourself, Auntie. How's your head?"

"It's a wonder what a shower will do. I'm getting the hang of a sit-down shower. It felt good to really wash off the grime from the last few days."

Savannah knew her aunt was speaking more about the incidents and their implications than the physical dirt.

"My head looks okay and it doesn't appear that I'll get a black eye. It's been two days and there's bruising only around the spot. I should be able to go

149

without the bandage by tomorrow evening. My hair will partially cover the gash."

"I'm glad it's healing up okay. No infection or anything," Savannah said. "Are you ready to go?" she asked. "I'll load your wheelchair in the car and come back and help you down the steps."

Savannah drove out of her aunt's driveway onto the main road. "Where to first?"

"Let's get the car washed. I'll treat you to an iced mocha while we wait. Do you remember where the car wash is?"

"Sure. Sounds good."

The two women drove in silence for a few blocks before Margaret said, "So Vannie, tell me—are you still okay with how things are between you and your young man, Travis?"

"Huh?"

"I mean, after thinking about your talk with him yesterday, are you still good with the situation?"

Savannah thought for a moment and then said, "Yes, I told you yesterday that it's over between us."

"Yeah, I know. But sometimes it's hard to let go. I'm just wondering…"

"The thing is, Auntie, we've been together on and off for about three years. We've had good times, but our relationship just never seemed easy for either of us. We'd break it off for a while, but it never lasted.

"Coming here, to a totally different environment and being distracted by all that's going on in your busy life, well, it has helped me to see our relationship more clearly. I began to realize that Travis and I were keeping such busy schedules that we weren't going out and meeting new people. We gravitated back to one another sort of out of convenience." She looked over at her aunt, her head cocked slightly. "Know what I mean?"

150

"Yes," Margaret said. "I think so."

"Travis admitted to me that there's a girl he'd like to get to know better at his gym. He's ready to move on and so am I. Michael has made me see that this is absolutely the right decision."

"Oooohhh," Margaret said playfully.

"Now I'm not saying he's the one. It's just that he's the first one who has affected me in a—well, you know—in a womanly way in a long time, and it made me realize that maybe there is a perfect match for me. I don't have to settle."

Margaret twisted her body toward her niece. "Oh no, Vannie, never settle."

"I can't tell you how freeing my conversation with Travis was and how therapeutic my time spent with you so far has been. I feel like I'm just starting to live and that there are definite possibilities for me in this world, more than just those in the small world I'd created for myself in LA. It wasn't all Travis—it was me, too. I was afraid to step outside my comfort zone, even though I wasn't all that comfortable, really. I mean, Travis is kind of immature. He's needy and he even admitted that my more independent nature bugged him a lot. Besides, he doesn't like cats. He and Rags never did make friends."

"You need say no more," Margaret said, slapping her knee with her palm and shaking her head. "There ain't no way we can tolerate someone who doesn't like cats!"

"Do you know what else, Auntie? You're not going to believe I dated someone like this for so long—but Travis smokes."

"Cigarettes?" Margaret asked, staring over at her niece as if she were in shock.

"'Fraid so." She sighed deeply before admitting,

"Yup, a smoker."

The women rode in silence for a few blocks when Margaret said, "You know, I think it's interesting that no one in our family ever took up smoking."

"Old Grandpa Forster smoked that pipe," Savannah reminded her.

"Oh yes. But I was talking about the Brannons. And your daddy's people didn't smoke; none of the other in-laws or outlaws smoked. Your sister doesn't smoke, does she? Any of your cousins?"

"Nope," Savannah said.

"Well, there's no way you would have married Trevor—or Travis—or whatever, if he was a smoker." She shook her fist in the air. "I would have stood up at your wedding and protested it on the grounds that we don't allow smokers in our family."

Savannah laughed out loud at the image. After a minute or so, she asked, "So Grandpa Forster was the only smoker in Tom's family?"

"Yes. And all he smoked was that pipe. I didn't let on to him then," Margaret said as if sharing a deep secret, "but I actually liked smelling the aroma of his tobacco." She thought for a moment, then turned toward her niece and said, "Wait, there was one other smoker in the family. That idiot nephew of Jed's, Joe Forster."

"Joe Forster smoked cigarettes? What kind?" Savannah asked.

Margaret looked confused. "What do you mean what kind? What do you know about cigarette brands?" Her demeanor shifted abruptly. "Oh, here's the car wash. Let's take the chair out and you can wheel me across the street to the coffee shop."

\*\*\*

Margaret sat at a small round table in the Coffee Bean while Savannah placed their order. Within a few minutes, Savannah returned with an iced blended mocha with soy and a chai latte. As she set the drinks on the table, she noticed that her aunt was just closing her cell phone. Margaret picked up her pen and a small notepad from the tabletop and tucked them into her purse. When Savannah looked inquisitively at her, she said, "Just getting a license plate number from Betty. I want to run it by Jim later."

After sitting with their drinks for a few moments, Savannah said, "Tell me more about Joe Forster, Auntie."

"For heaven sakes, Vannie. Why are you so obsessed with that creep?"

"Just curious."

Margaret took in a deep breath before she started to talk. "I didn't see him very often, which suited me just fine. He was deranged—you know, crazy—as far as I was concerned. I guess I first became aware of him when he was around seventeen. Like I said, he always gave me the creeps. Not too long after Tom and I moved in with Grandpa, Joe started coming around. He was about twenty-two then. Jed never seemed particularly pleased to see him coming—always wanted something—usually money, I think. I'd see him out with Grandpa smoking away—always smoking those cigarettes of his. They had filters on them and they came in a red and white box. I know because I used to have to clean them up after he left."

Savannah felt a knot in the pit of her stomach. She had goose bumps on her arms. But she wanted to hear more. She needed to know. She thought her aunt should know.

Margaret continued, "I'd provide ash cans, but he never used them. He'd sit on the porch with Grandpa or follow him around while he did odd jobs around the place and drop butts everywhere. If he finished a pack of cigarettes while he was there, he'd put some of the butts in the empty box and just leave it wherever. He didn't come often and didn't stay long, but I didn't like seeing him around the property at all. He always seemed to upset Grandpa—his being there."

Margaret took a long sip of her latte and then continued, "I don't know what happened, whether Grandpa and Joe had a falling-out or what, but after a while, Joe stopped coming around. Didn't see him for a couple of years before Grandpa died."

"So all Grandpa smoked was a pipe, huh?" Savannah asked.

"Yup. Grandpa didn't smoke cigarettes, but he did enjoy that pipe, especially when he took a drink of Scotch, which became more and more often when he got older. We discovered charred bottles in the barn after he died."

Savannah pushed her mocha to one side and looked across the table at her aunt. "I remember a lot of talk about Grandpa Forster and how he died in the fire. Did they ever decide what happened?"

"The detectives determined that he accidently started the fire with his pipe—maybe he dropped it or fell after drinking too much. One theory is that he fell out of the loft, hit his head and his pipe started the fire. That was their final report. But I was never altogether comfortable with it."

"Why not?" Savannah asked

Margaret ran her finger around the rim of her cup and said, "Well, I knew Grandpa was taking a nip
154

now and again and I knew he was doing it in private. He'd come in with his cheeks a little flushed and his pipe clenched between his teeth. But I never once saw him staggering drunk—enough that he would fall or start a fire without knowing it. Sure, he could have blacked out, had a stroke or something…I guess we'll never know."

"Auntie, what kind of cigarettes did you say Joe Forster smoked?"

Margaret glanced up at her niece and then said rather impatiently, "Oh, I don't know—those filtered kind in a box. What difference does it make to you, anyway, Savannah? Maybe Marlboro. But he was not a Marlboro man, I'll tell you. Eeeowwww." She shuddered at the thought of Joe Forster representing a brand of anything in a positive light. "Why are you so interested in Joe's brand of cigarettes?" She wanted to know.

"Well, Auntie, I might have some evidence."

"Evidence of what; what are you talking about?"

"Evidence of who killed Grandpa Forster—who burned him to death."

"What?" Margaret said as she pulled her cup away from her lips and dribbled a little of the golden liquid down the front of her white blouse. She set the cup down and grabbed a napkin. "Water; Vannie, get me some water, would you?"

Savannah pulled a bottle of water out of her large purse and handed it to her aunt. Once she had finished dabbing at the streak of chai latte with her dampened napkin, she looked pointedly at her niece and asked, "Now Vannie, what are you talking about?"

Savannah hesitated for just a moment and then she said, "Auntie, do you remember when we all came to stay at your house not too long after Grandpa Forster

155

died?"

"Sure, we were celebrating someone's birthday, or Thanksgiving, weren't we?"

"Yes, I believe so. Well, we kids found something that week."

"Found what?"

"Possibly a clue as to how Grandpa died."

"Okaayyyy," Margaret said with a suspicious tone.

"You know that old hollowed-out tree behind the barn where we liked to play?"

"Yes, it's still there. Why?"

"Well, we were playing cops-and-robbers or some such game using the tree as one of our hideouts and we found something. It was in a crevice in the tree stump."

"What, Vannie? What?" Margaret was listening intently, eager to hear more.

"A red-and-white cigarette box full of cigarette butts." Savannah hesitated before going on. "Now, I read a lot of detective stories then, and I figured out that someone had sat there waiting for Grandpa Forster to go into the barn and then he knocked him out and burned the barn down around him."

Margaret stared at her niece for a moment and then shook her head slowly back and forth saying, "You have some imagination, Savannah."

"Does this look like imagination?" She dug around in her purse for a few seconds and then pulled out a plastic bag containing a dirty, partially disintegrated cigarette package. "I took Rags for a walk around the property yesterday and found this right where we kids buried it some twenty years ago."

Margaret stared at the bag and its contents and then asked slowly and quietly, "Why did you hide it if

156

you thought it was a clue?"

"Because we weren't allowed to go near the barn. And when I asked questions about the fire, I was told to go out and play. As far as we kids were concerned, we would be in trouble if we even spoke of the incident, let alone show someone a clue we found so close to the barn," she explained.

Margaret sat silent, staring at her cup, thinking over what her niece had just revealed. Finally she spoke as if measuring her words, "Oddly enough, I thought about Joe when Grandpa died." She looked up at Savannah. "But I knew he was in jail. I'd read that he had been involved with a gang that was stealing farm machinery and selling the parts."

"When was he sentenced?"

"He'd been in for several months by then. His sentence was two years, I believe."

"His whereabouts at that time might be important," Savannah said. "Is it something we can check on?"

Margaret shrugged. "Yes, I can probably get the information from Jim. I want to talk to him, anyway." She thought for a moment and then said, "You know, that's just plain creepy to think that Joe might have killed his uncle. Why would he do it? Jed was the only one who gave him handouts."

"Where's Joe now?" Savannah asked.

"He's in a mental institution. There was an incident where he got himself arrested for something quite serious, as I recall—he was doing some work for a woman over in the next county. He wanted an advance on his pay—probably for drugs or something—and she refused to give it to him, so he beat her up. Her little dog tried to protect her and he killed the dog. It was determined that he was unfit to stand trial, so they put

157

him away in an institution. He's still there, as far as I know."

***

Savannah climbed behind the wheel of the Jeep, wrapped her hair in a knot, and turned the key. "Well, it's been another full day," she said. "Where to now, Auntie?"

"Home, James."

Deputy Jim had come through for Margaret. He was able to confirm that Joe Forster was out on the street the night his great-uncle burned to death in the fire. This information, along with Savannah's evidence, would surely cause authorities to reopen the case. The only problem was in determining when the package of cigarette butts was left behind. Since Joe was an occasional visitor to the Forster home, the defense would surely argue that it could have been left there sometime earlier.

As for the license plate number on the truck that Betty and Gil followed, Jim discovered which trucking company it was registered to and promised to follow up with some questions. Jim had told Margaret, however, "It's likely that someone took the truck without permission or the company rented it out for a job and the name on the paperwork is phony."

The most successful stop of the day was at animal regulations. Director, Bobbi Curtain confirmed that, indeed, they had received reports of missing horses. And neighbors in the foothills area had issued complaints about the condition of the horses at the Bray place. They were also familiar with the catnapping situation and were pleased to receive additional information from Margaret and Betty.

158

Bobbi Curtain told them, "With what you've learned so far, Ms. Forster and Ms. Gilbert, we should be able to act sooner rather than later, possibly saving many of the cats and horses. Imagine," she said, shaking her head in disbelief, "a ring of horse *and* cat thieves operating right here in the tri counties." A large woman with a plain round face and a mannish way of dressing, she thanked the women profusely when they prepared to leave, but not without an expected reprimand. "Ms. Forster and Ms. Gilbert," she said sternly, "I can't stress enough how dangerous this operation could be. You've already put yourselves at risk. I don't want you to do it again. Please, stay out of the way. We will handle it from here."

Margaret sank down a little in her wheelchair, looked up at the woman and said rather sheepishly, "Yes. I promise. Thank you, again."

***

"So, who are you going out with tonight? Somebody I know?" Margaret asked, a definite twinkle in her eye.

Savannah grinned. "Oh, I think you know him. Will you be okay here alone tonight?"

Margaret turned off her Kindle and set it aside. "Sure, I have two cats to keep me company and several mysteries loaded up and ready to read. Don't you worry about me."

"You'll probably be glad to have some time to yourself. You're not used to someone tagging along with you everywhere, are you?"

"No, not lately." Suddenly, she lurched forward and grabbed at something as it flew past. "Rags, what do you have, now?" she demanded.

"What was it?" Savannah asked, having seen

only a blur heading toward the staircase.

"It's Layla's pillow. Would you get that away from him?" Margaret insisted. "She loves that little pillow."

"Oh darn it. I'm sorry, Auntie. Raaaags! Bring that here." Savannah raced up the stairs after the errant cat. When she returned, she announced to her aunt in a flat tone, "I found his stash."

Margaret looked confused. "What?"

"He's been stashing things—the pillow—here it is, by the way, some of Layla's toys, a washcloth—he loves used washcloths, that cookie, and, oh yes, the cat from the meeting. And, this is a first. I found this." Savannah held up a small satin pouch with a zipper across the top.

"My coin purse!" Margaret exclaimed.

"And it's full of money." Savannah shook it so her aunt could hear the coins jingle.

"Hellloooo," Max announced opening the door and peering around it into the living room.

Savannah looked up. "Oh, hi Max."

"What's wrong with him?" he asked after entering the room. He pointed at Rags, who was sitting next to Savannah intently staring at the treasures she held in her hands.

"I found his stash, the thieving cat. Now, it seems, he's into stealing cash money," she said, tossing the pouch to her aunt.

Savannah eyed the tote bags looped over Max's arms. "Whatcha got there?"

"Dinner for two." He winked and headed for the kitchen.

"Auntie…" Savannah scolded when he was out of sight, "you little devil. You aren't going to be alone tonight at all. You have a dinner date."

160

"Yes, Max is cooking one of his gourmet pasta dishes for us. So where are you and Michael going?"

"Who said I was going anywhere with Michael?" Savannah teased.

"Oh come off it. You're not fooling anyone with those cow eyes you have for our veterinarian."

Savannah dropped her coy act. "I think we're going to an Italian place over in Straley. He says it has a great ambiance."

Margaret was quick to respond, "Romantic. That's what it is—romantic."

"Whatever." Savannah sloughed off her comment. "Just don't feel you have to wait up for us, okay?"

"Well, don't you be coming home too early, either," Margaret teased.

"Maybe you should hang a scarf on the doorknob if you want privacy."

"Huh?"

"Oh nothing. That's what we used to do in college. If a roommate had a guest and didn't want to be interrupted, we would…"

"Knock, knock!"

"It's Michael. See you later, Auntie," Savannah said as she grabbed her purse and coat and rushed toward the door.

"Savannah," Margaret called out.

"What?" She turned toward her aunt, who pointed down at her niece's bare feet.

"Don't you think you should wear shoes?"

* * *

"So, have you and Maggie been staying out of trouble?" Michael asked after they had driven a few blocks from the Forster place.

Savannah smiled. "What do you think? You know my aunt."

"I'm afraid so. She is a feisty one—great gal. One of my favorite people." He reached down and took Savannah's hand. "But I have a new favorite now," he said smiling over at her. "I've been wondering all day where you've been all my life."

Savannah became instantly aware of her heart beating in her chest. She felt a tidal wave of emotion. *Oh dear God, I have to get a grip. I'm not a giddy teenager. So why do I feel so vulnerable when I'm near him?* She took in the vision of his hand on hers. *I hope he can't feel me trembling at his very touch.* She glanced up at his perfect face. He was smiling.

"Well?" he said.

"Well, what?" she managed through the lump in her throat.

He lifted her hand to his lips and gently kissed it, taking his eyes off the road for a quick glimpse of the woman who sat next to him. "I said, where have you been all my life?"

Savannah shifted a little in her seat. "Michael, do you believe in fate?"

"As a matter of fact, I'm a firm believer in fate, destiny…whatever you want to call it. Things happen for a reason and there is a reason why you and I have been brought together. Don't you think so?" He gave her hand a gentle squeeze and glanced over at her again.

"Yes, I do. So your question about where I've been all your life is not relevant, is it?" she asked.

"Nope!" he agreed. "I'm just a little sad to think that you were on this earth all this time and out of my reach. Just imagine what it would be like if we'd met years ago."

"I believe that if we had met years ago, there

may never have been this moment. Don't you think?" She massaged his hand with her thumb.

He shook his head from side to side slowly. "You're absolutely right," he said. "We had to go through stuff before we were ready to meet one another. And now..." he took a deep breath.

"And now...what?" Savannah asked, still staring intently at Michael.

"And now, we've come together...as if it was meant to be."

They rode in silence for a while, holding hands and listening to Tim McGraw sing "It's Your Love" on the car radio. When the song ended, Savannah looked over and asked, "How's the little cat doing?"

"Great." Michael's voice caught. He cleared his throat and said, "She's coming along just fine. Scarlett may adopt her. She just lost her cat Buddy and she's grown rather fond of our latest project."

"Cool. Every cat should have a home. My heart just breaks for..." she started.

He squeezed her hand. "I know. I know."

And she knew he did.

Soon they arrived at Sapori D'Italia. Michael parked Savannah's red Honda in the lot behind the restaurant and promptly unfastened his seatbelt. He then released Savannah's, pulled her to him and slid the fingers of his left hand slowly down the side of her face. She lowered her eyes. *Surely, he feels me trembling at his touch.* She looked up at him as he gently lifted her chin. She could feel his breath on her mouth, closer and closer, until their lips met in a soft, sweet kiss.

Michael pulled back and stared at Savannah. *Can she see the pure passion I feel for her in my face?* He groaned and kissed her again, gently. She kissed him back.

Taking a deep breath, he leaned back, took the keys out of the ignition and said, "We'd better go in before..."

"I agree," Savannah said, pulling her coat around her, covering the little black dress she always packed when traveling...just in case. Tonight, she had used pearls to accent the daring neckline and wore her favorite designer heels.

Once inside the luxurious restaurant, Michael helped her remove her coat. "You look amazing," he whispered into her hair.

She smiled over at him, noticing that they were almost on equal ground height-wise when she wore her stiletto heels and marveling at how handsome he was in his blue dress shirt and soft grey blazer.

\*\*\*

"I had such a nice time, Michael. And thank you for dinner. It was excellent!" Savannah said as Michael pulled into the Forster driveway. "But I pay next time, okay?"

"Probably not," he responded as he opened the car door for her. "We're using your car and your gas, remember?"

"Well, that's only because you're ashamed to take a lady on a date in your veterinary truck," she reminded him.

Once Savannah stepped out of the car, he took hold of her arm and gently pulled her around to face him. Running his hands inside her coat, he placed them around her waist. He looked into her eyes and said, "You are beautiful in the moonlight." She moved closer until they were kissing—softly, at first and then hard and passionate.

164

*My God, I've got to control myself,* he thought and he pulled back. Savannah stared into his face, lips parted, breathing hard. She ran her right hand up his arm and placed it on the back of his neck, pulling him to her again for another passionate kiss.

Suddenly, he pulled away. He looked intently at Savannah and then embraced her. His voice was hushed and husky, "Savannah, I'm falling in love with you. I want you."

She could feel the warmth of his breath on her neck. "Yes, Michael," she whispered, "I want you, too—more than I can say." She pushed him away, looked into his eyes and continued, "But let's not rush it." She took his hand. "I want us to know each other before...well, before we..."

"Agreed," Michael said. "I feel exactly the same way." He then laughed and added, "Well, a part of me feels that way."

"And that's the part we need to listen to now, Michael."

He stepped back and took Savannah's hands. After staring at her for a few moments, he asked, "Hey are you going to the dance tomorrow night?"

"Sure am," she said. "You?"

"Absolutely. Do you have a date?"

"Um, no. I guess I'll play the field."

"Oh no you don't." Michael bent over in a deep bow and said, "Mademoiselle, will you do me the honor of..."

"Oh yes!" Savannah said exaggerating her enthusiasm.

He stood up and looked over at her. "But I didn't finish. Don't you want to know what I was going to say?" He took on a sullen look.

"Yes, I guess so," she said with guarded

anticipation.

He bowed again while saying, "Will you do me the honor of washing my cow?"

"What?" Savannah scrunched up her face in total confusion.

Michael burst out laughing, grabbed her shoulders in a big bear hug and whispered into her hair, "Of course, I want to be with you at the dance, you silly girl." He then kissed her on her hungry lips twice—three times—before reluctantly turning toward his truck. Savannah watched as he drove away, until he was out of sight.

# Chapter 7

"You are gorgeous!" Michael said when he got his first look at Savannah as she and Margaret arrived at the dancehall. But he didn't have to utter a word. His face said it all. "I thought you were at the pinnacle of your beauty when I picked you up last night for dinner. But tonight…" he paused, stared at her and shook his head slightly from side to side, "you are breathtaking."

"Thank you." She felt her face warming up and hoped the makeup would cover the encroaching pink on her cheeks. "I had such a nice time last night."

"Me, too." He then took her hands in his and held her at arm's length. "So did you girls go shopping today?" *I've never noticed just how lovely her skin is and that off-shoulder peasant blouse really shows it off,* he thought.

"No shopping. Between Aunt Margaret's closet and my suitcase, this is what we came up with."

"Stunning," he said, forgetting that he was supposed to be taking tickets for the first half- hour of the event.

"Excuse me, young man, is this where we sign up for the dance?"

Savannah looked up and her smile widened. "Hello, Dora." She walked toward the woman.

"Well, Savannah, I almost didn't recognize you without your blue jeans and ponytail." She reached out and put her hand on Savannah's arm, saying, "You clean up mighty nice, as my husband used to say. You'll have heads turning tonight, dear."

"She already has," Michael admitted as he watched Savannah hug Charlotte.

Smiling, and only slightly embarrassed, Savannah said, "Michael, this is Dora Lipton and

Charlotte, Dr. Michael Ivey."

"Oh, I've heard of you," Dora said enthusiastically. "You're a veterinarian, right?"

Michael nodded.

"I have a cat that's losing weight and no one can figure out why. I hear you are especially good with tough cases like Powder's."

"Well, there's got to be a reason—sure I'd be happy to take a look and see if he'll reveal the problem to me."

"Powderth getting thkinny," Charlotte said, worry taking over her round face. "He won't eat from my hand."

"Powder's one of Charlotte's favorites," Dora offered.

"And Thcooter and Bethany and...."

Savannah laughed out loud. "You love them all, don't you sweetie? You know what," she bent over and whispered in the girl's ear, "me too."

"Dora! Charlotte!" Margaret shouted just loud enough to be heard over the chatter in the large room. "How nice to see you. So glad you could make it. Come with me," she said as she wheeled her chair around. "I'll introduce you to some members of our group."

Savannah watched them walk away. Then, looking back at Michael, she said, "I have to go check coats. I'll catch up with you later."

***

After fulfilling her volunteer obligations, Savannah looked around the large room and spotted Margaret. She walked over and sat down next to her. "Well, it looks like you have a full house, Auntie! What a festive evening. The Alliance should make quite a haul on this

168

one," she said while watching the crowd. She noticed that Margaret was fanning herself with a program. "Would you like some punch?"

"Absolutely, yes. I'm parched. Thank you, Vannie."

Just then, Betty Gilbert walked up. She nodded to Savannah, who was headed toward the refreshment table, and then sidled over next to Margaret. "Great turn-out," she said. "The publicity really seemed to work this year."

"Yes, and the news about the missing cats. We've had more exposure in recent weeks and that helped, don't you think?"

"Most likely." Betty glanced around the room and then whispered, "Say Maggie, it looks like we've got a go for tomorrow night." She took another look around while speaking in a low voice. "Animal control and, I think, the authorities are showing up at Bray's with a search warrant."

"Wow! That's good news!" Margaret made her own assessment of who might or might not be listening in. "I made some inquiries today at local feed stores and discovered that there are some horses missing from some of the ranches and boarding stables in the communities around here. And one was even taken from a backyard."

Betty grimaced and shook her head.

"Who knows where they are now. I couldn't track the route with the horses you saw leaving the place the other night. But it looks as though they might be hauling them up to that horse slaughter house in British Columbia." Margaret sat silent for a few minutes—both women watching the dancers. She then turned to Betty and asked, "Do you know what the procedures will be and who will be involved?"

"Sure don't. They're taking it from here. But I'm pretty sure they'll report to us once it's all over."

Margaret sat with her thoughts for a few moments before saying, "I'd sure like to be a fly on the wall—or a mosquito on the pond—while this operation goes down, wouldn't you, Betty?"

"Oh, you betcha. It got personal when someone shot at you and when we observed the crooks in action."

While Margaret and Betty talked, Savannah approached the refreshment table. "Doesn't this punch look yummy?" she commented to whomever was in hearing distance, while ladling some of the liquid into two punch cups.

"Absolutely," Ida Stone responded. "How are you Savannah? And that wonderful cat of yours? I plum forgot to get Meowster from him when I left the other day."

"Oh hi, Ms. Stone…" Savannah said, replacing the ladle and turning toward her.

"Ida…"

"Ida," she repeated. "How are you? Great turnout, don't you think?" she said glancing around the room. "And such a pretty evening for a barn dance."

"Scuse me…" Savannah heard a man's gruff voice as someone bumped hard against her shoulder.

"Oh. That's okay," she said with a slight frown as she attempted to catch her balance. She turned in time to see someone wearing a red plaid flannel shirt disappear into the whirl of dancers. She was just glad that she wasn't holding the peach-colored drinks, lest they spill over her white blouse and Margaret's skinny skirt.

"Punch, my dear?" an older gentleman inquired as he reached for the two glass cups Savannah had poured.

"Yes," she heard his companion respond. Savannah looked over, intending to claim the punch. Instead, she just smiled at the couple.

Ida spoke up. "Savannah, this is one of our local city councilmen, Claude Pembroke and his wife, Phyllis." She paused. "This is Savannah, Margaret Forster's niece."

"Claude Pembroke nodded.

"Nice to meet you. Your aunt is a wonderful woman," Phyllis Pembroke said before she excused herself.

Savannah nodded as the couple turned and walked away and then she poured two more cups of punch. She made her way back to where Margaret was sitting in her wheelchair. Only she wasn't there.

*Oh, she is such a gad-about. This sort of shindig is right up her alley. On the other hand, I've never been much for parties and lots of commotion, but I am enjoying myself here tonight.*

"Want to dance?"

Savannah turned and saw Michael standing next to her. "Oh, are you finished with your ticket-taking stint?"

"Yes, and you have no more coats to check?"

"It's such a balmy evening few people are coming in with coats, so I was—well, fired. I'm free for the evening and," she looked up at Michael, saying rather breathlessly, "I would love to dance." She then looked down at the two cups of punch she held and asked, "Are you thirsty? This one's for Aunt Margaret, but I lost her. How about we drink these and I'll get her another one after we dance?"

\*\*\*

Margaret, in the meantime, had made her way to the restroom. She was pretty proud of how self-sufficient she had become when visiting restrooms away from home. As long as she had a wall, railing or bar to hold onto or lean against, she could manage on one foot for a limited time. Some public restrooms were tricky, though. There was the awkward process of opening the usually heavy door and getting through it on her own, either in the wheelchair or on crutches. Some restrooms didn't have enough room to accommodate a wheelchair. Since this experience with her broken foot, she had a greater awareness and admiration for folks who spend their lives in wheelchairs and even young mothers with children in strollers. *There's nothing like living in someone else's shoes for a while to give you a new perspective,* she thought.

She was quite pleased with herself that all went well during this bathroom visit, and it was mostly because she met people going in and coming out and they held the door for her. Such a relief. She pushed her wheels down the hallway toward the dancehall, eager for a glass of punch, when, suddenly, her chair stopped dead. She felt someone behind her and craned her neck to see who it was.

"Don't look back here."

"Who is it?" She tried to keep her voice steady. *Surely it's someone I know playing a little joke, but that gruff voice...it sounds so sinister.*

Before she turned away, she caught a glimpse of a rough, weathered hand on the push handles of her chair.

She looked straight ahead. She could see people in the large room at the end of the hallway dancing, talking, and laughing. All of a sudden, she felt hot breath on her neck. She smelled stale cigarette smoke.

172

"I want what's mine. That's why you will die tonight, Mrs. Forster," the man whispered loudly into her ear, speaking her name with an edge of bitterness and hate.

Just as suddenly as he had appeared, he was gone. Margaret turned in time to see a man dressed in jeans, a red plaid flannel shirt, and dark-blue baseball cap hurry out the side door.

"Maggie, there you are," Max said. "I haven't seen much of you all evening…Maggie what's wrong? You look frightened out of your wits."

"I was just threatened, Max," she said taking his hand in hers. "A man told me he's going to kill me. She stopped and took a few breaths. "He said he's going to kill me tonight," she said in a strained voice, obviously near tears.

"What man, where?" Max demanded.

"He just went out that door." Margaret pointed, as Max ran to the door. She watched him disappear into the night. "Max, no. Come back in here. Please, Max…" she said as she rolled toward the open door.

Max stepped back inside. "He's gone. That must have been him driving off in an old pickup truck." He ran his hand through his hair and looked sternly at Margaret. "Darn it, Maggie, this has gone too far. We must involve the sheriff. I'm going to look for Sheriff Jim now. I saw him earlier on the dance floor."

\*\*\*

Margaret held tight to Max's hand as she told the deputy the whole story. When she'd finished and she'd responded to Jim's questions as best she could, she looked earnestly at the deputy and said, "Gosh, I'm sorry for taking you away from the party, Jim. I know how much you and your wife enjoy dancing."

"Hey, like you guys with your cats, I'm pretty much always on call," he said. And then his tone grew more solemn, "And Maggie, from what you just told me about the threats and warnings you've been getting, we need to take this death threat seriously. I'm assigning a deputy to watch your house tonight while we check more deeply into what might be happening."

"Hello Deputy; Max," Savannah said enthusiastically as she and Michael walked up to Margaret carrying two cups full of punch. Her demeanor changed suddenly when she saw her aunt's face. "What's wrong, Auntie?"

Margaret looked down and wept into one hand—still holding Max's hand in the other. Savannah glanced from Margaret to Max and then to Deputy Jim, who was just walking away. "What's going on?"

Max was first to speak. "Your aunt got a threat."

"Oh my gosh, are you okay?" she asked as she sat in an empty chair next to Margaret. "What happened?"

"Can't we talk about it later?" Margaret asked, wiping her eyes with a napkin someone had handed her. "We're creating a spectacle here—let's just enjoy the evening, shall we? Now go out and dance, you two," she said looking over at Savannah and Michael.

Savannah hesitated. She then handed her aunt a cup of punch. "Well, here. Drink this. It's really good." She handed the other one to Max.

"Okay, thanks," Margaret said. When Savannah didn't move toward the dance floor, she urged, "Now go on, I'm okay. The danger's over…for now. Have fun. I don't want to disrupt the party. Please… go…," she said motioning with her hand.

Max watched as the couple joined dozens of other dancers on the floor. He noticed that Savannah

174

was torn. She had trouble focusing on the music and Michael at first. She kept glancing in her aunt's direction with a worried look on her face. Finally, Michael twirled her around and they disappeared into the crowd. Max looked over at Margaret. "Are you doing okay, Maggie?"

"Yes. Just stay near me, will you?"

"Always. Don't you worry about that." He squeezed her hand.

The two sat without speaking for a while and then Margaret said, "Wish I was out there dancing. Everyone's having such a good time. Look, even Charlotte's dancing with Savannah and Michael. How cute is that? Oh, I guess they had enough. They must be exhausted. Looks like they've headed over across the room for another punch refill. By the way, what time is it?" she asked.

"Nearly 11:30.

"Screeeeeeeam!!!!"

"What was that?" Margaret held onto Max's hand even tighter. "Vannie? Is Vannie all right?" Max could feel her trembling.

Within seconds, Savannah and Charlotte appeared next to Margaret. Savannah looked at her aunt and asked, "What happened?"

Margaret shook her head solemnly. "I don't know. I thought you might."

"No, Michael went to see. I wanted to get Charlotte away from the crowd that's forming over there." She glanced quickly toward the activity.

"Charlotte, there you are, dear," Dora said. She addressed Savannah, "It's getting late, I'd better get her home." She started to usher the child toward the door and then turned and nodded at the threesome. "This has been wonderful. Thank you all for making it special for

Charlotte…and for me."

Savannah waved to Charlotte and watched the pair disappear around the perimeter of the crowd. Just then, Michael joined the trio in an obvious rush. Breathlessly, he somberly reported, "Claude Pembroke is dead."

"My gosh, that's awful," Margaret said.

"What happened?" Max asked.

"They don't know. Not only that," Michael said, "his wife Phyllis is quite ill. Someone said they saw the couple leaning back against the wall as if they'd had too much to drink. They're taking her over to Community and, of course, he's going to the morgue. Such a shame," he said shaking his head. "They're a nice couple—always support events like this."

"Auntie, you look terrible. Did you know them well?"

"No, not really," Margaret said.

There was silence for a moment. Max studied Margaret's face, as if waiting for her to explain what had happened to her. He then turned to Savannah and said, "The threat she got tonight, Savannah, it was in-person this time."

"Oh no," Savannah gasped.

"Yes." Margaret explained, "Some man stopped me in the hallway and threatened me."

"What did he say?"

She hesitated and choked up. "He said I would die tonight."

"Oh my gosh. What does he look like, Auntie?" she asked looking around the room.

"He left. But he was wearing…" she looked Savannah in the eyes and said slowly, "a red flannel lumberjack shirt."

"And a dark baseball cap?" Savannah asked

176

sounding near hysteria. "Did he have a scraggly beard and moustache and longish hair and an ugly, ugly manner about him?"

"I didn't see his face, but that sounds like it could be him. Why, did he talk to you?"

Michael noticed how pale Savannah had suddenly become and led her to a nearby chair. "What's wrong, Savannah?" he asked.

"Auntie," she said as she sat at eye level with Margaret, "that guy was at the refreshment table real close to me a few hours ago. You know, when I went to get you some punch?"

Margaret nodded.

"Well, after I poured the punch, I set the cups down and spoke for a few minutes to Ida Stone. I felt a bump against me—it was him. He rushed off and about that time, Mr. Pembroke and his wife came up, took the two cups I'd poured and walked away. Auntie, he must have put poison in those cups right there without me knowing it!"

"Dear God," Margaret murmured.

Max stood up. "We need to tell all of this to Jim. I'm sure he's busy now. But I'm going to find him and let him know we have some details that might help him solve the murder. Savannah, Michael, will you stay with her?" he asked, motioning toward Margaret.

*** 

Margaret and Savannah were up early, and glad that the sun was out. A sheriff's deputy had been stationed outside the Forster home overnight, although they didn't think Margaret or Savannah were in danger, yet. As far as the killer knew, the two women were dead. The authorities agreed not to release news of Mr.

Pembroke's death or that of his wife, who died on the way to the hospital, for at least twenty-four hours, in order to give them a chance to do some investigation. They had a few suspects in mind—a couple of homeless men who had attempted a home-invasion robbery and a carjacking in recent years, and one Joe Forster—Margaret's nephew by marriage. He had been on the sheriff's radar ever since Margaret and Savannah brought the cigarette package in as possible evidence in Jed Forster's death.

"Did you sleep okay, Auntie?" Savannah asked.

"Not really. And Layla didn't help. She was extra affectionate last night. That might be because I've been gone a lot or because Rags is here or the deputy outside might have her concerned. She was just a cuddle bug, last night," Margaret said. "How about you?"

"It was a long night. I did sleep for a while. Maybe we can get a nap later."

"Oh, how cute is that?" Margaret said.

Savannah looked in the direction her aunt was pointing and saw Rags and Layla lying together in a shard of sunlight. He would reach out and pat her paw and then she would give his paw a couple of pats. Savannah giggled a little. "They're playing pat-a-cake."

After a few moments, Margaret looked up at Savannah. "I spoke to Max earlier; he and Michael have been summoned to help with the raid out at the Bray place tonight." She feigned an exaggerated pout. "Too bad we can't get in on the fun."

Savannah just rolled her eyes at her overly zealous aunt.

"They'll be responsible for catching as many cats as they can and bringing them to the clinic for evaluation and identification," Margaret explained.

178

"I suggested they take my car. With the seats down, they can fit in quite a few of those small plastic cat carriers. Some of them are designed to sit on top of one another—double-decker. They could conceivably bring out a dozen cats or so and the kitties will be warmer inside my SUV than in the bed of a pickup."

Savannah let out a long sigh. "That's going to be quite an adventure."

"Right-o. So they're coming by here around dusk. In a little while, we'll go over to Max's place and load up his extra carriers along with mine and they'll be all set to go when they get here."

Savannah smiled. "Oh, you just want to see Max again. I saw the way you two were snuggling last night," she teased.

Margaret took on a serious tone, "He is a wonderful, wonderful man." As far as Margaret was concerned, Max was a dear friend and she intended keeping it that way. She had found marriage far too complicated. Margaret liked the male companionship, but she was sure—pretty sure—that she never wanted it in a permanent way again. Besides, how permanent is any relationship? She had one divorce and one husband die on her. She wasn't about to go through any of that again.

*I sure do enjoy being with Max,* she thought, *whether we're making love or just working alongside each other. I've found myself thinking about Max more often—romantic thoughts. But I haven't found the time to figure out why, yet. Probably just a hormonal thing.*

\*\*\*

Later that day, Savannah walked into the living room where she found Margaret in her overstuffed chair reading. She yawned, raising both arms in the air and stretched. "Ahhh, that nap was wonderful. Did you get some sleep, Auntie?"

"Yes, I did. Then I got hungry and ate some of the fruit salad Helena brought over with a little yogurt. Hit the spot." She rubbed her stomach. "I shared some with the deputy. There's more if you want a bowl."

"Thanks, sounds good," Savannah said as she started toward the kitchen. Then she stopped and asked, "Have you heard anything about the sheriff's investigation?"

"No, they like to keep their secrets. I guess they got enough from us during that long drawn-out interrogation we went through last night."

Savannah crinkled up her nose. "Wasn't that grueling?" she agreed.

"Oh Savannah, just so you know, Deputy Ben has left for a while." Margaret looked at her watch. "Someone will take his place in a little while. Are you okay with that?"

"Do we have a choice? I think we all know who the killer is and they're probably watching him closely as we speak. I think we're okay," she replied. And then she said, "Oh, look at Rags. He's brought you something."

The two women watched as the leggy cat walked up to Margaret and dropped a pot holder at her feet.

"You crazy cat," Margaret said, reaching down to scratch him behind the ear. And then she perked up and looked toward the front window. "Oh, it sounds like the guys are here to pick up the car."

Savannah walked toward the front door, smiling at her aunt's obvious enthusiasm about seeing Max. She felt like a schoolgirl with a major crush at the thought
180

of seeing Michael again—even if briefly. But it wasn't Michael or Max at the door. Standing there, instead, glaring hatefully at her was a scroungy man dressed in jeans, a red plaid lumberjack shirt, and a dark- blue baseball cap.

# Chapter 8

Savannah felt a pang of terror and quickly closed the door. Before it latched, however, he caught it and pushed it open. Savannah turned and tried to run to get her phone, but he grabbed her by the arm and twisted it behind her back.

"Ouch! You let go of me, you monster!" she screamed.

"Oh my God!" Margaret said frozen in sheer panic. "Joe Forster."

"That's right, bitch. The rightful owner of this here property. Tonight, I take what's mine," he growled.

*The men will be here any minute and we'll be safe,* Margaret reasoned. *Oh why did we let the deputy go? It was quiet all day. We thought we'd be safe. They were supposed to pick this animal up this evening. But how will they catch him if he's here? This is awful—a plan gone terribly, terribly wrong.*

Savannah struggled hard, but his strength was more than she could overcome. *Maybe I can keep fighting him off until the men arrive,* she thought. *I don't see a weapon—oh wait. He has a knife sheath on his belt. I will try to keep him off guard so he can't get to it and maybe the guys or the deputy will show up in time.* In time for what, she wasn't sure. What did he have in mind?

In the process of struggling with the man, she knocked his baseball cap off. He reached for it, but missed and decided to let it go—he would pick it up later to cover his long, brown, thinning hair. For now, he had his hands full. He also dropped something he'd carried in and it rolled toward the ottoman.

He yanked Savannah's ponytail back. "Behave yourself, Missy," he said gruffly. "See this here bowie knife?" He pointed to the leather sheath snapped around a knife with a blade at least nine inches long. "And I'm not afraid to use it," he snarled.

Savannah heard her aunt scream. She glanced over and saw that Margaret was frozen in place—terror in her eyes and her hands up over her mouth.

It was no use. Savannah was no match for him. He was in control. When she stopped struggling, he let go of her hair and stepped behind her, holding her wrists together much too tightly with one hand. He pushed her face-down on the sofa and stretched to reach for the roll of duct tape he had dropped. He placed one knee in the middle of her back, removed is knife and cut a long piece of the tape, which he wrapped tightly around her wrists. As he pulled her up by one arm to a sitting position, she screamed out in pain and he cut another piece of tape and roughly pasted it over her mouth.

"That oughta shut ya up," he said as he stood there leering down at her—his eyes focusing on the shapely mounds under her sheer blouse. *No bra, huh? Nice,* he thought. And then, as if he'd suddenly snapped out of a daze, he said, with venom in his tone, "Now for you, Mrs. Tom Forster. Stand up!"

Savannah tried yelling through the tape. She wanted to tell him that she can't stand. *Don't make her stand, you idiot.*

"Stand up!" he shouted.

Margaret was no longer screaming. She looked up at the scruffy man, her breath coming in short gasps. "I can't."

"Yes you can, bitch." He pulled her up from the overstuffed chair and dropped her face-down across the ottoman. He stood over her and taped her wrists behind her back.

Margaret screamed and he rolled her over and slapped a piece of the silver tape across her mouth.

"Come on now; we're going for a ride." He yanked one of Margaret's arms and shouted, "Get up! Stand up!" Her shoulder hurt so much, she thought her arm would come out of the socket. He continued to pull on her arm as he led her outside, making her walk on her casted foot. Savannah tried to think quickly. What could she do to save them? While she looked around the room and contemplated an escape, she saw Rags saunter in. He looked at her as if she wore tape on her face every day. He then walked over to the dark-blue baseball cap, sniffed it, and picked it up, carrying it off down the hallway.

In a flash, Joe Forster was back. "Now you git up!" he said while yanking on Savannah's arm until she was standing. He half pulled and half pushed her out the front door, making sure to close it behind them, which Savannah was grateful for. She didn't want the cats to get out. But he had other motives. He didn't want any red flags indicating that someone had taken the women. This would give him more time to work his plan.

"Git in the truck!" he yelled at Savannah while jerking her toward the open door of the old dark-green pickup. She hesitated and he grabbed her just above the waist. She squirmed away from his touch. He grabbed her again and lifted her up onto the seat. Once she was seated next to Margaret, he stopped and looked her up and down—a nasty smirk on his ugly face—before slamming the door shut and rushing around to the driver's side. He quickly jumped up into the truck, started the engine and gunned it, speeding out of the driveway and onto the highway.

The women were terrified and uncomfortable. The jostling of the old truck made the pain in their

184

wrists and shoulders more intense and it was hard to breathe with their mouths covered. They both schemed about how they could escape this maniac, but succumbed to the fact that they were pretty much devoid of options. It was just about dark; no one would be able to see them—to see that an obvious kidnapping was in progress—unless he had to stop for gas. Margaret glanced at the gauge. *Nearly full.* What if they broke down in a well-lighted area? If only she had her hands free. She'd pull the keys out of the ignition. *Maybe I can kick the truck out of gear and wreck the transmission,* she thought. *Hell! There's no way I can get my foot up that high. Damn it all to Hell.*

Savannah visualized being able to reach her hands around to the side and open the truck door when he slowed for a stop sign or to turn. But her aunt might not be able to follow her escape. At least Savannah could get help. She stretched and strained, but the way he had her wrists taped, she didn't have enough reach to manage the door handle—unless she moved forward in her seat, which would make her effort obvious to their captor. But they were out of town now. No one was around. No traffic on the roadway. They were heading into a remote area.

They knew he was capable of killing. He had done it before. How had he known that they weren't dead as he had planned? The news was supposed to be squelched until tomorrow. Where was he taking them?

"It would've been easier if you'd just drank that punch last night. But oh no, you had to let those other people drink it and they died instead of you," he said, angrily pounding his palm on the steering wheel. "If it hadn't been for those men in the coffee shop this morning, I wouldn't know. People do flap their jaws, ya know. Good thing for me—bad thing for you." He laughed heartily. "I will git what's mine. I will have my own horse ranch. I won't have to work for that scumbag Bray no more."

*Bray?* Margaret thought. *We're headed for the Bray place. He works there. Yeah, that's about his speed—stealing cats and horses. Oh my gosh, the raid. We might be saved—or will we be dead by the time it starts?* Margaret's eyes began to fill with tears that spilled down her cheeks, over the silver tape, and into her lap.

It was getting darker. Soon Joe Forster turned off the highway onto a dirt road. As they bounced around in the rattle-trap truck, Savannah's shoulder hit the door hard. Pain shot through her shoulder and she tried to yell through the tape.

"You ladies enjoying the ride?" He laughed an evil laugh as he accelerated and turned the steering wheel quickly to the right and then to the left throwing the women into one another again and again.

Finally he pulled into the Bray driveway. Margaret and Savannah looked for signs of the authorities as he drove them past the main farmhouse around to the back where he stopped.

*No one's here,* Savannah thought. *No one knows we're here.*

Terror swept through Margaret as Joe Forster stepped out of the driver's side of the truck and walked around to the passenger door. Savannah quickly tried to push the door lock down with her chin. But it was too late. He yanked open the door and said, "Okay girlie, outta there." She groaned as he pulled on her arm and caused her to lose her footing and fall. He lifted her to her feet by one arm and then pushed her down to a sitting position on the ground telling her to stay there. He then reached inside the truck cab and started pulling on Margaret. She slid easily across the seat. She attempted to steady herself by standing with her good foot on the running board, but Joe Forster was too impatient to let her get her balance. He dragged her down to the ground, and she fell next to where Savannah sat. There was enough light that Margaret could see the fright in Savannah's eyes. *I'm so sorry, Vannie,* she thought, her eyes filling with blinding tears.

Forster used both hands to pick Margaret up to a standing position. He then reached with his right hand, grabbed Savannah's arm and jerked her to her feet. Holding both women by the arms, he pushed and pulled them along with him. Margaret, who was trying to walk on her cast, was awkward and slow and Joe yanked her forward every few steps.

Margaret's body was wracked with pain. It didn't help that she fell a half-dozen times as the trio made its way toward a small shed. *I'm going to die,* Margaret thought. *This is it! My life on earth is over. And Vannie. Look what I've done. I've managed to get that beautiful girl killed and why? I'm a foolish, self-centered, stubborn woman.*

She struggled to her feet one more time with Joe Forster pulling hard on her arm and she had a new thought. *We will get out of this alive. He's not going to get away with this. I won't let it happen.*

With her renewed sense of confidence, Margaret, once she was on her feet, turned to face Joe and, standing on her good foot, she kneed him hard in the crotch. She looked over at her niece whose eyes grew as big as saucers. Savannah saw this as an opportunity. He loosened his grip on the women and Savannah began kicking him with all her might.

It didn't take him long to recover and he came up with the knife in his hand. "Do you want to die sooner or later?" he asked, his eyes expressing the maliciousness of his very soul. "Now, both of you walk over to that shed!" he yelled.

The women did as they were told. He opened the door of the small shed and motioned for Margaret to get inside. That's when Savannah saw something scurry past her—a cat! One of the missing cats. She prayed that help would arrive in time to save her and Margaret from whatever evil plan Joe Forster had in his warped mind and to rescue the frightened cats.

Savannah started to dutifully follow Margaret inside the shed, when Joe pulled her back and shut the door—locking it from the outside with a bolt latch. This made Savannah lose her footing and she toppled over. *Damn, it's hard to balance without your arms. Especially when some jerk-off is pushing you around,* she thought, shooting a disgusted look toward him.

"Git up!" he said to Savannah while yanking her arm. She scrambled to her feet and he began leading her off away from the shed. She looked back and pulled back, hesitating—*Why is he taking me away from Aunt Margaret? Why did he leave Auntie in that shed by herself? Where is he taking me? God I'm scared. I've got to think of a way to escape—to save us. I'm not ready to die and I won't let it happen to Aunt Margaret!*

They approached a larger shed. He walked up a few steps, dragging Savannah along with him. He kicked the unlatched door open, and pushed her inside. *A bunkhouse*, she thought while looking around. He shoved her down on one of the cots and stood over her, leering. "I'm gonna git somethin' outta this," he said. He slipped off his boots, wrapped a wad of chaw from his mouth in a filthy bandana, and, before she could get out of the way, he laid down, partially on top of her. She became nauseated from his body odor and tobacco

188

breath. His hands were all over her. Her arms hurt like hell—as she laid on them with his weight on her. He nuzzled his face in her neck. She held her breath; turned her head; wanted to scream.

Suddenly, he raised up on his hands and looked at Savannah. "This aint' gonna be as much fun if I cain't kiss you," he said. He stood and pulled her up to a sitting position. He stared at her for a moment, revealing yellowed teeth through a grin. Then he reached over and ripped the tape off her face. "There now." He bent down to put his lips over hers. She shook her head. It felt like the skin around her mouth was on fire. He grabbed her hair and held her head still, while forcing a slobbery kiss on her lips.

She screamed as loud as she could and fought with every inch of her body to resist him.

"T'wont do you no good to scream—nobody who cares will hear ya," he said with a sinister laugh. Then his face twisted into something grotesque and he came at her again, forcing her against the bed his lips on hers. He breathed heavily into her neck and lay there moving himself up against her in a vulgar pulsating motion.

"Get off me, you scumbag!" Savannah gulped for air under the weight of his body.

He raised up on one elbow and put his free hand on her breast. "Mmmmm, nice," he said. I wanna see. I've been wantin' to see ever since I first touched you back at your aunt's—I mean *my*—house." He raised up and straddled her while attempting to unbutton her blouse. She lay still, feeling sick to her stomach, her head turned to one side and her eyes closed tight—a grimace on her face as he touched her over and over. *This isn't happening, it just can't be. It's a nightmare.* She tried to console herself.

"Hey, lookie at this girlie," he said. When she didn't respond, he slapped her across the face and shouted, "Look!"

She peered out through one eye and saw that he had unzipped his pants. She groaned in disgust. He climbed off her and reached for the button on her jeans waistband. Savannah flipped out. She began flailing her legs about, kicking at him, trying to plant one right in the crotch. But he had the advantage. She screamed and kicked and thrashed around until she landed on the floor on the opposite side of the bed from where he stood. *I can fit under that bed over there*, she thought and she rolled and scooted until she was deep underneath, up against the wall.

"You're not goin' to git away from me, girlie. Come back here, you wildcat." He quickly pulled himself together and fastened his jeans. He raced around the bed, leaned down and reached under the cot toward her. He felt around—nothing. He stood up and pulled the bed out. She rolled and scooted with the bed, staying under it. He became more and more irate. "Git outta there you blasted bitch. I'm gonna git what I want one way or tother, so you might as well settle down."

"COME OUT WITH YOUR HANDS UP!"

# Chapter 9

It was the authorities. The raid had begun. Savannah felt a new surge of hope—hope that they would find her and her aunt before the shooting commenced. If there would be shooting. According to any raid or showdown she'd watched on TV, there was always shooting. And she knew that, while she felt a sense of relief, the worst might not be over.

Joe Forster panicked for a moment. He didn't know what to do. *I sure don't care if my boss gits time for horse stealin'. I just work for him. I can git off by pleadin' ignorant. What can they do to me?* he thought. He then remembered his personal mission. *I don't care about Bray's problems. I have business of my own—a woman to kill.* He located his boots and quickly put them on. He then ran out the door. He could see a blinding light shining on the front of the main house, so he moved into the shadows and ran around to the back of the house. He rushed inside, his heart racing in his chest. He found Russell Bray pulling guns off the wall and loading them as fast as he could. "Git rid of the evidence!" he shouted at Joe.

"What evidence?" he asked.

"The damned horses!" Bray yelled. "Use the tractor—bury them in the canyon."

*Bury her in the canyon,* Joe repeated to himself. As Bray headed for the front door with two rifles in his hands, Joe raced out the back door toward the tractor Bray had purchased just for this purpose—to hide evidence—evidence of abuse and crime.

"I REPEAT: SHERIFF—COME OUT WITH YOUR HANDS UP!"

Joe ran toward the tractor. *I'll drive this thing around to where the shed is and push it with that old bitch into the canyon. No one will be the wiser. Then I'll circle back and slash that young girl. Such a shame I won't have time to...* he thought.

"Help! Help! I'm in here. Don't shoot!" Savannah screamed. It seemed like forever before she finally heard steps on the shallow wooden porch. She held her breath. *What if Joe Forster has come back?* She backed into the shadows inside the old bunkhouse and willed her heart to calm down, lest the intruder hear it beating hard in her chest.

"Michael!" she said, feeling deep relief as he entered the bunkhouse. "Oh, Michael!"

He rushed to her and embraced her while she sobbed into his shoulder. "My darling Savannah. What has he done to you?" His voice cracked.

"I'm okay—but my aunt's in danger. She's locked in a small shed on the other side of the house."

Michael let her go, saying, "I'll be right back."

She heard him shouting, "Savannah is here! Maggie's in a small shed around the side of the house!"

In just seconds, he walked back into the bunkhouse and over to where Savannah was waiting. He turned her around and, with the pocketknife he always carried, he cut the tape from her wrists. She rubbed them and then carefully and slowly began moving her shoulders around. *The pain—oh my gosh, the pain.* She tried, but could not make her fingers work to button her blouse. "Here, I'll do it," Michael said. He then took off his windbreaker and wrapped it tightly around her shoulders and pulled her into him again. "I love you, Savannah. The thought of losing you..." He choked up. "I want you, Savannah."

Savannah burst into tears, wrapped her arms around his waist as far as the excruciating pain would let her, and said, "I think I love you, too, Michael. It's

192

as if I've known you always."

Michael held Savannah away from him so he could look at her. "You have a dirty face," he said with a rather nervous chuckle. "And you're still the most beautiful creature I've ever seen." She blushed through the dirt and smiled. She reached up and began to rub one of her shoulders. "Here, let me," he said. And he began to massage both of her shoulders and moving them around, trying to get the circulation going and the muscles working again.

"Better?" he asked with a look of concern.

"Oh yes, I think much better. Thank you." Suddenly, her expression changed.

"What is it?" he asked as he looked into her eyes.

"Auntie. I am so scared to think about what he did to Auntie."

"Bang! Bang! Bang!" The two stood silent, wondering what was going on outside, but knowing it was too dangerous to step out.

"Got him," they heard someone outside say.

"I have to go see if she's okay," Savannah said moving toward the door. "Sounds like it's safe."

***

Joe had one thing on his mind: get rid of the woman who was the only obstacle keeping him from living his dream on his family land. He roared around the side of the house on the tractor. Yes, he knew he was supposed to be burying horses—especially those that came from BLM land and from those boarding stables and backyard stalls—*easy pickins*, he thought. *Free horses for the selling. Great idea.* Only when he runs his own ranch, he won't be as greedy as ole Bray and he won't get caught.

But now he had one focus—one last task he

had to do for his own future. He had to get rid of the only thing that stood in his way. The shed was within sight. He ran the tractor at full throttle up behind it and began pushing it—closer and closer to the edge of the canyon—the canyon that had hidden so many things Bray didn't want anyone to see. *That's the only thing my property over in Hammond don't have—a canyon. Maybe I'll dig a deep hole—make a pond or I'll have to find another way to git rid of problems,* he thought.

"Roar." He pushed the tractor hard against the shed to get it in position.

Just as they rounded the bend to where she thought Joe Forster had left her aunt imprisoned, Savannah gasped with fright. The shed was teetering on the edge of the deep canyon. "Oh nooooo," Savannah said as she watched the shed disappear over the edge.

And then the tractor began to shift in the dirt. It looked as if it were sinking. Joe tried desperately to drive it back up onto solid ground, but it was too late. He'd gone too far. He would jump free. But he'd have to hurry—the tractor was toppling over on the open side. He made a leap for it—but too late—the tractor rolled over crushing Joe Forster, and then continued rolling and tumbling down the deep ravine landing on top of the shed, demolishing it.

"My God! My God! Auntie!" Savannah cried.

# Chapter 10

"Oh don't be so dang dramatic, Vannie."

"What?" Savannah spun around and saw, there on the ground in the shadows, leaning up against a large rock, her aunt, in the arms of Max.

"Oh, Auntie Marg!" she shouted. She ran to her, bent down and the three of them had a group hug to beat all group hugs. Margaret and Savannah were crying and laughing all at once. "How did you...? What...?" Savannah stuttered.

"My hero," Margaret said, as she smiled at Max through tears, patting him on the chest.

"My fiancée," Max said, a wide grin on his face.

"What?" Savannah asked. "You finally said 'yes'?"

"How could I turn down a man who risked everything for me?" Margaret winked. And then she looked more closely at her niece. "Savannah, are you okay? You look awful," she said with obvious concern.

"Yeah, it was rough for a while—but, yes..." She looked over at Michael who was squatting down near them. "I'm okay."

By then a team of men and women were standing at the edge of the canyon looking down. Someone called out, "It's an all-clear!"

"That means you folks can get on with your work," a deputy said.

Michael stood up. "Come on, gang. We have cats to round up." He looked over at Max and suggested, "Let's make a human chair for Maggie and get her over to the work area."

"Oh yeah, a seat carry," Max said.

"By the way, Max," Margaret asked, "how did you know we were out here? Or did you even know we were missing? I guess I want to know, who tipped you off?"

"Rags," he said as he helped her to stand. "When we arrived and you two weren't there, we looked everywhere. I even checked for holes in your backyard," he said, obviously fighting back a rush of tears. He paused for a moment and then continued, "When we'd just about given up, we saw Rags in the spare room upstairs walking around with something in his mouth." He nodded toward the ravine. "It was this joker's hat."

"Yes, I remember knocking it off his head," Savannah said, while wiping her eyes again. "How'd you know it was his hat?" she asked.

"It had his name in it." Michael explained, "When you spend time in institutions—mental or prison—your name is in every stitch of clothing you own."

As Max held Margaret steady, he said, "We called Deputy Jim right away and he said they had traced Joe Forster to the Bray place. When he heard what we had to tell him, the sheriff bumped up the time they'd set for the raid. Otherwise," he choked up, "I'm not sure we would have gotten here in time."

"How about that?" Margaret chimed. "The cat and his klepto habits saved the day." Both she and Savannah wiped fresh tears from their eyes.

"Hop aboard, Maggie," Michael said as he and Max crossed arms and created a human chair for her.

Savannah tried to steady Margaret in an attempt to help her ease onto their arms.

"Ooooo," she moaned in pain.

Savannah winced. "So sorry. I know how you feel—sore all over."

"Just sit down," Max said gently. "We'll get you

over to where the car is and you can watch the show—ever try to herd cats?" he asked with a chuckle.

"Max, you know darn good and well some of the escapades we've been involved in together trying to round up cats. I want to do more than just watch," she said with a defiant pout. "I'm not an invalid. I can help."

Once they reached the car, the men lowered their arms so Margaret could stand on her good foot.

"Auntie, how's your foot? All of that walking he made you do…you could have a setback."

"That's for sure. Damn jerk," Margaret said, tearing up again.

"It's okay, Maggie. You're safe now," Max soothed.

From their location near the large barn, the foursome could see a lot of activity: Jeeps driving around the premises, men and women in camouflage talking on phones and handheld radios, people in jeans and jackets over near the horse pens. The body of Russell Bray lay on the porch covered by a yellow tarp. An officer was wrapping yellow tape around the porch pillars just above the steps. The commotion was a distance from the large barn where it was thought the cats were living.

Michael took charge: "Maggie, you sit here in the back of the car and get the carriers ready for the cats we bring. Max, you take the far side of the barn and the sheds over there—do you have a flashlight?"

"Yup."

"Savannah, put these gloves on and come with me. We'll see what we can find inside the barn."

It was just a few minutes before Margaret saw Savannah emerge holding a white-and-orange van cat. She had a carrier door open and held it steady while

Savannah slid the frightened cat inside. "Good job, Vannie," she said, lifting another carrier into position.

Michael walked up and pushed a large black cat into that carrier.

"Hey, one of the pictures we have of the missing cats shows a black one like that. Cool—somebody might be getting their pet back," Margaret said.

"Two tabbies," Max announced, as he rushed toward the car with the cats in his arms. "Small ones. They were huddled together; let's keep them together."

Margaret reached for a larger carrier and prepared it for the two new arrivals.
"What darlings," she cooed.

After a several more trips to the barn, Michael said, "I think that's it for now. How many is that, anyway?"

"With these two, eleven," Margaret said, amidst the sound of many meows in varying tones.

"Wait, where's Sally?" Savannah asked. "Has anyone seen Sally?" She peered into the carriers.

"Oh yes, that poor cat. Let's go in with flashlights and see if we can find her. She's gotta be scared out of her wits," Michael said.

"What kind of cat are we looking for?" Max asked.

"There's a picture of her in the car somewhere. She's a pastel calico with a lot of white."

After foraging around in the car, Max announced, "Here's the picture." He looked at it and then gasped, "Oh, God."

"What's wrong?" Margaret asked.

"I saw this cat. I don't think she made it."

Michael felt sick. "Show me, Max."

In a few minutes, Savannah and Margaret heard Michael calling out, "Clear a space for me to work."

They looked up and saw him rushing toward them with a limp cat in his arms.

Savannah pulled four carriers from the back of the car and set them on the ground out of the way. "You'll be okay, kitties," she purred to those in the carriers. She spread the sheet Michael had brought with him on the floor in the back of the SUV.

"Savannah, keep an eye on her," he said as he lay the cat down in front of her. She put her hands on Sally and felt a heart pumping faintly inside the quivering body. She pulled the sheet up over the cat and placed her hands around her gently to generate heat.

"Let's get some fluids into her pronto-quick," Michael said. "She's badly dehydrated." Once he had given her as much as he thought she could handle, with Max holding the flashlight and Savannah managing the little cat, Michael gave her a couple of injections. "One for any possible swelling," he said, "and one for pain. Savannah I'll need you to hold her. Wrap that towel around her. We've gotta get her temperature up."

"Then we're ready to go?" Max asked.

Michael looked around. "Yes, I think so."

"Well, let's see if we can stack some of these carriers to make room for all of us. Otherwise, animal control might have to take some of them to the clinic in their vehicles," Max said.

While Margaret sat in the front passenger seat, the others moved and stacked and shoved and figured until they were able to put the backseat in the SUV up for human passengers. There were two small carriers left over. "We can put them sideways on the seat next to us," Michael said. He smiled over at Savannah. "If you don't mind sitting close."

"I don't mind at all," she said with a flirtatious smile.

Just then a uniformed sheriff's deputy walked toward them. "When you're finished there, folks, I'd like to ask you some questions."

"Oh gosh, the ladies have been through so much, can't it wait? We have to get these cats to the clinic and look them over. Some will need treatment before we can call it a night. You understand, don't you, Deputy?" Michael asked.

"Sure. But I just need some basic information and statements now. We can finish up tomorrow after everyone's rested. With both men dead, it isn't like we need it for a trial. Just bookwork, you see."

"Okay," Margaret said, sighing. "Let's get this over with."

"I'm going to need from each of you a name, address, phone number where we can reach you, your association with either of the perps and…"

"Perps?" Savannah asked.

"Perpetrators—Mr. Bray and Mr. Forster."

"Oh."

"And I want to know what happened this evening. How did you ladies come to be out here when we arrived for the raid?"

Margaret and Savannah gave the short version, contact information was exchanged all around and soon the foursome was on its way home.

"Savannah," Margaret said amidst the sounds of cats howling and mewing and trying to claw their way out of the carriers.

"What, Auntie?"

"You will really have stories to tell when you get back home. Your mother is going to absolutely freak. And what will you tell your coworkers when you return to work? I'll bet they've never been involved in a cat rescue quite like this one."

200

"You've got that right, Auntie," Savannah said while looking out the window into the darkness. "This wasn't the quiet respite I was hoping for. Way too much excitement. But," she said, glancing up at the man who was holding her in his arms in the backseat, "some of it pleasant excitement."

"I'm trying to get Savannah to stay," Michael said, looking down at the cat she held in her lap.

"What?" Margaret craned her neck as far as she could.

"I can't," she said. "Not right now."

Margaret turned on the dome light so she could see Michael's face. "What's going on, Michael?"

"I want Savannah to come to work for me," he said. And then he added, "As a partner in my practice."

Margaret looked back and forth between the two. "Holy cow! You're serious. But how do you know if she's…" She hesitated.

"Whether she's a good vet?" he finished.

"Well, yes," she said.

"Auntie, have you no confidence?" Savannah asked feigning indignation.

"Cool down, ladies," Michael prompted. "With Savannah's permission, I spoke with her employer, Dr. Mason and I had her school records faxed to the office. This woman," he said looking over at her adoringly, "is an amazing veterinarian. Top of her class—vital in Mason's practice, which is one of the leading hospitals in California. In fact, he was going to ask her to hire on as a veterinarian as soon as she got back." He hesitated, cleared his throat and said, "But he can't offer her what I can."

Savannah pulled away to look at him. She and Margaret said in unison, "What?"

"Marriage." As soon as he said it, he wished he

hadn't. He could feel Savannah's body stiffen against him. He knew he was premature in his exuberance.

Savannah rode silently the rest of the way home. She kept her eyes on the limp cat she held to her chest, her head filled with thoughts—conflicting thoughts. *Marriage. That was an out-of-the-blue surprise. I mean, I think I love Michael and all, but marriage? Not now. Not yet. Can I ever do it? I haven't done a relationship right, yet. They've all been botched—or so it seems. I love the man and then I don't.*

She couldn't hold back the tears. It had been a horrendous night and now Michael had brought up the word that she fears more than anything. She wept quietly in the still of the night—a chorus of soft kitty mews and yeowls occasionally interrupting the stillness. No one seemed to notice. No one would blame her after the fear she'd experienced just hours before. In fact, each individual in the car was deep in thought about what had happened and all of the frightening what-ifs.

"I simply must, MUST take a shower," Savannah said when they pulled up in front of Margaret's house. "I just feel so—well, filthy doesn't quite describe it. Please, Michael? It'll be quick, I promise," she said, as she gently handed little Sally to Michael. "I'll be right there at the clinic with the carload of cats—the kit and caboodle," she said, botching an attempt at a joke.

"Okay," Michael said while exiting the car carefully with Sally in his arms. "I'll take this one with me." He looked back at Savannah. He wanted to say something more, but he stopped himself. He was aware that the marriage blurt had affected her and not in a good way.

Savannah stepped out of the car after him, noticed him standing there looking at her and she reached up and kissed him on the lips. "And the next kiss goes to Rags," Savannah said, as she quickly moved around the car to help her aunt out.

"Oh my gosh, Rags. My hero," Margaret said. "I'll never ever complain to him about a missing bra, shoe, earring, or anything again. He can do all the thievery he wants in my house and still be welcome. In fact, I think I'll keep him."

"Oh no you don't," Savannah was quick to say. She looked over and noticed Michael still standing there with Sally. "I'll be there in a quick minute, Michael. We have a whole lot of cats to examine and none of them sound very happy."

# Chapter 11

"So what time did you get home last night, Vannie?" Margaret asked as her niece strolled into the kitchen in search of a cup of coffee.

"Late—oh my gosh, it was late. We called Edie around two this morning to tell her the good news about Sally."

"Good news?" Margaret asked, excitement in her voice.

"Yes, she's going to be okay—for now. This was an awful setback for her. She probably would not have lived through the night. We found an abscess. Probably some of the other cats were picking on her. And she was severely dehydrated. But when I left this morning around three-thirty, Sally was up on all fours, lapping up a little 'kitty pablum,' as Michael calls it."

"I'm so happy for Edie. She must be beside herself with joy," Margaret said.

"Yes, we also found Samantha and Rascal. But, so far, there is no sign of Buster or Brillo. I think Max and Michael are going back up there today to see if we missed any cats. It's very likely. We may have to set out humane traps to catch those that are too scared by now." And then she changed the subject. "Did you make an appointment to have your foot x-rayed? At the very least, they'll want to change that filthy cast," Savannah said.

"Yes, we go in a few hours. I wanted to let you sleep. The sheriff suggested we both get checked out after our ordeal. Do you mind seeing my doctor? He said he would see us both."

"Oh, well, I guess so. Sure. Probably a good idea."

Margaret's voice took on a serious tone. "He

didn't…you know—hurt you…?" Margaret started.

"No. It got pretty ugly there for a while," Savannah said choking up. "But our rescuers got there in time, thank heavens."

*** 

"That's a nasty bruise, Savannah," Max said as he peered at her from across the small table on Margaret's expansive wrap-around porch. "Did you see that, Michael?" he asked.

"Yes, it's ugly. It must hurt like heck." He took his free hand and touched Savannah's face ever so gently. She held tight to his other hand.

"Yeah, it's tender," she responded. "And that's not the only one." She looked over at Margaret. "Auntie and I both have camouflage bodies," she said with a forced laugh.

"Yes, we're mottled like torties," Margaret added.

The foursome sipped lemonade late on Monday—the day after their ordeal.

"I'm glad the doc checked you ladies out," Max said. "Things could have been so much worse." He choked up. No one said anything for a few moments. Finally, Max looked over at Margaret and remarked, "Your new cast is quite…interesting."

Margaret lifted her multi-colored, mostly purple and pink cast up for everyone to admire. "Yeah, if I have to wear the thing for another four weeks, I figured I might as well make it festive."

Michael leaned over and studied the cast. "How in the world did you get the doctor to make it striped? I've never seen that done before."

"Oh, he had never done anything like this

before, either, but he was willing to have a little fun with it—to cheer me up, I think." And then she changed the subject. "What did you guys find out at the Bray place this afternoon?"

"Not much. Some of the cats will never be recovered—not with the predators in those hills hungry for cats. We found Brillo, but we couldn't get him," Max said with disappointment in his voice. "We left a couple of traps there. I'm sure it won't take long to trap him. There was no food or water anywhere around for the cats. They may have been drinking out of the horse trough, which we noticed was clean and filled today. I understand that the two troughs were virtually empty except for a little muddy water in the bottom, when the raid took place last night."

Margaret stared off into space. "Seems so long ago," she said.

No one spoke for a few moments. And then Savannah broke the ice, "When can Sally go home?"

Michael smiled. "She's home with Edie now. She's fairly alert, eating a little and what better prescription could I offer her than the comfort and safety of her home? That's where the real healing will take place."

"What a satisfying experience," Max said. "It is so heartening to be a part of something so worthwhile, don't you think, Maggie?" he asked as he squeezed her knee.

"Absolutely," she said. "Oh, Max, you said you talked to the board—when's our next meeting? We really do need to acknowledge those who were instrumental in the success of this rescue and get back to the business at hand—organizing our rescue groups so we're more effective."

"Is Wednesday okay with you? Will you feel up

206

to having the meeting here?"

"Sure. We don't have anything going Wednesday, do we Vannie?"

Savannah flashed a quick look at Michael. "Um, I'm thinking about going home this week, Auntie."

"What?" Michael appeared stunned. He straightened his posture and looked into Savannah's face.

She tried to avoid eye contact. "I have to go," she said. "We'll talk about it later, okay?"

In order to break the uncomfortable silence, Margaret said, "Wednesday's fine. I'd like to invite Dora and Charlotte." She looked over at Max and said, "I think we should award a special hero medal to Charlotte, don't you?"

"What a great idea!"

"Yes!"

"Wonderful!" the trio said in unison.

# Chapter 12

Margaret was just settling down into the overstuffed print chair, when Savannah stepped back into the house after walking Michael to his truck. "Now what's this about you leaving this week?" she asked

"I need to get back, but I won't leave until you feel okay on your own. You have so many friends. And there's Max and Helena. Since things have calmed down, don't you think you'll be all right here by yourself?"

"I would have done okay by myself this whole time," she responded with a bit of drama. And then she softened her tone and said, "I have really enjoyed having you here."

"You would not!" Savannah snapped.

"Would not what?"

"Get along okay by yourself."

Margaret gave her a sheepish grin and said, "Well, maybe not. But it has been a blast, hasn't it, Vannie?"

"Um…" She hesitated and then frowned a little. "Sure, if you want to call it that."

"Come on, when have you ever had more fun?"

"Maybe that day I got the root canal or the time I was attacked by angry bees and got all stung up… and then there was the time that pit bull I was working on…"

"Oh stop it!" Margaret laughed. "You needed a little excitement in your life—admit it! Besides, if you'd stayed at home doing your boring routine, you wouldn't have met Michael, right?"

"Michael." She sighed. And then she smiled. "You're right. I have really enjoyed myself…except for…"

"We're not talking about that. It's over. We're okay," Margaret reassured her. "I want to hear about what's going on with you and Michael. Do I sense apprehension? What's wrong, Vannie?"

Savannah plopped down on the ottoman where her aunt rested her broken foot. She looked down at her hands as she fought back tears. "I just don't know, Auntie. I think he's great. He really knocked me off my feet and I guess I'm trying to get my balance so I can make a good decision." She looked up and stared into Margaret's face. "Women can't just go around making choices based on emotion, now can they?"

"Why the hell not?"

Savannah cocked her head, a puzzled look on her face. "Um, well…is that how you make decisions? By the seat of your pants—depending on how you feel at the time?"

"Sometimes I do," Margaret said—a hint of smugness in her tone.

"And it works for you?"

"Do you see me complaining? Is my life so far off-track, Vannie? Really, now, is it?"

"Well, maybe it works for some people. But for me…"

"Are you sure you know what works for you? Is your life actually working the way you would like? What are your goals, anyway, Savannah?" Margaret stared intently at her niece for a moment and then spoke on, "You went to veterinary school. That's something to be mighty proud of. And it sounds like you did well. You've had some serious relationships. But you're not married, you have no children and you aren't even working as a veterinarian. It just seems to me that if you followed your passion more—let your emotions lead at least to some degree—you would be living with more purpose instead of living life from the outside looking in."

"Wow!" Savannah said after sitting with her thoughts for a good while. "All I can say, Auntie, is Wow! You've given me some things to think about, definitely. Could it be that I have it all wrong? That my clear-thinking, cautious way of approaching the important things in my life are keeping me from living it? Fascinating…" she said obviously caught up in her own thoughts.

And then she looked at her aunt and said, "Do you mind if I go for a walk? I'd like to get some exercise. I think it might help to work some of the soreness out, too."

"Sure, kiddo. I'm in the middle of a good book. Don't worry about me."

# Chapter 13

Michael picked Savannah up at 7:00 p.m. sharp, although she'd noticed him sitting in his truck in the driveway for several minutes before coming up the porch steps.

"Ready?" he asked when she opened the door to greet him. He looked around behind her and said, "Well, there's that famous hero cat. Hi Rags! Have you appeared on any talk shows, lately?" He took a closer look and asked Savannah, "What's that he has?"

"Oh, it's the cat from the meeting—Meowster. It has become his favorite contraband. He carries it around with him a lot and likes to sleep near it in the afternoon. I'm not sure he'll give it back to Ida. We may have to get her a new one," she said with a slight grimace.

Once the couple was seated in the cab of the truck, Michael reached over and took Savannah's hand. She welcomed his touch. "I've missed you," he said.

"We just saw each other a couple of hours ago," Savannah quipped.

"You know what I mean. And now I can't even hold you tightly because of your bruises."

"Says who?" Savannah asked playfully.

He smiled and pulled her close for a passionate kiss, which they both enjoyed immensely.

"Where are we going tonight?" he asked while nuzzling her neck.

"Well, I'm hungry—maybe that diner in town? I had breakfast there with Auntie one day." She paused for a few moments and then said, "Seems like years ago." She sat with her thoughts for a few seconds and then asked, "Do they serve a good dinner?"

"Yes, they do. But I'm afraid the atmosphere

isn't all that great."

"That's okay. After dinner," she said while running her fingers slowly along his neck, "I'd like to talk. Maybe we can go back to your place for a little dessert."

"I don't have anything for dessert..." Michael started in a serious tone. And then he noticed the look on Savannah's face and said, "Ohhhhh. Yes, dessert. Sure. I'd like that." He kissed her again and then started the truck, letting it run while they both got situated in their seatbelts.

***

"Hello Iris," Michael said when she walked up to their booth with menus and two glasses of water.

"Oh hi, Dr. Mike." She pointed the eraser end of a pencil toward Savannah and said, "... Margaret's niece—Savannah Jordan."

"Yes. Hello Iris."

"Wow, I see all kinds of hookups (if you pardon the expression) here in this place, but I never thought I'd see the two of you together," she said. And then as if catching herself making a stupid statement, she attempted to explain, "I mean, Dr. Mike, I rarely see you with a girl...er...a...that's not what I meant to say."

Iris blinked a couple of times, took a breath and said, "You know, you two make a gorgeous couple." And she hurriedly walked away.

"What was that about?" Savannah asked.

"I have no idea. I think poor Iris is just a tad overworked. She has a couple of teenagers still at home and she supports them by herself. She cleans offices at night. Mine included."

"But isn't she my aunt's age? She must have

gotten a late start having children if she has teenagers," Savannah said.

"Actually, one is hers and I guess he isn't a teenager anymore, but he lives off her as if he is. I think he's into drugs. And then she took on the responsibility of her last husband's kids when he ran off with a younger woman. Their mother is out of the picture. Iris is all they have and she treats them as if they were her own. They have a dog and I sometimes work a trade with her when the dog needs vaccines or food."

"Oh bartering. I believe in it, too. I'm afraid my current boss is pretty hard-nosed when it comes to people paying. He wants cash money and he'd rather pay cash money for services and stuff rather than fool around with any sort of bartering system. Do you barter your services often?"

"Just occasionally, depending on what the individual has for trade."

"Makes sense. You can't be giving away free services and products in exchange for things you can't use—crocheted baby booties, for example," Savannah said rather flippantly.

Michael looked across at Savannah for a few seconds and then said, "Crocheted booties? Where did that come from? I may very well want some crocheted booties at some point. In fact, I hope…"

"Have you decided?" Iris asked as she approached their table.

"Oh, I'm sorry, I haven't even looked at the menu," Savannah apologized.

"I recommend the Special tonight," Michael said. "They make a pretty good fish and chips. And their cole slaw is excellent."

"Sounds good," Savannah agreed.

"And two draft beers?" Michael gave Savannah

a questioning look.

She nodded.

Iris collected the menus. "I'll be right back with those beers."

Michael stared at Savannah and then said, "Don't you want to be married someday?"

"Sure, I think so." She thought about the question for a few minutes. "But you've been married. It doesn't sound like it was a fun ride for you. Why would you want to do it again?"

"Because I believe that marriage can be the most beautiful relationship ever with the right person. Don't you?"

"I suppose." She hesitated and then said, "But Michael, how do you know when it is the right person? I thought I was with the right person twice in my life and it turned out…"

"Turned out what? You aren't going to say the word 'failure,' are you?"

"Well, I'm not married, am I?" Savannah asked, not expecting an answer.

"And aren't you glad?"

Iris appeared again and set two chilled mugs of beer in front of the couple.

Savannah took a long sip, set the glass down, licked the foam from her upper lip and chuckled. "Yes, I'm really glad I didn't marry either of those yoyos."

"So where's the failure?" Michael asked. He thought about his next comment and then said, "Savannah, just because you dated with the idea of marriage, doesn't mean that you chose wrong or that you failed in some way. Dating is a prelude to marriage. Sometimes it ends in marriage and more often than not, it does not. That's why we date—in order to determine if we would be compatible and happy being

214

together with someone forever—whether we have the same values and goals. We don't—or shouldn't—go into dating anyone with such strong, well-defined expectations that when those expectations aren't met, we feel as though we've failed at life."

"Gosh, is that what I've been doing?" Savannah asked feeling a little off-kilter at the realization. "Have my expectations kept me from my dreams? I mean, you don't know how much time I've spent mourning my broken relationships." Finally she said in a quiet voice, "Wow, I always thought my girlfriends—and even my former boyfriends—were callous and in denial when they seemed to recover from break-ups so quickly and, seemingly, easily. But I was the one who was off base? Do you really think so, Michael?"

"Savannah, I'm not an expert, but it seems to me that you are just about as loyal as they come. You take your relationships and friendships more seriously than many people do in today's mixed-up world. And you hold onto things."

"Oh yes, I do hold on—big time. How does one get over that?" She looked Michael in the eyes and asked, "How did you get over your marriage breaking up, if you don't mind my asking?"

Michael thought before responding. "Well, Savannah, I was the one who ended the marriage. As it turns out, my high-school sweetheart wasn't ready for marriage. She married me just to get away from her dysfunctional family." He hesitated. "I guess I didn't see the big picture—although looking back, I can see that my own parents and a few friends tried to warn me. It's not easy to grow up in a dysfunctional family and not become a dysfunctional adult. Marcy didn't love me—I'm not sure she was capable of love at the time. When she got pregnant, I was the happiest man alive—on top of the world. But she began brooding. She'd been enjoying a night life—she was very social. And pregnancy wasn't in her plan.

"We were struggling financially. I was taking the prerequisites for veterinary school and working at night. She worked at night, too—at a popular club. Unbeknownst to me, she saved up her money and borrowed a little from her mother and had an abortion—without even consulting me."

Savannah could see the pain in Michael's face. She reached across the table and squeezed his hand. "I'm so sorry, Michael."

He gave her a faint smile, squeezed her hand in response and then sat back in his seat.

"Fish and chips," Iris interrupted. "Can I get you kids anything else?"

"No, we're okay, right, Savannah?"

"Yes," she replied. As Iris walked away, she said, "Let's eat, shall we? I want to hear more—I'm especially interested in knowing how you managed to get beyond all of that. But later, okay?"

"Sure," he said as he sucked down several swigs of beer. "This looks great. I'm hungry," he said with enthusiasm.

\*\*\*

Savannah looked over at Michael as they walked up the step to his house. "Thanks for dinner."        "Thanks for suggesting the diner. I enjoyed that," he replied as he unlocked the front door and held it open for her.

While Savannah was giving an overly excited Lexie and a curious Walter their proper greetings, Michael asked, "Would you like another beer? Or I have iced tea…soda…milk?"

216

"A nice glass or bottle of water sounds good to me." She smoothed the fur on Lexie's head and ears.

"That's easy," he said as he filled two glasses with ice cubes and filtered water. "Let's sit in the living room." Michael motioned for her to walk ahead of him.

"Who's this?" she asked upon seeing a pair of blue eyes peering out from under the cloth on a round table sitting in the corner of the room.

"Oh that's Buffy, a neighbor's cat. Mrs. Armstrong is traveling and I'm boarding Buffy, but I have to promise I won't put her in one of those *awful cages*," Michael said imitating how Mrs. Armstrong might say it. She's here so often, she's like part of the family," he said. "She gets along famously with these two. Being an only cat, she doesn't like much commotion. But once Lexie settles down, Buffy will be out demanding her share of the attention from us."

"Is she Siamese? Those eyes are incredible." Savannah leaned down trying to get a better look at the cat's face.

"Almost Himalayan." Michael set the glasses on coasters on a large wood-plank coffee table and motioned for Savannah to sit with him on the large dark-plum loose-pillow sofa.

"Almost Himalayan?"

"Yeah, like a cross between a Himalayan, a snowshoe, and maybe a ragdoll. She's quite stunning. You'll see her before the evening's over." He turned to Savannah and said, "Now, where were we when our dinner rudely interrupted our conversation?"

"I don't know if you want to revisit that period in your life, Michael. It must make you awfully sad."

"A little, sure. But it's in the past. As you said, it was a period in my life. It's over and I'm actually glad it happened—well most of it."

"Glad?"

"Yes, I believe that everything happens for a reason…that there is a plan—a bigger picture. We have free choice, of course, so we can accept or decline the various options that come into our lives. But I believe that we are somehow led—through gut or a higher power—I'm not sure—but we are led to make some of the choices we make because we need the experience in order to learn." He took a breath and then added, "I also believe that there are many wonderful gifts in the universe for us. All we have to do is choose to accept them."

"What?" Savannah asked, a puzzled look on her face.

"We may be the designer of our lives, but, in case you haven't noticed, we aren't in charge of the big picture. I didn't create Marcy or the circumstance of our meeting. That was something beyond my control, right? But I did choose to marry her. It didn't just happen. I had choices. She had choices." He stared into space before saying, "…although I don't think she realized it at the time."

He reached around behind Savannah and pulled her to him. "We had no control over the circumstances of our meeting one another, did we?"

"Well, no, I guess not."

"We didn't even decide to become attracted to one another, do you think?"

Savannah giggled a little and agreed with Michael's statement.

"But we did choose to spend time together this evening and I have made up my mind that I would like to be married to you—to spend the rest of my life with you—to have children together. That's what I want more than anything right now."

218

He could feel resistance in Savannah's body. *What is she thinking?* he wondered as they sat quietly together in the dimly lit room.

"Oh! Well, hello Buffy," she said as the lovely long-haired beauty reached a paw up and lightly clawed Savannah's leg. "You want some attention, huh, girl?" She leaned over and began to pet the little cat.

"Be careful, she's a wool sucker," Michael said as Buffy jumped up into Savannah's lap. "Hmmm, does she also eat ribbon and pieces of string off of frayed towels?"

"Oh, yes. Mrs. Armstrong has her hands full keeping things like that away from this one, especially when her little twin granddaughters come to visit with all of their hair bows, doll blankets, and stuff," he said, laughing. Taking on a more serious tone, he said, "I had to operate on Buffy once when she swallowed something she couldn't pass. The woman has done some research and found that there are some flower essence remedies that might help to reduce Buffy's stress and help remedy the problem. We have also experimented with a few stress-relieving meds. So far, we haven't made a lot of progress, but Buffy is only a year old, so maybe we'll hit on something."

"I know of a product. We've used it with success in LA. It's like a cat pacifier. Let me get the name of it for you. Buffy may like it instead of people's clothing and such," Savannah said.

Michael leaned forward so he could look Savannah in the eyes. "Now see, don't we make a good team?"

"Yeah, sure." A slight smile formed on her lips. After watching Buffy curl up and get comfortable on her lap, she began to pet the little cat. She then leaned back against Michael and said, "Michael, I do believe

I'm in love with you. I'm so grateful for what you did out there during the raid and impressed and…well, just awestruck. I have so enjoyed the time we've spent together. You are a wonderful, wonderful human being. Yes, I do want to get married and have a child—maybe two. The idea thrills me. I think the right man and a family would complete me. But I also think I'm… well…damaged goods."

"What? Now you're talking crazy, Savannah."

"Michael, please. I didn't call your deepest thoughts and beliefs crazy. Let me finish."

"Point well taken. So sorry. I'm listening," he said sheepishly.

"I obviously have some things to work out within myself before I can give of myself in the way a wife should be willing to do." She reached over and took his hand, intertwining her fingers with his. She then turned to face him and said, "I have some things to think about. I need to go home for a while. But I want to stay in touch. Can we do it that way?"

He looked her square in the eyes and asked gently, "Savannah, are you running away again?"

"From what?" she asked, shifting her body and causing Buffy to slide down between the two of them.

"From us, like you ran away from the situation with Travis."

"I didn't run away. He left. I only came here to help out my aunt." She noticed that her voice was raised and sounded a bit unnatural.

Buffy looked up at her as she spoke. She opened her mouth in a silent meow.

"Sure, Savannah, maybe that's the truth—at least that's what you believe. So that's *your* truth."

Buffy looked toward Michael now as he was speaking. She issued him the same silent meow.

220

"Yes, it is what I believe, so it is the truth."

"It is *your* truth. And I'm not saying there is anything wrong with it. It just is."

"Did you notice that?" Savannah said, looking down at Buffy.

"Yes, she's quite engrossed in our conversation."

"And she wants to be a part of it." Savannah laughed. She ruffled the fur behind one of Buffy's ears. "What a cutie."

The two sat in silence for a while just holding hands and watching the cat who so much wanted a connection to both of them.

Finally Michael said, "Savannah, I have to ask; in your gut, do you think you're leaving in order to forget me? Are you feeling trapped? Do you want to get away from me?"

"No, Michael. It's the opposite. I want to stay close. I want to be with you every minute. I want to experience everything about you and with you. As I said, I'm so off-kilter where you are concerned, I just feel a need to get my bearings before making a serious decision."

"Oh, Savannah," he said, pulling her toward him and holding her. "You feel as I do, only you just don't quite trust your feelings, do you?"

The cat wriggled her way out from between the couple and moved over to the coffee table. Savannah took advantage of the space and closed the gap between herself and Michael. "I think you're right," she said, now feeling a little weepy. "I don't think I trust myself. I've made so many mistakes."

"No!" Michael said sharply. This made Buffy react, thinking she was in some sort of trouble and she inadvertently bumped Michael's water glass and knocked it over. She jumped off the table before her feet got wet, but a few drops splashed on her coat and she sat in a corner for the next several minutes bathing herself.

"Sorry about that," Michael said as he rushed back into the living room from the kitchen. He handed Savannah a paper towel to wipe water off her shoes. He then used a towel to soak up the water that spilled over the coffee table.

"Hey, have you met Rags, the 'into everything cat?' This is nothing. Anyway, I think she got the worst of it." They both laughed.

*** 

"Will you be here for the meeting Wednesday?" Michael asked as he and Savannah pulled out of his driveway.

"I wouldn't miss it." She smiled. "I'm looking forward to it."

"Can I see you again before you leave? And when will you be back?" he asked.

"Yes, I'd like to see you while I'm here. Very much," she said, leaning across the seat and softly kissing him on the neck. "As far as my plans beyond that—I don't know. I will be back for Aunt Marg's and Max's wedding. I think they're planning it for next month."

"A whole month?" he asked.

She reached over and tapped the end of his nose. "You and I will be in touch a lot." She then pulled back a little. "I promise. Michael, I'm not saying 'no.' I'm saying 'not now.' I want to come to you complete. I need to be complete within myself before I can be the wife you deserve. Just so you know, I consider us a couple. It happened so fast—when I wasn't quite ready. From what you've told me, you seem to be good at following your gut. I have gut feelings, too, and maybe it's that I don't trust mine or that I'm just not as tuned in as you are. My gut says I need time. Will you give me that? In the meantime, Michael—yes I want to be with you. I want you in my life. I need you in my life."

He pulled up in front of Margaret's house, unbuckled his seatbelt, and then reached down and unbuckled Savannah's. He pulled her into a passionate kiss. Savannah relaxed completely. She did not want it to end. And she let Michael know this by returning the kiss over and over again.

# Chapter 14

"Auntie, I'm leaving tomorrow morning."

Margaret continued to hold her coffee mug up to her mouth, blowing across the top of it. Finally, she set it down on the table next to her chair, looked up at Savannah and said, "I'll sure miss you, Vannie. We've really shared some things, haven't we?" She wiped a tear from her cheek. She swallowed hard and then said, "But I understand why you need to go. I've known you since you were born and I know how you deal with things, Savannah." She reached both hands out toward the young woman. "You will be back. I'm sure of it."

Savannah moved forward, took her aunt's hands, and sat down on the ottoman. "Oh Auntie, I'm so in love with him. I just don't want to rush into anything."

"I know!" Margaret said, a superior tone to her voice. She let go of her niece's hands and leaned back in her chair. "You've always had to step back and look before you leap. It's your way." She then tilted her head and, with a knowing look, she said, "I've seen you miss some opportunities because of it, too."

"What opportunities?" Savannah insisted.

"Well, there was the time when you wanted that little rabbit from down the street. But you just weren't sure your cat would get along with her. You got so wrapped up in what was the right thing to do that you allowed that little rabbit to become that family's dinner."

"What? They ate her? I didn't know that. Oh, that's awful. I guess procrastination was a definite wrong choice that time."

"Sure was. And what about the time that sweet young man invited you to the high-school prom? You

224

thought yourself right out of that date."

"Oh yeah. Jason Turner. I ended up staying home—well, that was partly because I came down with the hives—probably due to the stress I felt because of my indecision. Another bad move on my part. But what about those times when I made snap decisions and they turned out bad?"

"When did you ever make a snap decision, Savannah Jordan? Tell me, I'm all ears."

"Well, when I joined the Brownies," Savannah said confident that this would make her point. "Remember, I got lost on our first outing and they had to bring in the search dogs?"

"Savannah, it wasn't the fact that you joined the Brownies that created the problem, it was your stubborn procrastination or indecisiveness—whatever you want to call it. You were the problem, my dear niece, when you waited too long to decide to return to camp and it got dark."

"Oh. Okay, well, anyway, I do want to go home, get my bearing, and think about it—and that's what I'm going to do. Tomorrow morning."

"Have you told Rags?"

"No, why?"

"I think he has a new friend."

Savannah looked over in time to see Rags lying on his back under a dining room chair, batting at Layla's long tail. She was peering over the edge of the chair seat trying to pat his long legs.

Savannah pulled out her cell phone and began taking pictures of the cats.

"Send me one of those, will you?"

"Sure." Then she became serious, saying, "Now Auntie, you will be okay, right?"

"Yes, absolutely. I have Helena coming three

times a week and her sister can help out if I need something when Helena isn't available. Max is a dear. I'll probably be over there more than at home, anyway. I can still work with the cats. I'm sure they've missed me. Antonio is here almost every day. He keeps an eye on things. He's a good man. Also some of my friends said they'd be on call to help out. One in particular is Edie—Sally's mom."

"Oh cool. She seems like a nice gal."

"Yes, and she wants to become a part of the Cat Alliance. She may be here this evening."

"Great, it will be good to see her again."

\*\*\*

"Come on in, Max," Savannah said after opening the door. She looked beyond him and motioned to the group of ladies from Ravenwood. "Hi Kitty, Clarice and… Anna, is it?"

"Yes, and you're Savannah?"

"Yes, is Gina with you?"

"She's coming with her mom."

"I'm so sorry about her Buster," Savannah said.

Kitty grabbed Savannah around the shoulders and began to cry as she hugged her tight. "You ladies are wonderful. Just wonderful," she said through her tears.

Clarice chimed in, "We are so grateful. And to think what you went through…"

"Horrible, just horrible," Anna said looking down at the floor and shaking her head slowly back and forth.

Savannah nodded sullenly and then she glanced up at someone behind the three women and smiled. "But we rescued most of the cats and it's mostly thanks

226

to this young lady. Charlotte is our hero," she said as the teen and Dora walked toward her. "She was brave enough to tell about something she overheard at school. She is the reason we found your cats."

Charlotte blushed and smiled, looking down at her feet. The three women rushed her and began thanking her profusely and telling her what a courageous girl she is.

Dora, sensing that the child was feeling a bit overwhelmed, thanked the women and steered Charlotte over to the refreshment table. She then found seats for the two of them set slightly apart from the others. Savannah watched this. She was pretty sure that Dora was protecting Charlotte from overstimulation. *Like Buffy,* she thought.

"Hello beautiful." Savannah felt her entire body tingle as she turned to face Michael.

"Hi, yourself," she said, standing on her tippy toes to give him a peck on the cheek.

*** 

The meeting started promptly. Max had brought five sheets of paper in different colors and taped them to a large board in the dining room. "I want everyone who is interested in cat rescue to sign their name, phone number and email address under the job task or skill set that most describes you or that you would most prefer doing. Where are your strengths? If you have multiple skills and aptitudes, put your name on more than one page. The committee will go over the names and come up with a model to present to the group for further discussion. If your expertise is cat socializing and behavior, for example, sign your name on the pink sheet. If you love being around cats, but your skills lie in the physical labor needed to sustain them—building cat trees, repairing pens, and so forth—sign up on the physical-labor sheet; I think it's blue. There's also medical and veterinary care, fundraising and so forth. Oh yes, and an important one, working with the public. This might be managing adoptions and volunteers, for example. If you're good at PR and marketing, sign up on the yellow sheet."

Numerous questions and some lively discussions followed.

Before the meeting started, Savannah had returned Meowster to Ida. But by the time the meeting was over, it was missing again. *Yes,* Savannah thought to herself, *I will have to replace that chenille cat.*

Charlotte fell in love with Rags and spent most of the evening on the floor playing with him.

Before adjourning the meeting, Ida called on Max and he gave a report about the raid at the Bray place. Gina and Edie had arrived by then. Edie broke into tears more than once as she continued to thank everyone for bringing her Sally back to her. Margaret expressed regret to Gina who lost her cat, Buster. Gina said, "We miss Buster, but, I'm just glad that Mom got Sally back. Thank you from the bottom of my heart for that gift."

Max announced: "The next item of business is to recognize some of the heroes. Betty and Gil, you went beyond the call of duty. We so appreciate your courage and caring."

The room echoed with applause.

He then said, "I have a very special award to give tonight." He looked over at the child who was sitting on the floor at Dora's feet with Rags. The room grew silent as he continued, "This is Charlotte. She is the very brave girl who listened carefully and shared

228

what she heard so that we knew where to find the cats. Without Charlotte, many of those cats might have died," he said choking up a little. "Charlotte, can you come up here for a minute?"

The girl looked up at Dora, who gave her a nod. She stood and walked toward Max hesitantly, smiling shyly the entire way. Max stood, took a shiny medal on a cord out of a box and held it up toward Charlotte, saying, "From the bottom of our hearts, Charlotte, we thank you for being the wonderful and special cat person that you are." He put the medal over Charlotte's head so it hung around her neck. Everyone in the room stood and applauded for a very long time. Some of the women teared up through their grateful smiles. Edie dabbed at her eyes while clapping one hand against her other forearm. Even Margaret stood with her crutches. Since her hands were occupied, she let out a shrill whistle.

Charlotte stood, looking down at the medal, smiling—glancing over at Dora from time to time. When the room quieted down, she held the medal out for others to see and said, "Thereth a cat on it. I like cath." She glanced over at Dora and then said, before walking back to her seat, "Thank you." Applause roared through the room again.

***

"I think that's it. I'm ready to go," Savannah said to Margaret, who was sitting on the porch clutching her robe around her. Helena was inside cleaning and preparing a few meals for Margaret. Rags was in the back window of Savannah's red Honda lying on a blanket, seemingly ready for the long drive home. "I'll see you in six weeks for your big day."

"It's not that big of a deal, Vannie. I've been married before, you know."

"Of course it's a big deal, Auntie." Savannah squatted down in front of her aunt and patted her hand. "Auntie are you crying?"

She wiped her eyes with the sleeve of her robe. "I'll miss you, kiddo, that's all."

Savannah reached up and hugged her aunt around the neck. "I'll be back."

"To stay, I hope."

"The jury's out on that question. We'll see what happens."

"How's Michael with all of this?" Margaret asked when Savannah stood up to leave.

"We're both sad. But we'll be in touch a lot. He's giving me my space to figure things out."

"Just don't take too long," Margaret scolded. "Men like Michael don't stay single long."

Savannah stared at her aunt for a moment. *Hmmm,* she thought, *I wonder if Michael has been dating much. It hasn't occurred to me that he might find someone while I'm away. I guess it could happen. In fact, it could very likely happen. Am I making the right decision to leave? Thinking back, I did see a couple of women keeping their eyes on Michael at the dance. I didn't pay much attention, other than to feel special because he was with me. I guess I am taking a chance of losing him by pulling away from him like this. But I can't do it any other way. I must go. I have to think. When I get married, it has to be the right thing at the right time.*

"I'll just have to take my chances," Savannah said in a weak voice. "See you soon, Auntie. Thank you

230

for everything."

"Thank *you*, Savannah. Be safe."

When she glanced up from inside her car to give one last wave, Savannah saw that Helena and Antonio had joined Margaret on the porch. Everyone waved enthusiastically and kept waving until they could no longer see Rags's face through the back window of the car.

# Chapter 15

"Oh Savannah, I can't tell you how good it is to have you home. I've missed you stopping by," Gladys said with tears in her eyes. After hugging her daughter tightly, she said, "Now, sit down and tell me how your job at the clinic is going. Have you been getting together with your biker girlfriends since you got back?"

"Mom, that's 'cycling,' not 'biking,'" Savannah corrected. "Yeah, I went out riding with Gwen a few days ago. Had dinner with Shelli and Stu. They're expecting a baby. The job is okay. Where's Brianna?" she asked looking around—hoping to get the focus off of herself.

"She'll be home late. She's working and then she has a class tonight. You haven't seen much of your sister since you've been back, have you? You both keep so busy."

"She spent the night at my place a couple of times this week, you know. So what's for dinner?"

"Your favorite, of course," Gladys said with a smile as she motioned for her daughter to follow her into the kitchen. "Texas hash. Do you want a green salad?"

"Yes, that would be great. Here, let me help," Savannah said as she opened the refrigerator in search of some greens. "Mom," she said as she cut up a few green onions to sprinkle on top of the lettuce and tomatoes, "can I ask you something?"

"Sure, honey," Gladys responded while checking the French bread she had browning under the broiler.

"How did you know that Dad was the one?"

Gladys turned to face her daughter. "What?"

"When you met Dad, how did you know he was the one?"

"Gosh, that's something I haven't thought about for a long time." She looked over at the salad as Savannah tossed it and said, "How about some artichoke hearts? The salad looks a little flat." She reached up and grabbed a small jar from a cupboard and handed it to her daughter.

Savannah opened the jar, drained the liquid and then cut pieces of the artichoke heart into the salad. She carried the bowl of salad over and set it on the table, where her mom was freshening a small bouquet of flowers from her garden. She stopped and sniffed the air. "Mom, is something burning?"

"The bread," Gladys said, rushing toward the stove. "Will I ever learn to make garlic bread?"

"It wouldn't be like home if the garlic bread wasn't burned, Mom. It's your trademark, isn't it?"

Both women laughed. Gladys scraped burned bits off the French bread and put it on a plate, saying, "I think it'll be okay."

"Looks fine to me."

Gladys set the casserole on the table, poured two glasses of water, turned on the coffee pot and sat down to eat. "There's berry cobbler for dessert," she announced.

"Oh yum. I'll save room," Savannah said. And then she looked over at her mother. "It's so nice to be here, Mom." She laughed. "... burnt toast and all."

"Okay now," Gladys said after eating a good portion of her salad and half piece of bread, "how did I know your dad was the one, you ask?"

Savannah set her fork down and listened intently.

"I didn't know. If you want the truth, I simply

didn't know. I don't think we ever know what our future will be, Savannah. Do you? Really? We just make the best choices we can and try to make our lives work within the choices we make. You're thirty-two years old. Isn't that what you've learned?"

"Apparently not," Savannah responded.

"What do you mean? Do you think life comes with guarantees? Well it doesn't." Gladys took a sip of water, set the glass down and then continued, "I didn't know that we would be as happy as we were. I didn't know that we would be blessed with two lovely children. I didn't know that your dad would die and leave me so soon." She looked off into space for a few seconds and then said, "And would I do it all again if I had known the whole outcome?" She looked Savannah in the eyes and said with conviction, "Absolutely."

The two women continued eating without talking for a while. And then Gladys asked her daughter, "Why the questions, Savannah? Have you met someone?"

Savannah poked her fork at what was left of her meal and then looked up and said, "I *have* met someone, Mom. He's wonderful—knocked me right off my feet. He's handsome. He's smart. He's a veterinarian!" she exclaimed.

"Do you love him?"

"Well, I've just known him for three weeks and for part of that time, we've only communicated by phone and email. I knew Travis for several months before we became a couple and it turned out to be a mistake, as you know."

"Mistake?" her mother repeated. "Why do you think it was a mistake? Because you ultimately broke up? Savannah this does not mean that your relationship was a mistake. It just means that there's something else

234

out there for you. This was one of those life experiences that helps to build character, to teach you some lessons that you need in order to prepare for the experiences in your future."

"Wow! Now isn't that profound. In fact, I think that's exactly what Michael was trying to tell me the last time I saw him."

"Savannah, do you know how your father and I met?" Not waiting for an answer, she said, "I was working at a diner in town. I was just nineteen and still pretty darn wet behind the ears. I'd lived a sheltered life, you might say, and had not done much dating. Oh, there were a few puppy crushes—is that what you call them?—in high school. But then I met your dad. He had just returned from college and was in the process of taking over his father's business. He came into the restaurant where I'd been working for only a few weeks and we really hit it off. There was just something about him. And he was obviously infatuated with me. He was eight years older than me. Well, we had a whirlwind romance, you might say and we married the following year...without my parents' blessing, actually."

Savannah looked stunned. "What? I never heard this story. According to Auntie Marg, you have no sense of adventure. But marrying behind your parents' back— now that seems a bit adventurous to me."

"Yes, well, you might say that. But my point is, Savannah, I knew I was in love with your father and wanted to spend the rest of my life with him after our second date."

"I thought you said you didn't know. Now I'm confused."

"Well, honey, there is the heart knowing and the head knowing. I was clear about what my heart wanted. And I guess it's what my head wanted, too. But

235

I was still not privy to how life would actually be once we were married and had children. Circumstances can change. Things happen. I can tell you all sorts of stories about people I know who were met by obstacles and made new choices. You're always at liberty to make new choices, dear."

Gladys continued, "For example, when your dad got sick, that wasn't something I knew would happen. I never even considered it as a possibility. Yeah, yeah, they include it in your wedding vows. But who takes that seriously? We all think it's not going to happen to us and if it does, love will see us through." She took a sip of water, cleared her throat and continued, "Well, when he got sick, I had options. It was certainly a new circumstance. Things had changed without my permission. My expectations of a long, healthy and happy life together had been completely thwarted. My choice was to stick by your father and take care of him for as long as I had the opportunity to do so."

She looked long and hard at her daughter and then said, "Savannah, don't allow yourself to miss out on a beautiful life with a wonderful man because you can't be absolutely sure that the marriage or the man will live up to your every expectation all the time in all ways. There are no absolutes and there are no guarantees."

# Chapter 16

When Savannah left her mother's home that evening and headed toward her apartment, she had a lot to think about. She was surprised that what her mother told her was so much in alignment with what Michael had said to her. *I guess I've had it all wrong. I've been afraid to live—too cautious. I mean, even my mother has taken risks and been glad she did.*

She didn't call Michael that evening. She turned off her phone and she and Rags went to bed early. Six hours later, she awoke with a start. She was sweating profusely and breathing hard. She looked at the clock. It was 3:00 a.m. And then she remembered her dream. She could see Michael off in the distance. He held his hand out for her. She tried to walk toward him, but each step she took placed her farther away from him. He was disappearing into a crowd of beautiful women. In her last glimpse of him, he was turning away from her, putting his arm around another woman and walking through a tunnel. At that point, she began calling out to him, "Michael, Michael. Don't leave me." But it was too late. The window of opportunity had closed for Savannah.

Suddenly, she knew what she had to do. Although she had made a tentative date with Gwen to ride down to the beach that afternoon, she felt a greater need to take care of something within herself. She got up out of her bed and fed Rags. She showered, threw on some jeans and a sweatshirt and pulled her hair back in a ponytail. She put a few toiletries and clean clothes in her backpack, grabbed a jacket, and jumped in her car. Luckily, she had filled it with gas the day before. She would call Brianna and ask her to feed Rags for the next couple of days.

Savannah headed north on Highway 101 and drove until it got light. She stopped above Santa Barbara for a bite to eat and then continued north, catching Highway 1 just outside of Morro Bay. It was midday when she reached Big Sur.

Even Big Sur made her think of Michael. She recalled one glorious evening together when they talked about their favorite places. She was blown away to learn that they actually shared a couple of favorite spots. Both of them had spent brief periods in Alaska and each of them had a strong desire to return. And then there was this cove in Big Sur where Savannah had spent time with her family over the years. Michael thought he knew the spot, as he used to go there when he was in college to get away from the grind, take in the wonders of nature and to think. As she trekked down the rocky path toward the beach, she was glad to see that it was secluded. She bundled her jacket tightly around herself against the wind and began to walk out onto the sand. It was then that she spotted someone standing a distance away. She stopped. *Probably a resident out for a walk,* she thought.

She found her favorite brooding/thinking spot and sat down on an old log. She was engrossed in watching the waves rush in and slowly back out. The foam formations appearing and disappearing mesmerized her—she found it almost hypnotic. *I'm glad I came,* she thought. *This place is so beautiful—so peaceful.*

"Savannah?"

# Chapter 17

*What? My God, who's that? Am I hearing things?* she thought as she turned toward the voice.

"Michael! What are you doing here?"

"Thinking. The same as you are," he said. "I thought I would feel closer to you if I was in your favorite place." He walked around in front of Savannah, took her hands and said, "I miss you."

"Oh Michael." Savannah stood and threw herself into his arms in one quick motion. "I can't get you out of my mind." She kissed him over and over.

"Well good."

She pulled away from him, looked hard into his face and then kissed him so passionately both of them were weak-kneed for a few moments. "Michael," she said as she nuzzled into his neck, "I want us to be together."

He held her away from him and stared into her face expectantly. "Do you mean…?"

"Yes…er…no, well, I mean…"

"What Savannah? A man can only take so much. What are you thinking? What do you want?" he asked while sitting down on the log and pulling her gently down with him.

"Michael, I came here to think about us, my life, my goals, my stupid expectations and to try to figure out what to do. When I saw you just now, it all became quite clear to me. If you will agree, this is what I'd like to do."

"Yes?" Michael waited trying not to let his boyish impatience show.

"I'd like to spend time with you in some sort of normal dating situation. Does this sound hokey to you or like I'm afraid to face how we feel about each other?"

"No," he said hesitantly. "No, I guess not, really. I want you to be as ready for marriage with me as I am ready to marry you, Savannah and I'm willing to do whatever it takes. If you need more time, then let's take more time."

"But I want us to spend that time together as much as possible," she said.

He looked over at her. "Do you want to move up to Hammond now?"

"I'm thinking about it," she said. "I've realized that I don't have anything in LA to hold me. There's my mom and my sister and a few friends. But I'm not attached to the job. I'm not interested in going clubbing and my married friends are too busy to bother with me at this point in their lives. Brianna is off to medical school most of the year in Cleveland and my mother, it so happens, has carved out a fairly nice life for herself. She even took Aunt Marg's advice and joined a singles group. Wait until I tell Auntie!"

She took in a deep breath, massaged Michael's hands with her own, and said, "I'm ready to move on, Michael. Sight unseen, no crystal ball, and with no guarantees, I'm ready to commit to you, if you don't mind that we take baby steps," she added, just as he was ready to comment.

"Baby steps, giant leaps…it doesn't matter, as long as we can be together, my love." He wrapped both arms around her and they sat quietly for a while watching the ocean waves and listening to the wind whistle through the twisted cypress trees on the cliff above them.

Finally, Michael whispered in Savannah's ear, "Where do we start?"

She looked over at him. "I'd like to take you

up on your offer of a veterinary position whenever you want me to begin."

"Yesterday."

"Funny boy," she laughed. "I think it's too soon to involve lawyers and get something in writing, don't you?"

"Yeah, I guess. But you can come to work for me. I have a proposal and wage schedule already worked up. Come home with me now and we'll talk about it," he said in a husky voice into her neck.

"Nice try," she said. "No, I'm going home to LA tomorrow."

"Tomorrow?" he asked pulling back—a look of expectancy on his face.

"Yes, I thought I'd stay for the weekend since I'm here." She watched him, as if waiting for him to make the next move.

"I packed my overnight bag, too." He searched her eyes for a sign of what might come of the weekend. "I know a cozy little motel off the beaten path with a great view of the ocean and nothing distracting like TV," he said hopefully. And then he added, "We can share a room. But the rooms have only one bed."

"It sounds lovely, Michael," she said as she rubbed her hand softly over his.

\*\*\*

"I'll be there next weekend," Savannah said into the phone.

"Oh Vannie, I'm thrilled that you're coming. You can help me pick out a wedding dress." Margaret sounded almost giddy. "And you can help me plan my honeymoon. Max wants me to choose the place and I don't know where we should go. I can't even decide what flavor cake to order. But guess what? I'll have my cast off for the wedding. In fact, it comes off a week before, so I can practice my dance steps," she said, laughing.

"Well, I'll help where I can, but I'll be working at Michael's clinic starting next Monday. I have rotating days off and we're both off on Sunday. I sure appreciate you letting me stay with you while I look for an apartment."

"You don't need to look for an apartment. Just stay here. I'll be moving in over at Max's anyway. I'm selling the place. But not right away. You'll probably be staying a lot of nights at Michael's right?"

"Oh, I don't think so, Auntie. We've decided to go slow, so there will be no premature living together," Savannah said. "Thank you for the offer of your place. I've become quite attached to my room upstairs. Rags and I would love to come back there. I'll pay you rent while I'm there."

"You'll do no such thing—at least not until after the wedding."

# Chapter 18

"It's your wedding day, Auntie," Savannah said as she stood behind Margaret, smiling at her through the mirror on her dressing table. "Are you ready?"

"Oh, I guess as ready as I'll ever be."

"You have only an hour. The family should be here any time. What are you going to do with your hair?"

Margaret held something up for Savannah to see. "I bought this foo-foo hairdo thingy—otherwise I'll wear it like I always do. How can you change a do that is cut to be a bob?"

"I love your foo-foo hairdo thingy," Savannah said with a laugh. She looked more closely at her aunt's hair. "I can help you put it in." She pulled Margaret's hair back off her face on one side. "How about we put it here for a dramatic look…like this?"

"Ohhhh, I like it. Good idea," Margaret said. Then she looked up at Savannah. "Can you help me with makeup? You do such a good job with your own. I want to look like you."

She smiled. "I think your new husband would rather you look like you, Auntie. But sure, let's give your face a little color."

In the meantime, Helena and Martha were in the kitchen putting the finishing touches on the hors d'oeuvres trays for the reception that would follow the nuptials. Antonio and Juan had built an arbor out in Margaret's backyard over which they wove two climbing rose bushes. Lavender. Margaret wanted lavender roses and Esperanza shopped until she found a shade as close to lavender as possible. The party-rental people had set up the tables for the reception and the chairs for the service.

***

It was a lovely service. Michael, Max's son, and a college friend stood up with the groom and both of Margaret's sisters and Savannah stood up with Margaret. Her brother walked her down the aisle and Brianna was in charge of the guest book. Max's two grandsons carried the ring. Charlotte, still proudly wearing her medal, was the flower girl.

After the wedding, the happy couple would stay home and spend a few days with the family that had travelled to share in their happiness. And then they were heading to the beach communities of California. Savannah had made reservations for them at the secluded motel in Big Sur where she and Michael had stayed weeks earlier.

"Oh there you are Savannah. Sorry we didn't get to visit before the service—talk about a grand entrance. Rose and I almost missed the whole thing."

"Hi, Mom. I saw you come in just in time to line up with us. What happened?"

"Stuck in traffic—you know how it goes...but we got here. I'm so glad to see you. You look lovely."

"You, too, Mom," she said as she reached out for a hug. "Hi Sis," she said hugging Brianna hard. "Good to see you Sis Doc."

"You, too, Sis Vet."

Both girls giggled.

"Who's this?" Brianna asked her sister.

"Oh, I'm so sorry. This, my dear mother, is your future son-in-law. Brianna, meet your new brother," she quipped. "This is Michael Ivey, my fiancé."

"Really!!?" all three of them said at the same time.

244

She turned to Michael and said, "Yes, my darling. Yes."

# More Books in the Klepto Cat Mystery Series.

## Book Two—*Cat Eye Witness*

The second book in the series, Cat-Eye Witness follows Savannah and Michael as they work together in his veterinary practice and, in the midst of a murder investigation, plan their wedding. Since Margaret moved into Max's home after their marriage, Savannah is caretaking her aunt's large, old, two-story home next door until they find a buyer. With Margaret's blessings, Savannah opens the home to a fundraiser to help the abused horses rescued from the same people who were stealing cats. And, before the afternoon is over, the funds collected go missing and someone is murdered in an upstairs bedroom.

Suspicion surrounds Iris, a local waitress, Margaret's former classmate and Savannah's new best friend. The only witness to the murder is Rags, Savannah's cat. With the assistance of a cat psychic and Rags's good friend, Charlotte (the young girl with Downs), the cat helps to "paw" the killer…but not before an attempt is made on his life. The case is solved only after Rags comes face-to-face with the killer.

Detective Craig Sledge is new to this book as is Damon, Iris's errant son. Sledge finds this to be one of the muddiest, most confusing cases he has ever worked, with inconsistent clues and no apparent motive. He's constantly surprised, perplexed and impressed by the cat's uncanny ability to come up with clues he and his men have missed.

In this story, one of the rescued horses needs help foaling and a there's a night of high drama at the ole corral. This causes Savannah to renew her deep interest in horses and riding, which ultimately serves to

246

help her bond with a very important surprise character who finds his way into hers and Michael's life just as they prepare to repeat their wedding vows.

Some say this is a love story with a mystery in the background.


Book Three—**Sleight of Paw**

Michael Ivey, the local veterinarian and Savannah's new husband, is violently attacked by an enraged client and then later accused of this man's murder. The evidence quickly stacks up against Michael, until Rags, Savannah's kleptomaniac cat, starts digging up new clues. Coinciding with the details of this challenge is the discovery that the old house, which the couple purchased from Savannah's aunt, is cursed. Is this why the couple has not been blessed with a child?

Savannah's sister Brianna comes for a visit. She teams up with the Iveys' vet tech, Bud, to discover how to break the gypsy spell and they fall hard for each other. Will their courtship be strengthened or weakened by a frightening carjacking incident?

Detective Craig Sledge is prominent in this story as the lead investigator in the murder case. As usual, he engages in some creative tactics to get the information and the confessions he's after. He has also become embedded in Savannah's friend, Iris's family. He's dating Iris and helping with her son, Damon's rehabilitation in prison.

matilijapress.com
PLFry620@yahoo.com

Made in the USA
San Bernardino, CA
28 June 2014